living with regret

Lisa De Jong

living with regret

CHAPTER one

June 3, 2013

I ATTEMPT TO OPEN my eyes, but I can't. It's like that moment when you realize you're stuck in some nightmare and can't wake up. My arms and legs won't budge … the weight of them is too much. No matter how much I try, nothing happens … and all I hear is that sound. The same tone repeats every couple seconds, making me even more anxious to escape the solitary insanity.

Beep.

Beep.

I wonder where the hell I am, and why that stupid noise won't stop. I just want it replaced by silence or voices—something normal. Where's Cory? I'd give anything to hear his voice right now, or even my parents'. And this bed, or whatever I'm on, isn't very comfortable. My head feels like it was repeatedly slammed against cement. It throbs, and I hate it, but the pain is the only thing that gives me any hope I'm still here, and this isn't some horrible afterlife state I'm living in.

Beep.

Beep.

This is frustrating. My life is about control. I always have to be in control. This isn't working. I keep waking up like this. Unable to move. Unable to see. Unable to remember.

"Rachel. Everything's fine, baby." Mom. Has she been here this whole time?

I nod, or at least I think I do. It's hard to tell in this weird half awake, half asleep state. My mind is functioning, but my body … that's another story.

"You've been sleeping for a while. Be careful, baby." Why can't I see her? Why is she telling me to be careful? Nothing makes sense. Where the hell am I? I'd give anything just to ask one question.

Time passes, and the room is quiet again. Where did Mom go? Where's Cory? Before I fell asleep, or whatever this is, I was studying with him on the couch. I remember that much … at least I think I do. I'm not sure what's real anymore.

"Cory," I mouth, but no sound comes out. I hear footsteps. Loud, heavy rubber against hard floors coming closer. My heart beats faster … I feel it all the way up to my ears.

The footsteps stop next to where I lay, and a cool hand wraps around my wrist. I have no idea what's going on, and if I could, I'd pull my hand away. I'd escape from here and run straight toward normal. Hopefully, normal is a place that still exists.

"Get some rest," a soothing, unfamiliar female voice says from above. The cool hand unwraps itself from my wrist. I attempt to curl my fingers, to quietly beg for her not to leave me, but just like everything else, it's impossible. With every passing second, I hear less, feel less. "That's it, you'll feel better soon."

When I wake again, my body is still frozen in place, but everything hurts a little less. It might be because I just woke up, or thanks to whatever the lady with the noisy shoes gives me when she comes in.

The annoying beeping sound still plays loudly, but other than that, the room is like church during prayer. Maybe that's what I need to do in order to get out of this state, to fully wake up. Maybe God hasn't heard me because I haven't asked him the way I should. Maybe the only thing I have left is a prayer.

I want to beg God to let me wake up so I can see the world again. I want to tell him how sorry I am for whatever I did to deserve this and promise to never do it again. I'd do anything he asked me to just to get out of here, to see Cory and my mom. I want to hear their voices, see their familiar faces.

There's nothing I want more than to open my eyes ... for this all to end. Until then, I let myself get lost in the last thing I remember before I wound up here. It gives me something to look forward to, a time I want to go back to. A life I want to return to.

"What's your last final?" Cory asks, tracing his finger along my bare thigh. After four years, I should know better than to study near him in short shorts, or any shorts really. I guess I keep wearing them because I like the attention he gives me. I like that after all this time he still touches me like he can't get enough.

"Statistics," I answer, batting his hand away. I don't bother looking up; there's no need because I have every inch of him memorized. He looks all California boy—light brown hair, naturally highlighted with a few streaks of blond—but he was born right here in Iowa. His clear blue eyes mesmerize me even when I'm not looking into them. Today, they shine even brighter than usual because of the green shirt he wears ... not that I was staring earlier or anything.

His finger returns, inching up higher, so high all I can do is close my eyes. Screw statistics. Not like I'm going to use them later in life anyway. "Take a break for a few minutes," he whispers, his lips not far from my ear. "You've had your nose buried in a book for weeks."

What he's proposing sounds so good, but I shouldn't. Not really.

"I can't." My breath hitches when he traces the line of my panties. He's a master manipulator, but in the best way. He goes up just a little higher, one finger slipping under the thin cotton.

"You sure?"

"The test, Cory. I need to pass the test."

He groans, but his hand continues to work at my delicate skin. "That's all you seem to care about anymore. Just give me five minutes. Please."

I want to give in. God knows having him inside me would release the tension that finals have left.

Looking at the clock on the DVD player, I realize I only have forty-five minutes before my last final. Cory is my greatest temptation, but he'll have to wait until class is over. Then I'll have a whole summer to be with him just like this or any other way he wants me.

"After class. I promise."

His warm finger brushes against my center. He's driving me so freaking crazy. "Are you sure? Because your wet panties are telling a different story."

"As soon as this last test is done, I'm yours. Any way you want me," I say, hearing the desire in my voice. I've never been good at hiding it. Not when it comes to Cory.

"I'm going to hold you to that," he says, pulling his hand from under my shorts. He looks at me, eyes burning like fire, then kisses me in a way that's decisive and possessive. Soft. Then firm. Then hard. There's no doubt in my mind I'm going to finish my test quickly so I can run right back here. From the grin on his face, he knows it, too.

That's where the memory ends … it's the last thing I remember. How did I get from there to here?

My eyelids flutter just enough to break open to the light around me. Bright fluorescents shine from large rectangles in the ceiling. It's too much to handle at once, so I choose darkness again while I attempt to move my fingers. It works this time—a little bit.

My body still aches all over. Like a powerful, unyielding wave crashing into it, the pain leaves no part of me untouched. It's worse than the time I fell off my bike, colliding hard with the pavement. And the time I fell from the tree in the back yard while trying to free my kite from its branches. It's worse than anything I've ever experienced.

With every second that goes by, the darkness becomes lonelier. My mind is a fucking mess, like a five hundred piece jigsaw puzzle spread across the floor. I wish I could go back in time, to when everything was normal. It's easy to forget the miracle behind normal because we're so used to living in it. I will never take it for granted again.

I'm going to get back there. I'm going to see Cory again and spend the rest of the summer swimming in the lake. This has to be temporary. I need everything to be okay.

After a few minutes, I open my eyes to the light again. The stale white and baby blue walls confirm my worst fear. The uncomfortable rock I've been lying on is nothing but a hospital bed. The room's cold and smells of antiseptic; and strange, plastic machines surround me, one making that sound that has held my sanity hostage for God knows how long.

Scanning the room even further, I see Mom sitting in an old, mauve-colored waiting room chair not far from my bed. Her usual perfectly-in-place blond bob is a mess, and it's the first time I've seen her out of the house without make-up. And sweats. She's wearing a pair of black sweatpants and a gray sweatshirt.

Her head rests on her arm, her eyes tightly closed. Even sleeping, she looks tired.

"Mom," I whisper, feeling the painful burn in my throat. It's like someone took a knife and scratched along its edges, but when she doesn't move, I know I have to try again no matter how much it hurts. "Mom!"

Her eyelids lift just enough to get a glimpse of me. She straightens quickly, resting one hand on my arm and the other against my cheek. They're so cold, but it feels good. Yet another sign that I'm still here. That this is something real and not part of a dream.

5

"How are you feeling?" She looks at me with the saddest eyes.

"Water," I reply, "Please."

She nods, running the backs of her fingers along my forehead. "Let me get the nurse."

While I wait for her, I glance around the room. There are flower arrangements on the windowsill and the small table next to the bed. Most of them are full of my favorite: Gerbera daisies. Usually they lift my mood, bringing cheerfulness to the worst of days, but I'm too locked in a state of confusion to feel the brightness that would normally be radiating within me.

Maybe I should be screaming for answers. The reason for being here, the reason for the excruciating pain that runs down the entire length of my body, but I'm pretty sure—based on everything I see before me—I don't want to know.

Ignorance isn't always bliss, though, and somehow, this all needs to make sense.

The door swings open, and a nurse in green hospital scrubs enters followed closely by my mom. "You're awake," the nurse says, checking the fluid in my IV. I follow the line down to the top of my bruised hand. "I can't give you any water until the doctor gets here, but would you like some ice chips?"

I nod slightly, willing to take whatever she'll give me. This is worse than any sore throat I've ever had in my twenty years.

"Okay, I'll be right back."

She starts to walk away, but I'm not done with her yet.

"Wait." My voice is lost, like the morning after cheering at a football game. I'm convinced I swallowed shards of glass at some point. "Can you turn that machine off? The one that keeps beeping."

A sad smile curves her lips. "I wish I could, but we have to keep them on for at least a few more days," she says in a soothing tone. That's not exactly what I wanted to hear, but at least it's just a few more days.

After the door shuts behind her, I turn back to Mom. There's so much I need to know, but I don't know if I'm necessarily ready to hear it. Waking up in a hospital without any memory of how you got there isn't something that happens every day.

"Why am I here?" Those four little words are almost impossible for me to say, but the answer is so important.

"Get some rest. We can talk when you're feeling better," she answers, her voice like a soft lullaby. The back of her fingers slide across my cheek, smoothing a few strands of hair off my face. It's comforting, but it doesn't take away my curiosity. There's no way I'm going back to sleep without some answers.

"No. Tell me now."

She closes her eyes and slowly shakes her head before looking back down at me, defeated. "There was an accident." The last word leaves me with a sinking feeling, and the fact that she's having trouble looking me in the eye says a lot.

"What kind of accident?"

She swallows visibly, moving her eyes to mine. She hesitates, reaching her fingers up to touch my cheek yet again. Mom is never like this—showing me this much affection—and it's scaring the hell out of me.

"Car." Her voice is so low, it's almost as if she didn't intend for me to hear her.

"What? What happened?" Tears well in my eyes. There's something she's not telling me; it's written on her face in large print.

"You were driving and went down an embankment. You hit a tree head on." She stops, tears now spilling over. Her fingers brush my hair, carefully tucking it behind my ear. "We're lucky to have you back, baby."

Closing my eyes tightly, I try to remember. How could I not remember crashing into a tree? How is it possible to go through something like that and not remember a single thing? Then it hits me like a thousand bricks … Cory. Rarely do I do anything without Cory. Sometimes I go out with the girls, or hang out at home when he has plans, but it's rare for us to be apart. For almost five years, he's been my heartbeat … the one thing that keeps me going.

"Mom, where's Cory?" My voice cracks as the sinking feeling takes over. If he knew I was here, he'd be by my side. I know he wouldn't leave me alone. He's not perfect, but he loves me.

"Rachel, maybe you should get some rest. Your body's been through a lot." Her tone could wilt a flower. So much is being said without actually saying the words.

I shake my head, trying my best to push down the feelings inside, but it hurts so freaking much. It's like someone took my skull and repeatedly banged it against the wall. Between that and not knowing why the hell I'm here, I'd almost prefer to go back to sleep again. Lying here, anticipating the worst, isn't helping. Why won't she just tell me where Cory is? I need her to tell me the truth, even if it sends me into a world of all-consuming misery. "Where's Cory?" I pause, trying hard to catch my breath. "Tell me ... please."

She falls forward onto the bed, resting her elbows against the edge and gripping my hand between hers. Her warm lips touch my knuckles before she looks up at me again. The pain shows like a dark cloud in her eyes as she opens her mouth then closes it. "He didn't make it," she cries, touching her lips to my skin again. "I'm so, so sorry, baby girl."

Everything stops. My heart included.

"What?" I choke, not even sure if the word actually came out.

Mom closes her eyes tightly, slowly shaking her head. "Cory didn't survive the crash ... I'm sorry."

The one part of my future I felt sure of is gone. With the words '*He didn't make it,*' the movie of my life has been put on pause ... and I don't see any reason to finish it.

Not without him.

Lost, I stare up at the white ceiling tiles trying to breathe air into my weighted chest. My body shakes, and my throat isn't the cause of my pain anymore. The excruciating ache in my heart overrides everything else. It's like someone took a pitchfork and pierced through it, over and over again, until it was filled with open wounds. Then, because that wasn't enough, salt was poured right over top. Unyielding, it's the worst pain I've ever felt. The worst pain I think anyone could ever feel.

My hands and jaw tingle, and the room spins. Nothing feels right with the world anymore.

This can't be happening.

Why him and not me?

I want to remember something—anything—about what happened, but I can't. Things like this aren't supposed to happen to people like me. It's as if I'm stuck watching one of those movies where something so horrible happens that you say to yourself there's no way that would happen in real life. This is my life, and it's so fucking real right now that I wish I could just un-live it.

Warm tears slide down my face, but I don't bother to wipe them away. My mind is spinning so quickly, but nothing really matters anymore.

How did I end up here? The only thing I recall is studying for my college statistics exam with him on the couch. I don't remember going to class, much less getting into a car. This would be easier to believe if it made even an ounce of sense.

"I don't get it," I cry, "I was on my way to class."

She shakes her head, sympathetic eyes narrowing in on me. "No, you got home from school that afternoon. The police mentioned that you were on your way home from a party when it happened."

There's so much I'm missing. So much I don't remember. Closing my eyes, I try, but there's nothing.

"How long?" I whisper, swallowing hard.

"How long what?"

"Have I been here?"

"Seventeen Days."

The darkness was a much better place. Sometimes it's better not to know … I want to fall back into naivety, but it's too late. What's done can't be undone.

CHAPTER *two*

SINCE MY MOM LEFT TO shower a few minutes ago, my eyes have been locked on the door. I thought that, after a while, I'd wake up and find out this has all been a bad dream … the worst kind of nightmare that digs itself deep into the skin until the line between reality and imagination is blurred.

I'm shut inside an empty, sterile room, devoid of any soul. There are floors of rooms in this hospital that look exactly like this. It's a place where people are left to heal their wounded or weakened bodies, but the atmosphere is doing little for my mangled, torn heart. The machines I'm hooked up to ensure that it's beating, but it can't detect the large, hollow hole that's now in the center.

This isn't my life. This isn't what I had planned. Cory and I had been together since we were freshmen in high school. We were supposed to get married after college and move back to our small town to live happily ever after. He was my future … all I could see when I opened my eyes every morning. All I could think about when I closed my eyes every night.

Now, all I have are memories. He'll never be here smiling down at me. I will never be able to wrap my arms around him or press my lips to his again. Never again will he grab my hand in his or whisper things that shouldn't be said out loud in my ear.

As much as I hate it, this is my new life. A sick, twisted version of hell that no one really deserves.

I think back to the day Cory first asked me out. He was that guy ... the one who girls have in mind when they get dressed for school in the morning. The one you can't help but smile at when you walk past, but you tuck your hair behind your ear casually, hoping he doesn't notice that you're staring.

I'd gone to the first high school party with my friend, Madison. It was a night I'd never forget.

"Will you quit pulling at your skirt already? It's supposed to be that short," Madison says, pushing my hand from the hem I'd been tugging at since we walked into the packed house.

"I can't believe you made me wear this."

She rolls her eyes. "You shouldn't hide your body ... especially those legs."

Shaking my head, I follow behind her as we weave our way through the crowd. The good thing about growing up in a small town is I pretty much know everyone here, but it's still a who's who of our high school. I don't think we should even be here.

I spot Sam, my next-door neighbor across the room and start toward him. "Where are you going?" Madison asks, wrapping her hand around my forearm.

"I'm going to go talk to Sam."

"Seriously, Rachel. You shouldn't be hanging around him."

"Why?" I ask, waving in his direction.

"You don't want to be the girl who's seen with him. People will talk. They'll make assumptions."

Sam's quiet and has an aura of darkness that follows him wherever he goes. It might be the black leather jacket he wears or the classic car he drives. Whatever it is, most of the girls in our high school find it irresistible, and while some have had their shot with him, it never goes beyond a night in the backseat of his Camaro. I asked him about it once, and he told me life's simpler if you don't let yourself get too attached to anyone. It seemed honest because I'm the only person he's really ever attached himself to.

People in town talk about him like he's a destined felon, simply because his dad went down that path when he was younger. It didn't matter that it was almost twenty years ago when his dad had one minor theft conviction and way before they even moved here. I guess, in their minds, crime is a genetic, chronic disease but they don't know Sam like I do. Over the last seven years, I've spent more time with him than I have anyone in this crowded house—Madison included.

Before I have a chance to argue with her, I feel a hand squeeze my shoulder, and I spin around. Cory Connors stands behind me with a cocky grin spread across his handsome face. His eyes are even bluer than I'd thought, and his light brown hair is sun-kissed from spending hours outside this summer. He's the definition of perfect.

"Hey, it's Rachel, right?" he says in his deep, masculine voice. It floats through my mind like sugar, coating every part of me in happiness.

"Yeah," I say, trying to pry my eyes from his full pink lips. They're hard to look at without imagining what they'd feel like on mine. Not that I'd really know what that feels like since I've never been kissed. I think about it a lot, though. A whole lot.

His grin widens as he follows the path of my eyes. "What are you looking at?"

I swallow the lump in my throat, shifting my focus up. "Umm ... nothing. I mean. I was—"

He laughs. "Hey, I was only teasing." He reaches his hand up toward my face but quickly pulls it back. "Did you just get here?"

I nod, still shocked that Cory is actually talking to me. I'm afraid if I say too much, it's all going to come out wrong. And this is probably the one and only time he's ever going to talk to me. I have to make it count.

"I was just heading outside if you want to come with me," he says, interrupting my thoughts.

I'm frozen in place, staring into his glassy blues. This is my chance, but I'm not sure I'm ready for it. "I don't know."

Madison pushes against my back, practically sending me straight into his chest. "I'll just wait in here, Rachel."

Before I have time to argue, he wraps his hand around mine and pulls me toward the back of the old farmhouse. As I follow close behind, I glance around the packed room noticing all the sets of eyes on us. Most notably is Sam, whose hooded eyes follow me. When I see him pushing back against the wall, I shake my head. He's always been my protector, but he's a senior and won't be around next year. I need to learn to navigate through life on my own. He stops, his eyes narrowing in on me, but I quickly look away before he convinces me otherwise.

"Rachel!" he yells from behind me before I can get too far.

I turn my head, taking in his parted lips and pained eyes. For a second, I think about ditching Cory and disappearing with Sam, but I don't. I told myself high school was going to be about me taking chances. Sam isn't a risk ... he's always been the one to catch me.

I pull my lower lip between my teeth and smile, burying the nervous butterflies deeper in my stomach. Sam understands what I'm trying to tell him right away. Dejected, he lowers his eyes and rubs his hand along his strong jaw.

Unable to watch, I focus on Cory. Letting him lead me through the crowd again. The voice in my head keeps telling me Sam will ask me to stay. If he says the words, I will. He doesn't, though.

When Cory and I step outside, he still doesn't let go of my hand. I don't pull it away either because it feels too good. "Are you having fun?" he asks, so close I can feel his warm breath against my cheek.

I open my mouth, but quickly close it again, trying my best to compose myself. The last thing I want to do is sound like a complete idiot the minute I'm alone with the god of our freshman class. "I just got here," I finally reply, gazing up at him. He's lit only by the moonlight, and Cory under the moonlight is something to be seen.

"Well, you're staying for a while, aren't you?" He smiles, and I swear I've never seen dimples like his.

I nod, feeling his warm finger brush against the skin below my ear. "Good." His voice is soft but smooth, like melted butter. Warm tingles run the entire length of my body. Everything about this suddenly feels right.

We'd been together ever since that night. He was my first date, first kiss, and first love. I let him have everything because I thought he'd be my only. Things have changed now, and nothing will ever be the same. Everything I thought, felt, wanted is gone, and I'd do anything to have him back.

It should have been me who didn't make it out of that car. Living without him is going to be worse than not living at all.

The door clicks, and another nurse walks in with my medical chart in hand. Her expression becomes sympathetic when she sees my tear-stained cheeks.

"How are you feeling, Rachel?"

I shake my head, unable to put into words what is going through my mind. Why would someone even ask me that?

"Are you in pain?" she asks, fastening the blood pressure cuff around my arm.

I nod, turning my attention out the window on the other side of the room. I'm not sure if it's the physical or emotional pain that runs deeper, but I'm not going to explain that to her. She wouldn't understand … no one would.

After taking my vitals, she smoothes my long blonde hair away from my face … the way my mother had done just hours ago. "I'm going to give you something to help you sleep. You need to get some rest."

My eyelids grow heavy just minutes after she leaves, and before I have time to object, temporary relief finds me. It doesn't last long, though, and my mind drifts off to the land of memories and confusion again. The same scenes continue to play, and I let them. I wish there was a way to climb into them, to go back in time.

When I wake up, the room is dark. Blinking the sleep away, I glance around the quiet space in search of my mom. She should have been back hours ago. I need her, more than I ever have before.

The whole time I slept, I heard Cory calling my name. I tried to run after him, but I couldn't catch him. It was foggy and dark, but I could still see him looking back at me every once in a while. It fueled me to move faster, but the distance between us didn't close. Now that I'm awake, I realize it was just a dream. I'll never touch Cory again; my whole life will be spent chasing those memories, but not being able to catch them.

"Rachel." I glance over, spotting Madison standing in the corner of the room. Her shoulder-length brown hair is pinned back away from her face. She looks tired, much the same way Mom did before.

When I don't respond, she moves closer, curling her fingers around my forearm. Madison's been my best friend for as long as I can remember. Our moms were best friends, and we've done everything together since we were babies: baths, swimming and dance lessons, and family trips. We understand each other, especially the pressure our parents put on us to be the best at everything. We both did everything we could to get straight A's in school, and if it weren't for calculus, I would have accomplished it. We joined every committee we could, just like our mothers had in their high school days: prom, yearbook, and homecoming. Looking back at it now, it was exhausting. I lost a lot of myself trying to be what my parents wanted me to be. It doesn't seem worth it now.

She takes the seat next to my bed, watching me carefully. "You look like you're doing better than the last time I saw you." I wonder when that was, but I don't ask. It doesn't matter. "How are you feeling?"

I look away from her. It's a stupid question—one I'm so tired of hearing. How does she think I am? I woke up with no memory of what put me here and just found out my boyfriend is dead. I know it happened. I'm not in denial, but I'm also not ready to talk about it. It makes it that much more real.

"I used some of your photos to put together a slide show for the funeral. I saved it for when you're ready to watch it," she says quietly, leaning her cheek against the side of the bed.

Funeral. The thought never crossed my mind, but there had to have been a funeral. One I didn't get to attend. Anger floods me, but I quickly push it away. No one's going to wait seventeen days for a funeral, yet I know it was my chance to say my goodbyes … a chance I won't get now unless I find a way to do it on my own. It's not fair … but none of this is fair.

"How are his parents doing?" I whisper. The words almost stick in my throat. Cory was their only son, the youngest of three kids. He was his father's pride and joy. In his eyes, Cory could do no wrong. It's how most of our small town viewed Cory. It's exactly how I saw him … how I *still* see him.

"About as good as you'd expect given the circumstances. I can't imagine what it would be like to lose a child—your only son."

More tears slip from my eyes. "I can't believe this is happening."

"How much do you remember?" she asks, looking down at the bleached white sheets.

A thought hits me. Maybe she can fill in the gaps. Maybe she remembers something about that night that I don't. "Not much. Can you help me? I need to know something—anything."

"I didn't get home from school until the morning after," she says, glancing down at her fingers.

"I thought you were coming home the same day Cory and I did. I remember talking to you about it. Did your plans change?" I'm so confused. Maybe I imagined that too. Being stuck in a permanent fog really sucks.

She stands, folding her arms over her chest. She can't seem to look at me so she stares out the window instead. "I told you not to drink so much at parties, Rachel. I wish … I wish someone had stopped you."

"What?" I watch her as she briefly looks at me then turns away again. It doesn't even matter that she didn't answer my question. "What do you mean by that? Tell me."

Her hand slides down, covering mine, but her eyes drift away. "You were driving that night. When they found you, there was alcohol in your system."

My vision blurs, and the room spins even faster than it was before. Cory's not just dead … I killed him. I'm the reason he's not here.

Choices. We make them every day, but this one … this one is one I'll live to regret forever.

CHAPTER three

BY THE TIME THE doctor finally makes it into my room to check me over, the gray skies have been replaced by night skies. I should know because my eyes have been fixated on the window since Madison left a couple hours ago. There was so much more I wanted to ask her, but it was all lost after she told me I'd been drinking. Everything ended there, and she left soon after without saying more than a goodbye.

My throat still burns, but the water I asked for hours ago is the last thing on my mind. Besides, I deserve the pain ... after what I've done, I deserve much more than this.

"How are you feeling?" he asks, pulling his stethoscope from around his neck. He's a middle-aged, balding man who wears a worried, pensive expression on his face.

"Why does everyone keep asking me that? I'm here, aren't I?"

"And you're lucky. I saw pictures of your car in the newspaper." I don't even want to think about what that looked like. I wouldn't be able to handle it, knowing the fear that Cory probably felt in his last minutes. I wonder what he was thinking. Did we say anything to each other? I wish I could remember that much. I hope I told him I love him. That's what I'd want to say, if I had the choice.

The doctor presses the cold metal to my chest, listening to my heartbeat. I wonder if he hears my heart breaking, and if a heart under the weight of misery sounds different than one with a normal beat.

"You sound good. How's the throat?"

"Hurts," I whisper. Everything hurts. Pure, freaking agony lives inside every part of me.

"I'll have the nurse bring you some water. Is there anything else I can get you?" Why is he being so nice to me? I need someone to yell at me, to tell me this is my fault … it should have been me. I need someone to justify what I feel inside. To rip me apart the way I've been ripping myself apart the last couple hours.

Shaking my head, I focus on the window again. Darkness … that's all I need. I should've stayed there when I had it. It wasn't my favorite place, but it was better than this.

"Okay. Tomorrow we're going to run some tests to see how your brain is healing, and then I should have a better idea of when you'll get to go home. Hopefully it won't be too much longer."

It dawns on me that no one has explained what my prognosis is or why I've been sleeping for seventeen days. "What happened? I mean, why have I been here for so long?"

"You hit your head pretty hard, had some serious swelling, so we had to put you in a medically-induced coma so you could heal. We expect you to make a full recovery," he says, a sad smile forming.

All I can do is nod as he lightly pats my knee. A full recovery means nothing to me. I'll never go back to the life I had before all this.

When he's finally gone, I let my tears fall on my pillow, remembering more of what I've lost. Everything I lost…

"I swear you were the prettiest girl in that room," Cory says, pulling me out onto the golf course. There was a fundraiser that both our families attended tonight, and now that our parents have had a few drinks, we manage to sneak out. Stolen moments are few and far between at these things …

it's all about keeping up appearances. Fake smiles. Forced conversations.

"I bet you say that to all the girls," I tease, following him out to our spot in the trees. We've been together for almost three years, and one of the best parts has been discovering our little hideaways.

He stops, gripping my hips to pull my body close. "I'm pretty sure there's only one girl who gets my attention. I think you know her—blond hair, blue eyes."

Biting my lower lip, I stare at his mouth. "Sounds familiar. Tell me a little more."

He nuzzles his nose against my neck, pressing his lips to the skin below my ear. "She's funny and smart. She also has really nice legs ... I love her legs," he whispers, his warm breath reaching my ear. He walks us back a couple steps until my body leans against the tree, his fingers brushing against my bare thighs.

Cory charmed the pants off me after we dated for a year, and we haven't stopped since. Every moment we get alone is spent this way. Sixteen may have been a little young, but once hormones got ahold of me, they didn't let go.

"You're not so bad yourself," I say, wrapping my arms around his neck. He slides his hands down my sides, curling his fingers under the hem of my dress to bring it up. My breath hitches as he presses his fingers between my legs, tracing small circles where he knows drives me crazy.

Maybe we should be afraid that someone will walk out here and find us, but we've done it a few times before. During the day, this course is full of people, but at night it's complete solitude.

"Not so bad?" He grins, leaning in to kiss me.

"You're all right." He presses one finger into me, forcing a groan from my lips.

"What was that, Rachel? I don't think I heard you right." His lips press against my collarbone as another finger enters me.

I can barely breathe, much less talk, but he's not going to let it go; he never does. "You're perfect," I gasp, feeling my walls clench around him. Every ounce of stress and tension *leaves my body, giving me the relief I crave. He doesn't move until I've come back down, a withering girl under his control. It never takes him long to get my body to react, and he knows it.*

I wrap my arms tightly around his neck, capturing his lips with mine. His fingers are still inside me, and it's so tempting to beg him for another round. It's always good the first time, but the second is always better. I want to be greedy. I want to beg for more, but I hold back, hoping to get another taste of him later.

"Have you talked to your parents about Southern Iowa yet?" he asks, withdrawing his fingers from me.

"I'm in," I say with a huge smile on my face.

"Seriously?"

"Seriously," I answer, leaning in to kiss his lips.

He lifts my feet from the ground and spins me, not caring that my skirt is still up around my waist. "You're stuck with me now."

"There's no one else I'd rather be stuck to."

Things between Cory and I weren't perfect during our first year at Southern Iowa. We had different priorities, and we'd each changed in our new surroundings. We didn't have the risk or excitement that came with sneaking around. Things were just … different. Cory asked for a break shortly after Christmas, but I fought for us with everything I had. We planned on forever, and I didn't want to let that go. He gave in to me, and I wonder now if it cost him everything. Did we have a fight that night? Is that why I was drinking?

Things had been better that last month, but we were still fighting more than normal. I thought with a summer spent at home, we'd remember what it was that drew us together in the first place. Why we were inseparable for so many years.

Now, I'll never know. All I do know is I would have fought for him … no matter what. He meant so much to me. In a way, he'd come to define me. I was always where Cory was. I was happiest when I could breathe the same air as him. Now, when I have the strength, I'm going to be starting with a blank slate. I'm going to have to figure out who I am without him.

The door clicks open. After one day, I'm already dreading that sound. I don't want to talk to anyone … I want to stay lost in the good memories of Cory. Sometimes just thinking about him allows me to believe he's still here. It's my own world of pretend, and I just want to be left to play in it.

"The doctor ok'd clear liquids. I have water and apple juice. I can also get you a 7-Up if you'd prefer." It's a different nurse than I had before.

"Thanks," I mumble, wiping tears from my cheek.

She grips my wrist, pressing her fingertip to my pulse point. "Things get easier … with time," she says, looking down at her watch.

"I don't think that's possible. I didn't even get to say goodbye," I cry, staring up at the white ceiling tiles. The longer I'm stuck on my back, the more I wonder why they make the ceilings like this. They're baron, depressing. The last thing anyone in a place like this needs is something to worsen his or her already depressed mood.

The nurse remains quiet as she continues her work, keeping her eyes down. She's the first person who's been in this room today who hasn't asked me how I'm feeling, and for that, I'm grateful.

"Your mom was here earlier while you were sleeping. She went home for the night but said to call if you need her."

I just stare, feeling out of sorts. There's a numbness where my heart used to be.

"Before she left, she told me you know about the accident, and I want you to know I'm right outside if you need anything. All you have to do is push the red call button."

Still, I say nothing. This woman doesn't know what I feel. There's no way she can read what's going on in my head. It's just an illusion people use to get others to talk.

"I know you're probably thinking it's better to keep it all inside because no one's going to understand, but that's not true."

My brows furrow as I watch her check the wraps they'd put on my legs to prevent clotting. They make my skin itch, but that's the least of my worries.

"My husband died a few years back. Farming accident," she continues, checking the fluids in my IV.

"I'm sorry," I whisper.

"It's the worst thing I've ever been through. Didn't think I'd make it, but I did." She stops, pulling my covers up. "He's always here," she says, placing her hand over her heart.

"But I did it. I'm the reason he's not here," I choke, my chest noticeably rising and falling.

Her hand touches my forearm—cool and comforting. "Forgiving yourself is going to be your biggest hurdle in letting go. Just remember no amount of guilt or punishment will bring him back."

My cries shake my body and soul, quickly turning to sobs. I knew the downpour would come eventually, but hearing another person confirm that Cory's not coming back undoes me.

"Let it out, honey. It's the only way you're ever going to feel better. I think it was at least a month before I let myself have a good cry, and it was the most miserable month of my life," she says, patting my arm.

Even if I wanted to respond, I couldn't. My heart's been shredded and spread across the floor. I'm just waiting for someone to come and walk on it. I deserve to hear the hate I feel within myself.

CHAPTER *four*

June 9, 2013

IT'S BEEN SIX DAYS since I woke up. Six days since this broken, crappy new life started … a sad, empty version of what I used to have.

It brings me back to when I was younger, to the first time my life was lonely. My dad always worked hard, trying case after case as the county attorney. He was often gone before I woke up in the morning and came home late in the evening, many times after I'd already gone to bed. Since I've been here, I realize he hasn't changed one bit. He's only visited me twice, and our time together is full of excuses about why he hasn't visited more. I know I'm never going to be able to change him, so I keep my mouth shut and make a mental note of what not to do when I have kids—not that it's likely to happen now.

Mom, on the other hand, was always busy keeping up appearances, a member of the church board and the PTA. Everyone thought we were a perfect family, but they could only see what was on the outside. They didn't see the hollow loneliness within me. The girl who craved attention like an addict craves their next fix. All I ever wanted was a little bit of their time. I wanted them to get to know who I was, not who they wanted me to be.

We lived on a ranch, a property my dad inherited from my great grandfather. We had a few horses, and when I was six, my parents let me get a puppy, which I named Toby. We were inseparable, and I was grateful for him because he filled a small part of the void my loneliness had created. I remember one day in particular … the day I met Sam. I was only eight.

Mom has some of the church ladies over for afternoon coffee. She made me put on this hideous floral dress with a pink bow across the front this morning just for the occasion. I hate it, and after she finishes parading me around like a pony at the fair, Toby and I slip outside to hide away.

It's a sunny day so we decide to take a walk, ending up in the grassy field next to our property. There isn't much to it— just a vast open area with extra tall grass bordered by a line of trees and a tiny creek. The best part is it's hidden from the road and difficult to see from my house. It's a perfect hiding place, just Toby and me out in the middle of nowhere.

Deciding to defy my mom's plea stay clean, I lay back in the grass, letting the sun beat down on my skin. I close my eyes and get lost in the serenity of summer, not opening them until I hear footsteps coming close. I never expected anyone to come out here.

My heart races, especially after Toby starts barking because he wouldn't do it if it were just Mom or Dad. They've told me time and time again not to come out here where they can't see me, and of course, something really bad is going to happen to me on the first day I choose not to listen.

Maybe if I lie still, whoever it is won't see me. Actually, who am I kidding? Toby just gave us away, and I'm as good as dead. It's probably one of the strangers they always warn us to stay away from in school. What am I supposed to do now? If they offer me candy, I'm definitely not going to take it.

"What do you think you're doing out here?" From the voice, I know it's just a kid, but I'm still too afraid to open my eyes. I've always been a little shy; Mom points it out to me all the time when I hide behind her in church.

"I don't need to tickle you to make sure you're still breathing, do I?" he adds.

With the threat looming over my head, I finally open my eyes. Most boys are gross, but this one is different. He's cute, like one of those boys from the Disney Channel. He has to be a couple years older than me because he's so tall, and his blond hair is long, curling around his ears. Even though I hate boys, I don't mind looking at this one.

"That gets 'em every time," he jokes, crouching down beside me.

"What's your name?"

He shrugs. "Do you really want to know or were you just looking for something to say?"

"Just wondering if I should run. If you offer me candy, I'm out of here," I reply, using my arms to sit up.

"You're safe. My name's Sam by the way. I just moved in next door." Since I live out in the country, next door doesn't really mean next door ... the nearest house is almost a half-mile away, so neighbors are harder to keep tabs on.

"My name's Rachel. I live right back there," I say, pointing my finger back toward our property. I've lived in the same house all my life, a huge two-story white traditional with a wrap-around porch. "How did you know I was over here?"

He lies back in the grass, much like I'd been when he walked up. "I didn't."

"Oh, do you come out here a lot?"

"Nah, I walked out here yesterday and noticed how quiet it was. Seemed like a good place to come when I needed a break from my dad."

Lying back in the grass, I'm careful not to get too close to him. I can't believe I'm staying here, but if he really wanted to harm me, he probably would have done it by now. "I'm hiding from my mom."

I turn my head, noticing his eyes are on me. I can't take the serious way he looks at me so I look up to the blinding blue sky.

"What's with the dress?" he asks.

"I had to play dress up for my mom's friends. And for your information, I hate this stupid dress," I say, pulling at the pink bow that wraps around my waist.

"If you say so."

25

We remain quiet for several minutes, enjoying the sounds and sights of nature. It's serene, almost like we're living in a whole different world by ourselves. It feels strange because I barely know this kid, but it also doesn't faze me like it probably should.

After a while, I just can't take the silence anymore. "Why did you need a break from your dad?" It's none of my business, but I'm still curious.

He blows out an audible breath, rolling onto his side. "You sure do ask a lot of questions."

"Not any more than you do," I shoot back quickly. I've always been quick on my feet; you have to be when your dad's a lawyer.

"Point taken," he says, rubbing his hand over his jaw. "My dad drinks a lot, and I think he hates this place, which is just making it worse."

"I'm sorry. Where did you move here from?"

"Washington."

"Hmm, there's probably not as much to do here."

He laughs. "That's an understatement. We've moved a lot, though, so I'm used to it."

"What does your dad do?" I ask.

"He builds things out of wood, mostly cabinets and furniture. What about your mom? What does she do?"

I shrug. "Throws parties and stuff, I guess."

We spend the rest of the afternoon talking about the places he's lived and what he liked to do at each place. He also tells me the reason his dad drinks all the time is because his mom died soon after giving birth to him. Even though my mom makes me a little crazy, I can't imagine what it would be like without her. It makes me sad, but Sam doesn't seem as bothered. He says it's hard to miss someone you've never really known, but he also admits he wishes he knew what it was like to have a mom.

After a couple hours, I hear my mom yelling my name from across the field and sit up from the spot where my body had molded itself in the grass.

"Are you going to come back out here tomorrow?" Sam asks, tucking his hands in the pockets of his khaki shorts.

I smile, thinking about the possibility of hanging out with him again. He's easy to talk to compared to other people I know. "What time?"

His expression matches mine. "How about two o'clock? My dad usually disappears into his shop by then."

I start walking backward, finding it difficult to look away from my new friend. "Bye," I say, finally willing myself to turn around.

"Hey, Rachel!"

I look back, noticing he hasn't moved at all from where I left him. His smile hasn't fallen one bit.

"Wear shorts tomorrow, and we can stick our feet in the creek."

"I'll see what I can do." I wave and take off running to my house with a grin on my face that hadn't been there in a long time.

That was the first time I spent the afternoon with Sam Shea. I used to escape with Sam, but I haven't been to the field since I was fifteen. I've driven past countless times, watching the trees go by in my rearview mirror. It used to be a place for me to run to when I needed to pretend that the pressures in life didn't exist. It's easy to see why my mind would go there again. I wish it were that easy to escape from this.

The door clicks, taking me away from my memory. That happens more than I'd like these days.

A police officer walks into my room, taking slow, hesitant steps toward the chair next to my bed. I'm not surprised he's here … just that it took this long. I killed Cory. I'm the reason he's never going to take another breath, and I deserve whatever I have coming, even though it scares me to death.

I've already condemned myself to a life in emotional prison, which might be just as bad, if not worse, than any small cell. And maybe by talking to him, I'll be able to fill in some of the gaps in my memory. Maybe he knows something that no one else is telling me.

"Miss Clark, I'm Officer Elroy." He stops, watching me carefully before he clears his throat and continues, "I've spoken to your mom, and she told me that you don't remember anything about the night of the accident, but I need to take a formal statement. Is now a good time?"

I look away, focusing my attention out the window. Rain hits it, rolling down the glass, giving texture to the gray sky. It seems like it rains most days now, which is fitting to my mood. "Is there ever a good time for something like this?" I finally ask.

"I guess not," he replies, grabbing my attention again. He rubs his hand along his jaw. He's older, probably my dad's age, and his hair is speckled with gray, a sign that he's lived through a lot in life. "Look, can you tell me the last thing you remember, before the accident?"

Closing my eyes tightly, I recount the last memories I have of Cory. They really don't explain much about how I got here. "The last thing I remember is sitting on Cory's couch in his apartment. I had one more test to take before my freshman year was over, and then we were going to head back home. He was watching baseball ... that's the last thing I remember."

"Was that the day of the party?" He scribbles in his notepad.

"I don't know. I don't remember talking about or going to any parties. What was the date of the accident? I don't even know."

"The accident was during the early hours of May seventeenth."

I swallow, tears pricking my eyes. "Yes, it was the morning of the sixteenth. It was the last day of the semester." I've forgotten almost twenty-four hours of my life. How is that even possible?

He opens his mouth to ask me another question, but the door swings open and my dad comes barreling through with his briefcase in his hand. "Rachel, don't say another word!"

"She's not under arrest," the officer replies, clicking his pen a couple times.

"Not yet." My dad's jaw works back and forth as he stares between Officer Elroy and me. I've always thought my dad was handsome with his chestnut brown hair, tinted with just a touch of red, and deep green eyes, but time spent in the courtroom has weathered him over the past couple years.

"I was taking her statement."

Dad throws his briefcase on the end of my bed, eyes full of rage as he stares at the officer. "Read me everything she said, and Rachel, if he says one thing that's out of line, I need to know."

I open my mouth to tell him it doesn't matter because I don't remember anything, but he holds his hand up to silence me. Officer Elroy repeats what I told him to perfection, appearing annoyed with the whole process. When he's done, Dad looks at me again. "Did he leave anything out?"

"No," I whisper, ready for this to end. Officer Elroy should just arrest me. I deserve it.

Dad nods, shoving his hands in the front pockets of his trousers. "If you have any other questions for my daughter, you'll ask them with me by her side. Do you understand?"

"Loud and clear."

"Good. Now, if you have anything further, you can continue; if not, get out."

Elroy's face reddens as he shakes his head. My dad is a shark, and he knows it. Everyone in town knows it. "Do you remember anything at all from the party that night?"

"No." My voice is meek. The tension in this room is too thick. Suffocating.

Elroy glares at my dad, but his expression softens as he looks down at me. "I'm going to let you get some rest, but I'll leave you my card in case anything comes to mind." He pauses, nodding at my dad. "When she's released, I'm going to want to talk to her some more. I'm sure I don't have to tell you that, though."

I close my eyes, wishing I could disappear. That's all I want … to go wherever Cory is and put an end to this nightmare.

"I'll be ready for it," Dad says, narrowing his eyes.

"Rachel, I'll be in touch," Officer Elroy says quietly as he stands, lightly patting my hand. He should hate me … why is he treating me like a china doll?

"Through me," Dad remarks as Elroy disappears out the door.

Dad's gaze stays locked on the door long after it closes. Things are uncomfortable between us; just like the other two times he's visited since I woke up. It's usually during his lunch break when he knows he doesn't have much time. It's an easy out for him. Mom says he's worried about me, but I wonder if he's more worried about himself and his reputation. His good name has always meant so much to him.

He glances down at his watch before giving me the attention I've long craved. "I need to get going. I have a case this afternoon." He leans down, kissing my cheek. "If he, or anyone else from the sheriff's office, comes back, you call me. Don't say a word."

I nod, seeing a glimpse of sympathy in his eyes. I must be imagining things, though, because that's not what Dad's about. He's a dictator, not an understanding man.

"I'll check in on you later," he says as he starts toward the door. It's a lie, a nicety he says every time he leaves but never follows through on. By now, he should know I see through it. More empty words … I've had a lifetime of those.

Before he opens the door, I yell out to him. "Dad!"

He looks back, a curious expression on his face.

"Dad, I'm scared." My voice is low yet loud enough for him to hear. I don't know why I choose to tell him … maybe it's because I know he won't do anything with my broken honesty. He doesn't know how to deal with it.

"It's going to be okay. I'm not going to let anything happen to you," he says, looking down at the plain white tile floors.

I wish our relationship were such that I could tell him that's not what I'm talking about. It's not punishment I'm afraid of … it's life without Cory. It's living every day wondering what happened and hating myself because I'm responsible for all of this. His death. My pain. It's all on me.

"Okay," I whisper, fixing my attention on the window again. It's hopeless. Everything feels empty, and broken, and no one seems to stay long enough to help me through it.

Life is like a sealed cardboard box. Some are full of wanted treasures, but others are just empty. That's mine. I struggled for years to remove the heavy tape and shook it in hopes of feeling something, but it's hollow. No feeling. No hope. Just empty.

CHAPTER *five*

June 17, 2013

I WAS ABLE TO GET out of bed for the first time today. It took two nurses, and more time than I'd like to admit, but I took my first shower and got to use a real bathroom. It wasn't much, but it was the first hint of normalcy I've had in a while.

Now, I'm back in bed, staring at the familiar walls. This is what prison would be like ... nothing to do but get lost in my own thoughts. That's what the whole punishment is about—making you think about what you've done until it completely eats you up inside.

Mom's here for her daily visit. I don't mind it. In fact, I think I've talked to her more the last couple weeks than I have the last five years. It's sad if you think about it. Some days, I wish she would stay longer than just a couple hours, but on others, I look forward to my time alone. It gives me time to sort through my emotions, to try to remember anything about the last day of Cory's life. So far, I haven't had any success, but it's not going to stop me from trying.

"How are you doing?" she asks, coming to stand beside my bed.

"Tired. They let me take a shower earlier."

"You look good." She smiles, running my hair between her fingers.

"Must be the clean hair."

"They say you should be able to leave in a week or so. Your ribs are healing, and the swelling in your brain has gone down."

I nod. Maybe the news of my impending release should make me happy, but I feel nothing.

"Madison says to tell you hi. She's been working and hasn't been able to make it back up to see you."

Madison doesn't need an excuse. I know she hates me. The whole town probably hates me. Cory was the town's golden boy. Everyone loved him. I still can't escape the weird feeling I was left with when she did visit; like there was something she wasn't telling me. You can sense those things when you've known someone for so long.

"I'll bring you some of your clothes from home tomorrow. That might help. Did you want any books or magazines?"

Back in middle school, I used to write poetry, but I haven't written any in a long time. When weaved right, poetry is like therapy. One line leads to another, much like a therapist leads you to finding your own truth. It's something I really need to find my way back to right now. "There's a pink notebook in the table next to my bed. Can you bring it?"

She smiles. "Of course. By the way, they finally sent your replacement phone." She pulls a cell phone from her purse, handing it to me. "They even put your contacts in for you."

I've been addicted to my cellphone since I got it on my twelfth birthday. Now, as I look at it, I don't see any of its purpose. Cory's gone. Madison hates me. It's almost worthless.

"Thank you," I whisper as she places it next to me on the bed.

"Well, I should be going. We're having a luncheon at the church, and I'm in charge of the sandwiches." She stands, pulling her purse strap over her shoulder. There've been days when I've felt she should spend more time here with me, but I understand her need to return to something normal, mostly because it's something I crave.

Before she leaves, she adds, "The boy next door asked me about you yesterday. He was dropping off some shelves he did for me."

The thought of him makes a lump form in my throat. "Sam?"

She nods.

"What did he say?"

Her eyebrows pull in. Pensive … that's always how she's felt about my relationship with Sam. "He asked how you were doing. I told him you're as good as can be expected, given the circumstances."

Sam's never been the boy next door; in a literal sense, yes, but not figuratively. His dad ran a small woodworking shop out of a shed on their property, and mostly kept to himself, with the exception of his nightly trip to the town's only bar. Sam didn't say much about him except for he treated him all right, making sure he was fed and clothed, but he also didn't spend the time with Sam that he needed. He'd work all day then disappear into a bottle of booze. And when Sam talked about his mom's death, I felt that maybe my home life wasn't nearly as bad as I thought. He had it much worse. At least my family pretended to care.

Sam was rough around the edges, even back then, with a temper that was easily fueled and a heart that was easily wounded. I saw it, little by little, but I understood where it was coming from. He has so much frustration and hurt that he's never dealt with, but it doesn't make him a bad person. He was just my Sam—the boy who would do anything for me.

My mom didn't like him then, said I shouldn't spend time with him, but he was different with me. We'd talk for hours about our pasts, our dreams for the future. He didn't shut me out. I was just as much his soft place to land as he was mine.

While I sat in Sunday school every weekend, he'd work with his dad in his shop. After lunch is when we'd make our escape, meeting in our spot. There were weeks he'd have detention at school because of fights on the playground or talking back to his teacher, and his dad would ground him. Those were his worst weeks … and mine. Those were the weeks my cardboard box stayed empty. Sometimes I think he tried harder to stay out of trouble just to be with me out there. I wanted to save him … he was my purpose. Days I could put a smile on his face were the best days.

Sam didn't care for school; it wasn't his thing. He didn't care for rules either, especially the ones he didn't agree with. My parents made a rule the summer I turned thirteen.

Stay away from Sam.

He was sixteen. They didn't think it was right to be around him, and according to them, 'that boy was bad news.' It didn't end our friendship. The field was our safe place. Our solace from it all. I still remember the last time we met out there … before I started seeing Cory.

*"I didn't think you were going to make it out here today,"
Sam says as I walk up behind him. He doesn't even have to
look back to know it's me.*

*"We had people over for a barbeque after church. The last
family just left." I sit down at the edge of the creek, sticking my
feet in the warm water. Out here is where all my worries and
life's craziness fall away. That's even truer when Sam's with
me.*

"Are you ready for school tomorrow?"

*I shrug, digging my fingers into the tall green grass. "Not
really. Going to high school seems intimidating. I'm starting at
the bottom again, you know?"*

*His shoulder brushes mine. "I made it through three years
without a scratch. You'll breeze right through."*

*"You don't know that." Sam always acts like he knows
everything but he doesn't. He just likes to pretend he does.
Typical boy.*

*"Do you remember when your mom took you shopping for
your first bra after your tenth birthday? Or when you got your
braces on? Oh, and we can't forget when your dad made you
read the law journal after you stayed out here too late.
Remember that?"*

I nod.

*He continues, "You didn't think you'd ever make it through
any of that but you're still perched on the edge of this creek."*

*Rolling my eyes, I watch as the wind creates small ripples
in the water. Sam literally knows everything about me. He*

34

listens even when I think he's not. Whether I'm talking about an action packed movie or an outfit my mom made me wear, he soaks in all of it. I do the same for him—hanging on his every word. "Are you ready to go back to school?"

"Hell no!" he shouts, tossing a small rock into the water. "I'm ready for this year to be over. So I can go on with the rest of my life."

"Yeah? What are you going to do?" Sam hates school, but he also hates working for his dad. I don't think he even knows what his future looks like.

"I have nine months to figure that out." My eyes are still on the water but I feel him looking at me. I take a few seconds before meeting them with my own. The way the sun hits his face makes his brown eyes sparkle. They're easily my favorite things about Sam. "You'll be here for another four years so that gives me something to look forward to."

The way he looks at me is different, or at least, I'm reading it that way. His eyes hold me. I couldn't let go of his stare even if I wanted to. I should say something, break the spell, but I can't.

He leans in slowly. The closer he comes, the more I think he might kiss me, and I quickly realize that I want him to. I like Sam. He's one of my best friends, but there's something deeper I have missed until just now. The longer he looks at me, the more I feel it in my veins.

Sam Shea is my everything and maybe more.

Before we touch, he stops, reaching up to brush my hair behind my ear. "Is that better?" he asks, leaning back.

A ball of disappointment wedges itself in my throat. I wanted that kiss, like really, really wanted it, but Sam didn't feel the same. Maybe I imagined everything. The way he looked at me. The lust in his eyes. Maybe I'm just too young for any of this.

I nod, biting down on my lower lip to push back tears. I hate being a girl sometimes.

Cory and I started dating shortly after. That's when things changed because Cory and Sam couldn't exist together. Now, I regret ever losing Sam as a friend. He became an acquaintance, someone I said *Hi* to whenever we crossed paths. He became a painful memory – not because of what happened between us – but what I lost when I left him behind. Young love clouded my judgment, and I'd do anything to have Sam back in my life. I need someone who will listen to me, and who won't pass judgment along the way.

"All right, honey, I'm going to head out. I'll stop back after dinner," Mom says softly. She gently squeezes my hand then disappears from the room.

After a few minutes of staring at the door, I pick up my phone and scan my contacts. Toward the top are Cory, Madison, Kate, Mom, Dad, and as I scroll down, I see Sam's name. I haven't talked to him in a long time. I don't even know if he still has the same phone number, but I yearn for a piece of the past. I crave something normal and simple, and thinking of him reminds me of a time when things were just that.

He brought me out of my darkness back then, and I wonder if he ever misses those times, because I think I brought him out of the darkness, too. I wonder if he thinks about me at all. When you're young, the phases of life change so fast. Immaturity overrides common sense. Looking back, I wish I'd still made time for Sam after beginning my relationship with Cory. He meant too much for me to just leave him behind.

My phone rings for the first time since I've been here, startling me. I pull it from the bedside table, seeing Kate's name on the display.

I answer, bringing the phone to my ear. "Hello."

"Hey, Rachel. It's so good to hear your voice," Kate says. She sounds like she could cry.

"It's nice to hear yours too." I mean it. Kate reminds me that some of the better parts of life still exist. I met her before college started. Our friendship didn't get off to a great start because she initially thought I was dating the guy she loved. After we cleared the air, we became great friends. She's kind and doesn't get into all the bullshit that some girls our age get into. She's also the only person who might get what I'm feeling right now.

"I'm sorry I didn't call sooner. I talked to your mom right after the accident. She's been keeping me up to date."

"It's not a big deal. I haven't felt much like talking anyway," I say honestly.

"I'd ask how you're doing, but that's probably a stupid question."

"Thank you for the flowers." I stare at the purple flowers she sent me. They're different than the daisies that fill my room.

"You're welcome. I'm just glad you got to see them finally."

Just like that, a new idea hits me. Maybe Kate was with me that day … before I left school. Maybe she can tell me something that would help explain how I got here. "Did you see me that morning?" I ask, feeling a little hope. If someone could just fill in some of the missing pieces.

"No," she replies, sadness etched in her voice. "I wish I could help."

"It's okay. I just feel like I'm sitting around waiting for something that may never happen. It's so frustrating."

"It'll come with time."

"I hope so."

We talk a few more minutes, about my prognosis mostly. I can tell she's purposely avoiding anything that has to do with Cory, and for that, I'm grateful.

"I need to get ready for work, but I'll call again soon."

"Thank you … for everything, Kate."

"I'm here no matter what. You'd do the same for me." And I would.

After I hang up, I look around the room for something to do, to keep my mind off things. This morning, Mom brought me the pink notebook I asked for yesterday. It's setting on the table beside my bed, begging to be picked up.

After she left to go run a few errands earlier, I flipped through it, reading old poetry I'd written years before. I see now that I wasn't very good at it, but it always made me feel better, a way of healing my heart in the privacy of my bedroom. At times when I felt like I had no one, I could arrange words on paper and feel like someone was listening.

I'd written them after fights with my mom and dad.

When Sam was grounded and couldn't meet me on our days in the field.

The day Toby ran onto the road in front of our house and was hit by a truck.

A lot of pain and bad memories are held in this notebook.

Finding an empty page, I pull my pen off the table and stare at the thin blue lines. I write one word then cross it out. It's hard to find the starting verse for this one. This isn't just another situation I need to sort through … it's a turning point, a life changer.

Closing my eyes, I try to pull my thoughts together. They don't come—only tears. I remember the way Cory smelled of spice and citrus. I used to nestle my nose in the crook of his neck and breathe him in. He had this thing he liked to do where he lightly tugged on my hair to get my attention. I'll always remember the little things. He made me feel cared for and loved. Always teasing. Always smiling. That was my Cory.

When I hear the door open, I don't bother opening my eyes. So many people come in and out of my room every day that I'm immune to it now. It's usually Mom or one of the nurses. Dad was just here yesterday so I know it's not him; he fulfilled his obligation for the next couple days. I feel a cool brush of air against the tearstains on my cheeks as the sound of rubber soles on the floor becomes louder—something else I'm used to now. Maybe I should wipe my tears away, but I don't. At this point, I don't even care who sees me like this.

My ears follow the footsteps until they stop near my bed. I'm expecting to hear the customary "How are you feeling?" from one of the many medical personnel who comes in and out of my room almost hourly. Instead, a warm, calloused hand covers mine. Suddenly, I'm that eight-year-old girl back in the fields. It's been years since I felt his touch, but I remember it like it was yesterday. He always held my hand to help me climb out of the creek after we'd been swimming. There were also a few times, while we stared up into the night sky, he had wrapped his fingers around mine as we talked for hours. His skin was rough from hours in the shop, but it felt right.

"Hi," he whispers. His voice holds as much pain as I feel. He was never a fan of Cory's, but he feels what I feel. It's always been like that for us. It's almost as if five years hasn't passed since the last time we laid in the tall, green grass.

Finally opening my eyes, I fixate on Sam. His blond hair is longer than it used to be, falling onto his forehead, but his eyes are just as brown as I remember. They've always calmed me, but right now, they're just making my tears fall faster. He's a symbol of what life used to be like.

"Hey," he says, squeezing my fingers between his. "It's going to be okay."

Without any sense of control, I fist the front of his T-shirt and pull him down until he's close enough so I can wrap my arms around his neck. He stiffens before relaxing into me, his cheek pressed to mine. "I missed you," I say, holding him tightly.

"I'm here now," he whispers, his warm breath tickling my ear. "I'm not going anywhere."

"I never thought you'd come."

"I didn't think you'd want me here." He stops, lifting his head to look in my eyes. "I wanted to come to you as soon as I heard about the accident, but I didn't know how you'd react ... it's been so long, Rachel."

"Too long," I say, trying to draw off the warmth in his eyes. Sometimes just knowing someone is there for you makes everything better.

"I almost had to pay the nurse to get in here. I guess your mom didn't add me to the list of approved visitors," he says, running his thumb along the exposed part of my forearm. He scans the room, taking in the medical equipment that surrounds me. His eyes follow the IV line down to my hand, to the large green and yellow bruise that covers it. I hate the pity on his face. I don't deserve it.

"You obviously found a way in," I say to bring his attention back up to my face.

He looks up, smiling sadly. "Nothing was going to stop me."

For a few seconds, I just stare at him, still surprised that he's even here. It almost feels as if no time has passed at all. I want to blurt out everything, unleash the pain from my soul. I want to tell him I'm sorry for leaving him behind. Losing someone you love makes you look at everything differently. It brings heartache, but it also brings regret.

"Sam?"

"Yeah?"

"I'm so scared and confused. How does something like this happen, and I don't remember a thing? So many people have come and gone from this room, but no one has been able to tell me anything. Someone's got to know something," I cry.

Sam inhales a deep breath, peering up at the ceiling then back to me. "You don't remember anything?"

"No," I choke, wiping fresh tears from my cheeks. "Can you help me? It's a small town; someone's had to say something. I don't even remember going to a party or anything from that night."

"I wish I could, but no one's saying much about the accident. No one I talk to anyway. Besides, some things are better left buried. Maybe that's why you can't remember." He stops, running his fingers through his hair. "I want to see you through this, and I'll do whatever it takes to make this better."

I nod, taking some comfort from his presence.

He pulls the lone guest chair closer to the bed, wrapping his warm hand around mine again. "Get some rest, Rachel. I'll stay until you fall asleep."

When I was younger, I filled that empty cardboard box with Sam, and once I started seeing Cory, there wasn't room for him anymore. It's not that I didn't want him there … Cory wasn't willing to share the space. Now, I need Sam again. I think I've always needed him, and I can't believe he's here now. *Please don't let this be a dream.*

CHAPTER *six*

June 23, 2013

"READY TO GET OUT OF HERE, TODAY?"

I stare up at Sam, giving him the most honest answer I can. "I have mixed feelings about it. It'll be nice to see something besides these four walls, but I know there's going to be things outside of here—in the car, my house and room—that remind me of him. I don't know if I'm ready for that."

He squeezes my hand. "Do you remember when my dad died?"

I nod. I will never forget that day; it was during Sam's senior year. The same year our friendship began to dissipate. He hadn't called in weeks, and when my phone finally lit up with his name, I smiled. I missed him, but he'd made it clear that he thought I deserved better than Cory. His call was the last thing I expected. The reason for his call was even less predictable—his father had a heart attack.

"I didn't sleep in our house again after that. I couldn't because it held memories, good and bad. I worked day and night to finish the apartment above the shop. I didn't cry a single tear ... I had it in my mind that I never would, but as soon as I went in the house to get my clothes and furniture, I fell apart. I needed it. I needed the memories." He pauses, running his thumb over my knuckles. "Let yourself grieve,

Rachel, because, in the end, it's the only way you're going to heal."

I know he's right, but it's going to be painful. I don't think I'm ready. It's easier to stay in a certain state of denial, to let him live in my dreams hoping it might actually be real.

When I don't respond, he continues, "Someone said something to me not long after that still plays in my head every single day. He said, 'We've all been given a life, but we have to make a conscious decision to live it.' And you know what? He was right. It's not easy, but it's what you're going to need to do."

His words make sense. Too much sense. I remember seeing him so stoic at his father's funeral. All I kept thinking was how if he didn't cry—let out some emotion—he was going to fall apart in the worst way. I gave him a hug that day, told him I was sorry, but he sort of disappeared after that. I always wondered if he'd let himself feel the loss. I feel better knowing he did.

Just as I'm about to respond, Mom walks in, dressed in a pair of black slacks with a perfectly pressed white silk shirt tucked into them. She's gone back to looking perfect every day… her life has resumed while mine is stuck somewhere between hell and a hard place.

"What's he doing here?" she asks as soon as she sees Sam sitting next to me. He has stopped by after work every day since that first day he was here, but he came in earlier today because I wanted him here for this. When I was younger, on the days it was just Sam and I, life was good. I felt safe, and he could always put a smile on my face. Worries didn't exist, not in those moments. I think, by having him with me, maybe today won't sting so much. Getting out of here and having to face my old life is going to suck, there's no doubt about that.

"I asked him to come."

She opens her mouth but bites back her words, considering them carefully while looking between the two of us. "Sam, can you give me a minute with my daughter?"

He looks at me, concern showing all over his face. Our conversation before she walked in wasn't light, and we didn't get the opportunity to finish it. I nod, letting him know I'll be okay. I've dealt with my family's judgment and guidance for years, and this is the least of my worries today. Besides, there's nothing she can say that's going to make me turn him away.

As he stands, his hand squeezes mine. My mom watches the whole thing, her disdain written all over her face. A few weeks ago, her behavior might have caused an argument between us, but my body and heart have been drained of all energy. She can think what she wants to think about Sam, but it really doesn't matter to me.

I listen for the familiar click, curling the hospital sheets between my fingers. I hate when people pass judgment on others based on their family's social standing or things they've heard around town—something that's especially bad in our small town. It's like deciding not to read a book because of its cover … there are so many beautiful, meaningful words I would have missed out on if I'd done that.

"Rachel, what are you doing?" Mom asks, rubbing her fingers across her forehead. I'm annoyed that she is so bothered by Sam being here. There are bigger things to worry about.

"What do you want me to say, Mom? I need him here."

"I don't think that's such a good idea. Not with the police coming. Do you understand that you could still be facing charges?" She says the last part like it's a disease. One she wants to run away from. She hasn't come out and said it, but I feel like an embarrassment to my family. Being a potential felon doesn't really fit the prim and proper image my parents created, but that doesn't matter to me, not when I consider what I did to get myself here.

"They're not going to tack a charge on for hanging out with Sam Shea."

She opens her mouth, but as soon as her eyes connect with mine, she stops, her eyes warming. "Your father's going to be here soon. I just think it might be better if it's just the three of us."

"I need him here," I whisper.

She shakes her head. "Your father—"

"I'll take care of him." All the little fears I once had have been forgotten, because I've faced my greatest. I didn't even know what my greatest worry was until just days ago. It shows how quickly things can change, and how those things change people. Before this all happened, I did whatever I had to do to keep my parents happy, especially Dad. Things like that just don't matter anymore.

When Sam walks back in, he ignores the way my mom's nose wrinkles as her whole body recoils. It only worsens when he takes the seat next to me and rests his hand on my forearm. He's been doing that since he arrived earlier. Talking to me, lightly touching my arm or squeezing my hand. It feels nice … it's helping keep at least a part of my mind off of what's to come today.

All that comfort fades when Dad joins us. Mom may not be Sam's biggest fan, but my dad flat out doesn't like him. He's never really talked to him, but his perceptions of him aren't good. He's the type of guy who hates foreign cars even though he's never driven one. The minute he spots Sam, I know this is going to be a battle.

"Sam, I think it's time for you to go home. This is a family thing." He stands at the end of my bed like a statue of authority. I'm almost scared into submission, but the thought of being here alone with my parents fuels me.

"He's not going anywhere," I say quietly, pleading with my eyes. If we were just at home, he'd push the subject, but I know he won't here. There are too many people within earshot. His reputation, and everything he's built from it, means too much to him.

"I'm not leaving her," Sam adds, squeezing my hand tightly. Sam pretty much despises my dad and everything he stands for. He's also one of the few people in town my dad doesn't have any hold over. Not much scares Sam.

Not surprisingly, Dad ignores him, and the way his jaw works back and forth tells me he's not ready to give up just yet. I'm not going to either. "Do you have any idea how important today is? You could still be in a lot of trouble, Rachel."

I'm being released from the hospital shortly, and my first stop will be the police station. Dad says I probably won't be booked on any charges because my blood alcohol content was under the legal limit. I'm ready to get it over with, and if I am to be punished, I'm ready to take what God has coming for me. It doesn't mean I'm not scared.

"That's exactly why I need him here. This day isn't about you. It's about me, and I want him here."

He shakes his head, glancing to Mom then back to me. "Fine, but when they dismiss you, he needs to go home," he says through gritted teeth. I don't miss how he doesn't seem to care that Sam can hear him. I don't miss the fact that he didn't ask how I was doing when he walked in. I'm about to be thrust back into a life that only half exists; I realize that now more than ever.

"Keith," Mom says, placing her hand on Dad's shoulder. "Let's go get some coffee. Rachel doesn't need all of us in here watching over her."

Dad runs his hands through his hair, staring Sam down for a few seconds before answering. "We can grab a quick cup. I want to be up here in case that officer decides to stop by."

Mom grabs hold of his arm and gives him the look of adoration that always melts his ice-cold exterior. *If only she did that a little more often.* They disappear out the door without another look in my direction. It's a few minutes of freedom that I'll gladly take at this point.

"Is that your going home outfit?" Sam asks, pointing to the royal blue velour sweat suit Mom brought for me. I know he's just trying to lighten the mood we created before.

"Classy sweats. Mom picked them," I say, pulling on the zipper.

"Yeah, getting caught leaving here in regular sweats would be horrible." He laughs, but I can't join him, not with all this stuff going on in my head.

He reads me like a children's book, folding his fingers over mine. "Everything's going to be okay. You know that, right?"

I shrug, feeling tears well in my eyes. "Nothing can ever be the same, so right now, I have a hard time believing that."

"I'm only thinking about today. You're going to get out of here, and tonight, you're going to sleep in your own bed without all these machines around you."

"Do you really think I deserve something to look forward to? Because I don't."

Sam leans in, grasping both of my hands in his. "Don't talk like that. You're lucky to be here ... don't take that for granted."

I try to pull my hand away, but he tightens his grip. "You're wrong. I don't deserve it, Sam. I just wish I could remember something because I never drive after I've been drinking. Never. If I could just remember, to make sense of it all, I'd have some peace, but this sucks. This whole thing sucks."

"I wish there was something I could do to make this better for you."

It's a struggle to even swallow, much less talk. "I wish it would have been me instead of him."

Sam shakes his head, squeezing my hand a little tighter. "I swear if you don't stop talking like that, I'm going to walk out that door, Rachel. Neither of us knows what caused that accident, and I'm not going to let you beat yourself up about something that's probably not even your fault."

It's hard to look at him when he's angry. The vein in the side of his neck sticks out, pulsing with every word. His cheekbones turn a couple shades of red. It's a sign that he's not saying everything he wants to say to me. He's been doing that since we were kids.

"But if I wasn't behind the wheel of the car—"

"Stop! And what if things had been different? What if he was driving the car, and he was here right now? Would you want him to think like this? Would you want him to live like this?"

"No," I say honestly, tears brimming. Sam doesn't pour sugar on anything. It's his best and worst quality.

"There's a reason you're here. You may not be able to see it now, but you weren't left to live a pathetic life. And I'm not going to let you."

I nod, wiping the tears from my cheeks.

"And just as a side note, I wasn't really going to walk out the door a minute ago." He smiles sadly, gently brushing his thumb across my cheekbone to clear away fresh tears. It's hard to not feel at least a little better, especially when he's being normal Sam.

"I knew you were lying." I sniffle.

"No, you didn't. You should have seen your face."

"Whatever."

He laughs. It's deep, and his eyes sparkle at the same time. Nothing more genuine than that. There aren't very many people who've heard it; he shows the masses his darker, mysterious side—the one that hides who he really is.

"Hey, Sam?"

"Yeah?"

"I'm glad you cried after your dad died. I was really worried about you, especially when you wouldn't return my calls." I called three times a day for over a week before he texted me a simple *I'm fine.* I got the point—he didn't want anything to do with me. Or that's what I thought.

I learned a long time ago he doesn't like to get close to people. In a way, he prefers the solitude, because it was what he grew up with. His dad was busy in his shop or drinking, and he never knew his mom. I think I'm the only one he's ever connected with on a deeper level, and I have no idea why he picked me. But in a way, I left him too.

The sound that's all so familiar to me rings through the air, and my parents walk in, each with a cup of coffee in their hands. "Are you okay?" Mom asks, quickening her steps to the bed.

"Yeah, we were just talking."

Dad scowls, focusing his chronic negativity in Sam's direction. "Maybe, now's a good time for him to leave."

I open my mouth to argue, but Sam beats me to it. "I have to get back to work anyway." Looking up, a burst of panic shoots through me. He's the one thing that's keeping me some version of sane. His sympathetic eyes connect with mine, and some of my anxiety fades when he winks. Him leaving will be better for both of us.

I nod, keeping my attention on him as long as I can. When his hand is pressed against the door, he turns and signals to me that he'll call later. It's something to look forward to. That's going to be the key to getting through this.

47

CHAPTER seven

I HAVEN'T SEEN MY house in weeks, but as we pull into the driveway, everything looks the same as I remember. I only wish I could see the last day I spent with Cory as clearly. I'd tried so hard every day I laid in that hospital room, but I haven't been able to come up with anything. It's the most frustrating feeling in the whole world.

When the car comes to a stop in front of the porch, Dad quickly jumps out and opens my door. When we walked out of the police station, I expected him to say he had to return to work, but he surprised me by offering to drive me home in his car.

"Grab onto my arm," he says, bending so he's within my reach. I've gotten better on my feet, but I still need assistance because my balance isn't where it needs to be. The doctor says with a few more weeks of physical therapy appointments, I should be good to go.

We take a few small steps together until my toes touch the stairs that lead to the front door. "Do you think you can handle these, or should I carry you?"

"I can walk," I reply, lifting my right foot to the top of the first step. It's not as easy as I thought it would be, but I'm stubborn. Besides, there's only three.

The whole process takes forever, and by the time we finally reach the door, my body is exhausted. It's definitely going to take some time before I can get back to normal activities.

As Dad closes the door behind us, I take in the two-story entryway and expansive living room. It's pristine, highlighted by a wooden spiral staircase. Everything in here is exactly how I remembered it. Beautiful. Classic. Extravagant. If only everything in life could stay like this.

"Your mother was going to make up a space for you in the family room so you don't have to go up the steps. Is there anything you want from your bedroom?"

"No! I mean ... I don't want to sleep down here. I need my own space." It comes out harsher than I intended, but I need time to think, and I'm not going to be able to get that down here with everyone around me.

"Fine, Rachel, but when we're not home, I want you downstairs in case anything happens," he says, rubbing his fingers along his forehead.

"Which is all day every day," I say under my breath.

"What?"

"Nothing. Can you take me up to my room? Please."

Just as he's about to help me to my room, Mom walks through the front door with a bag of groceries in her hand. "I didn't think you guys would beat me here."

"Things went pretty quickly at the police station. She has a good lawyer," Dad says, smiling almost as if I'm not even here. He met his goal for the day. It doesn't matter how shitty I feel ... making it out of the police station was the least of my worries.

Mom pats his shoulder and heads for the kitchen, yelling back at us as she goes. "Did you show her where she's sleeping?"

"She wants to sleep in her room. I'm going to help her up now."

"Okay, I'm standing right here! Quit talking about me like I'm not in the room!" I yell, feeling weeks of frustration coming to the surface.

Dad looks down at me, brows furrowed. He's probably wondering where his sweet, obedient daughter went. He needs to get used to this version of me because the old one's never coming back. "Let's get you upstairs so you can get some rest."

The process doesn't seem as bad this time, even though it's more steps, because I'm driven to have some alone time. Neither of us says a word, and by the time we reach the top, Mom's right behind us with a bottle of water and a plate of her homemade chocolate chip cookies. There used to be a time when I'd devour them on sight, but I could care less right now. This is an emotional mess that carbs can't fix.

When I'm standing safely at the threshold to my room, Mom hurries inside to put my snack on the table next to my bed while Dad excuses himself to return to work.

"I'll be home for supper," he announces as he walks down the hall. I kind of doubt it since he rarely is. Today's not going to be any different.

The first thing that catches my eye when I look into my room is the bulletin board above my desk. It symbolizes years of memories … years of Cory. There's a picture from our first date, our first dance, our first Christmas, and all the ones after. Everything on that board made me happy at one point. Everything on that board symbolizes, in full color, what I no longer have.

"Are you okay?" Mom asks when I don't move from the spot in the doorway.

"No," I say honestly, feeling warm tears slide down my cheeks.

"Do you want to talk about it?"

"No, just help me to my bed. Please." I choke back my emotion when I notice the picture on my nightstand. It was the day of our high school graduation. We were both so happy, with no idea of what was to come one year later. We'd both had our graduation parties the night before, so after the ceremony was over, we headed to the parties of a few of our friends. I'd felt like all arrows were pointing my life in the right direction, especially when he took me out to the lake after the last party and we talked, well into the morning hours, about the future. And now I realize, too many lives are cut too short. There's no notice, but if you live every day like it matters, like what you do or say really means something, there should never be regret.

When we met with the police earlier, they mentioned they wouldn't be filing charges unless new information forced them to do so. I don't think it matters where I am at this point. It's not going to change the sadness that's drowning my soul.

He's been gone for thirty-seven days, but every one seems just as bad as the last. They don't get easier. I don't think about him any less. The worst day of my life is on constant replay.

Mom holds my arm until I'm comfortably seated on the bed.

"Can I get you anything?"

"No," I say, shaking my head. "I just need to be alone."

"Okay," she says softly, pulling the pink blanket my grandma knitted from the end of the bed. She covers my bare feet, knowing I'm usually cold whenever the air conditioner is turned on.

When she walks out of the room, I stare up at the ceiling, needing a break from the images of him. But there's no break; the images live in me, day in and day out. I fight them, not because I don't want to remember, but because they punish me. My guilt has become a demon, tormenting me whether I'm awake or asleep.

Contrition.

Remorse.

Shame.

I want to repent, but I can't see through the fog long enough to even begin that process. I've wondered if things would be different if I could remember the details of that night, but I know it wouldn't change a thing. It'd still be my fault. Nothing's going to change that.

Drawing on the little bit of strength I still have inside of me, I glance at the photo by my bed again. Cory was always smiling in our pictures. The sun was bright on graduation day, letting the brown speckle show in his blue eyes. His light brown hair curled in the humid air, but that was when I liked him most. Clear eyes. Curls. Dimples. That's when he felt like he was mine. I can tell by the way I'm looking at him in the picture, I was thinking the same thing then … he was the axis to my world.

Now, I just feel like I've been stranded on an island, and the worst part is I was the one steering the ship that got me here. I just want to go back to my old life … to *our* old life. It wasn't perfect—nothing's ever perfect—but it was better than this.

My phone vibrates in my purse, bringing me back to reality. Looking at the name on the screen brings me some relief, like listening to the soft, calming melody of a song.

"Hey," I say, swiping my sleeve against my cheek.

"Hey, are you home?" his voice is soft, like he's trying hard not to wake someone. It's how he's talked to me since the first day he came to the hospital.

"Yeah."

In a way, being home is worse than being at the hospital. Sure, the scenery is better, and the bed is more comfortable, but having Sam here isn't really an option. The hospital room felt more like mine than this room ever will.

"What are you doing?"

"Crying."

I wear my feelings on my sleeve in vibrant color. People who hide them expend too much energy that could be spent solving their problems and living in the goodness that life offers. I've never questioned that until now. What if the problem isn't fixable? What if this is all that's left of my life?

A minute or so goes by before he replies. I'm sure he's listening to my soft whimpers, trying to find the right thing to say. Sam doesn't run from conflict, but he doesn't technically embrace it either.

"Do you want me to come over?" he finally asks, even quieter than before.

Do I want him to? God, yes. He's the only person who'd be able to wipe these tears from my eyes with more than his sleeve. Waking up in the hospital and learning what happened to Cory was like a rainstorm, and Sam's been my rainbow. If you'd asked me weeks ago if I'd ever be friends with him again—like this—I would have seen no chance, but life has a way of bringing people back to us when we need them most.

If I were anywhere but this house, I'd invite him over in a heartbeat. He gives me an escape from the prison my mind has locked me in.

"I'm tired, but can you pick me up tomorrow. After you get off work?"

"Aren't you supposed to stay in bed?"

"Please. There's somewhere I need to go, and you're the only person who I trust to take me there."

He sighs. "Rachel—"

"Please," I whisper. "The doctor said to limit my activities, and if that's the only thing I do tomorrow, I'll be okay. It's not far."

"Six-thirty, but Rachel, I'm going to make sure you're home by eight."

There's something I've wanted to do since I found out what happened to Cory. Something I *need* to do.

"Thank you," I say, feeling relieved.

"Get some sleep."

"Night."

I'm about to hang up when the smooth baritone of his voice stops me. "If you get lonely tonight, look up at the sky. The Big Dipper was still there the last time I looked."

"I almost forgot about that."

"I didn't." The only thing I hear is the sound of his breathing as I glance in the direction of the window. I hadn't thought about the stars since we were kids.

"Get some rest. I'll see you tomorrow." I hear the smile in his voice.

"Goodnight, Sam."

When I finally hang up, there's the hint of a smile on my lips. As kids, we hated when we had to separate and go back to our lonely, quiet homes. Sam came up with this idea that we'd look up at the night sky and find the Big Dipper. He said if we both did it, it was almost like we were together, even when we weren't. I haven't done it since elementary school, but the fact that he remembers brings warmth to my chest that's been missing for a while.

Rising from my bed, I brace my hand against the wall as I take small steps toward the window. The Big Dipper isn't the most exciting of constellations, but it was easily identifiable for us. It's just seven stars, but they shine so brightly, standing out in the endless night sky. Looking up, I spot them easily and lower myself to my knees to fight the weakness in my legs.

With my chin resting atop my hands on the windowsill, I close my eyes and go back to better times, but memories that once brought a smile to my face only make my tears fall once again. I guess this is what it's like living with regret.

CHAPTER eight

June 24, 2013

TODAY'S NOT GOING TO be easy, but I'm the only one who knows that, because I haven't let anyone else in on my plan for tonight. There are some things that just have to be done, no matter how much they're going to hurt.

"Are you going to be okay if I go into town for a couple hours?" Mom asks as she breezes through the living room. The woman has never worked a day in her life, but she never stops. If she's not cleaning or cooking, she's running into town. This errand. That meeting. This event. It never stops.

"I'll be fine," I answer, looking up from my book.

This morning she actually sat next to me for an hour trying to make plans for the rest of my summer. Inside I was screaming because, with the giant storm cloud hanging over my head, it's hard to plan any sort of future, especially if it involves fun.

"Your father has a trial today so he won't be home until late, but I'll fix us dinner when I get home. Is there anything you're hungry for?"

Clearing my throat, I look up at her anxiously. "Actually, Sam's going to pick me up after work and get me out of the house for a couple hours."

She stops picking up, or whatever she was doing, and glances over at me. "It's way too soon for you to be going out. You're supposed to be resting."

"Jesus, Mom, I'm not going out to the freaking bar."

Her lips part as she turns and focuses her attention out the window. I've never been a big drinker, but now that one night will forever define me. She's probably sat around wondering how many other times I've drank. How many times did I put the lives of others at risk? Honestly, that was the first time, and that's what's making it so hard to believe.

"There's somewhere I need to go," I whisper, waiting for her to turn back around.

When she does, her eyes are full of unshed tears. "I can take you. I have to decorate the church for the fundraiser this weekend, but that can wait."

Her defeated appearance softens me, at least enough to ease up on the battle—put my weapons away. "I'm sorry, Mom. I need to do this with Sam. It's hard to explain, but it's something I need." *My soul needs.*

"Okay." She nods, crossing her arms over her chest. "If you start to feel sick or weak, I want you to come home right away."

"He promised to have me home by eight."

Without another word, she disappears out the screen door with her purse in hand. It's always been my opinion that some people go to church because they believe, and others go to keep up appearances. For my mom, I think it's about social standing and companionship. It's an expectation fueled by her selfish need to be the best at everything. It's about belonging and being my dad's perfect wife. I, myself, have always gone because it was an expectation. I heard the sermons, but I didn't really listen. I was a believer who didn't understand exactly what it was she was supposed to believe in.

My family only prays when we have people over for dinner. My eyes have scanned past the Bible on the bookshelf many times, but I've never picked it up. We've never been forced to believe that a life exists after this one.

I've seen things through a different pair of glasses the last few weeks. I want Cory to be in a better place than this. It's the only thing that puts my mind at ease, keeping my guilt from boiling over. Belief is my salvation … my hope that there might some day be forgiveness, that maybe one day I'll get to join him where he's at.

My heart rate picks up the minute I hear Sam's old Camaro pull into my drive. That thing has always been like an alarm bell, alerting everyone in town to where he is or where he's heading. Today, it's just a sign that I'm one step closer to the goodbye I've waited weeks for.

I hear his heavy boots on the front porch right before he knocks on the screen door. "Come in!" I yell, smoothing down my long pink and cream printed skirt, which I paired with a matching pink tank. For this, I feel I should look nice, as if Cory might actually be able to see me … maybe he can.

Sam steps in with his hand braced against the door to keep it from slamming. He looks like he always does in faded blue jeans and a tight white T-shirt. It's simple, but he wears it well on his fit build. As soon as his eyes find me, the hint of a smile appears at the corner of his lips. "Suddenly, I feel underdressed, but you look nice. Are you going to tell me where I'm taking you?"

"The cemetery," I whisper, watching the easy-going expression fall from his face.

He nods, shoving his hands in his front pockets. He knows; that's what's so easy about being around Sam. He just gets me.

"Do you need some help getting out to the car?"

"Just an arm. My balance isn't quite right yet."

When he comes to stand in front of me, I grip the hand he offers and move to my feet with a small shoebox tucked under my arm. "Tell me if I'm going too fast."

We weave our way through the living room furniture and out the front door. I feel feather light with most of my weight being held by him. That's how our friendship's always been. He's always been strong when I've been weak. Sometimes I wonder if he has a tin coating around his heart, or if he just hides things well.

"Does your mom know where you're going?" he asks as we walk across the porch.

"She knows I'm with you. That's all she needs to know."

"I'm sure that put her mind at ease," he teases, helping me down the three front steps.

"Things aren't like they used to be when we were kids. I don't need anyone's permission."

He opens the passenger door, slowly lowering me in. "I guess not."

When he pulls my seatbelt across my lap, I grip his forearm, stopping him. "I can do that."

"I know," he says, pulling his arm back.

Sam's a protector, a doer. He takes what he wants because it's the only way he's going to get it. His father was always hard-nosed, not the nurturing type we all crave as kids. He didn't come home to fresh cookies after school or wake up to pancakes in the morning. He started working in his father's shop about the same time he entered elementary school, while other kids were busy watching cartoons and playing video games. I think that's what makes him different. His father made him fly before he even knew he had wings. I think Sam's tried to show me how to do the same a few times, but I'm not a quick study.

After my door clicks shut, I rest my forehead against the window and take in the smell of the old Camaro. I've only been in it one other time, and besides the loud roar of the engine, the distinctive smell is all I remember. It reminds me of my grandpa, a mixture of brut and peppermint. It doesn't sound all that great, but it's the most soothing smell in the world. It makes me wish Grandpa was still here to make this all better.

"Are you sure you're up for this?" he asks as he climbs into his seat and revs the engine.

"Cory is out there, and I need to show him that he's not alone. That I'm here," I say quietly, feeling the seat vibrate beneath me as he puts the car in drive.

He reaches over, his eyes finding mine as he brushes his finger against my jaw. "It's not your fault. I'm going to keep telling you that until I feel like you really believe it."

I don't believe him … not yet. Probably not ever. This summer could have been so different—time at the lake, barbeques, and long rides through the country with the windows down. Where I'm going now … this is my fault.

By the way his eyes narrow on me, I know he's seeing through me. "We're going to talk about this again. I promise you that," he says, turning the car onto the main road.

The ride is quiet as I watch familiar houses go by, but I'm not really paying attention to the details. It's a distraction, a way to look occupied. I need it to be this way so I can gather myself. *This isn't going to be easy*, I think to myself as I look down at the shoebox that sits on my lap … it's a box of memories I want to leave with Cory. It's going to hurt so freaking much, but I owe him a proper goodbye.

Every story has a beginning, middle, and end. Cory was supposed to be my middle and end. Now, I don't know what part he plays. Maybe my life was meant to be a series of short stories. And every story gets its own conclusion. This one doesn't have a happy ending … it ends in goodbye, and I want it to be perfect. I need him to know how much he meant to me. How much he still means to me.

It doesn't take long until we're pulling up next to the cemetery. It's tucked away in the trees on the outskirts of town, giving some solitude to mourners who need a quiet, tranquil place to say goodbye.

Closing my eyes, I cradle the shoebox and say a silent prayer. It's a call for strength, courage, and understanding, because this might be the hardest thing I've ever done in my life.

"Ready?" Sam asks, unbuckling his seatbelt.

"Yeah. I, ah, I just need help getting to his grave."

I chose Sam to bring me here because I knew he'd understand my need for space. People tend to think we need a shoulder when we're sad, but in my opinion, the only way to deal with sadness is to hit it head on.

My mom wouldn't have let me cry alone, but Sam gets it. He knows I need him here for support, but that I also need some space to mourn. I have things to say, things I don't want to share with anyone but Cory.

We make our way over to a large gray tombstone. This time, the weight builds in my chest, another heavy brick added with each step. Things are bad when you're not even sure you deserve a second chance. I'm ready to beg, to do whatever it takes so I can have one.

Seeing Cory's gravestone makes everything feel that much more real. I hadn't envisioned what it would look like, but it's simply stated.

CORY CONNORS
BELOVED SON, BROTHER AND FRIEND.
AUGUST 2, 1994 TO MAY 17, 2013

For days, I've thought about what I'd say to him in this moment, but now that I'm here, that's all washed away. Pain pierces my chest, down deeper than I imagined it ever could. The worst loss I've ever experienced is now in front of me, in full color, and I'd do anything to turn back time and put him right back in my arms where he belongs. Even if I could just see him, his smile and his boy-like dimples, everything would be so much better. I don't think I ever took him for granted because I always fought for him and gave him everything I had, but if I could have him back right now, I'd find a way to make things better.

I'd always say good morning with a smile on my face.

I'd end every argument with an 'I'm sorry' even if it wasn't mine to concede.

I'd kiss him in the need-you-want-you way at least once a day.

And I'd never fall asleep without saying good night. That's what this feels like ... going to sleep without a good night.

This is the reason why people hate goodbyes.

I kneel in front of the grave and look up at Sam whose own face looks like a mirror of my sadness. He was never Cory's biggest fan, but he has a heart. One that recognizes that someone lost his life too soon. I wonder if deep down inside he thinks it's my fault like everyone else but can see past it because of the close relationship we once shared. He knows the good parts of me and can forgive the bad.

"Can you give me a few minutes?"

He nods toward his car, taking a couple steps back. "I'll wait by my car. Signal when you're ready, and I'll help you back."

"Thanks," I whisper, turning to the grave. The ground around it still looks freshly dug, and a few flowers decorate the front ... they're his mom's favorite: white daisies. Thinking of his mom without him just causes another onslaught of tears.

"I miss you. Every day I tell myself that it will get better, but it doesn't. I wake up thinking about you. I spend my days thinking about how much I love you, and my nights fighting all of it. And when I'm trying to sleep, I drown in my own guilt because I'm the reason you're not here. I'm the reason your life was cut short, and there's not a damn thing I can do to change that."

Tears slip down along my chin. It's a hot, humid June day, but it might as well be raining.

Opening the shoebox, I eye its contents, second-guessing whether I want to leave them out here for the world to see and judge. In the end, I know I have to leave a piece of myself—a piece of us—with him. It's part of letting go. The first thing I pull out is the bracelet he bought for me after the first time we said 'I love you' to each other.

"I have something for you," he says, pulling a small white box from his front pocket.

My hand comes up to cover my mouth, holding back the girlish excitement that wants to escape. He slowly lifts the lid, giving me an eyeful of the simple silver bracelet it holds. The chain is thick with a plate nestled in the center that reads LOVE. It's beautiful.

"Can you put it on for me?" I ask, holding out my wrist.

"Do you like it?"

"No, I love it." I bite my lower lip to keep my smile from growing any bigger.

"There's something I want to show you first." Turning the
plate in his fingers he shows me the engraving on the back. It's
our initials C + R.

"It's perfect," I whisper, watching as he pulls the chain
against my wrist and clasps it between his fingertips.

*When he's done, he turns it so the plate is at the top. "When
I saw it, I thought of you. Now, when you see it, you'll think of
me."*

"I always think of you." Standing up on my tiptoes, I press
my lips to his cheek. It's the first time I've ever felt like our
future is forever.

The only time I took that bracelet off was to shower or swim.
It was just as much a part of me as he was, but I feel like it
belongs to him. So that it doesn't get swept away or stolen, I dig
up a small mound of dirt and drop it in before covering it up.

Next, I pull out a picture of us. Not just any picture, but a
copy of my favorite. It was the summer between our junior and
senior years, and we'd gone swimming with a group of friends.
I was in a royal blue bikini my mom warned me not to wear,
and he was in his black swim trunks. We both look happy, like
we could live out in the water for the rest of our lives and not
have a care in the world. It was when we were at our best,
before life started to get in our way. I prop it against his grave,
knowing it won't last long out in the elements, yet wanting him
to have it anyway.

Last is a promise in the form of a small diamond ring. He'd
given it to me on the evening of my eighteenth birthday, and at
the time, I thought the story of my life had been written. Cory.
Me. College. Wedding. House. Kids. At one point, it was all I
thought about.

"Are you coming?" he asks, laying a blanket out on his
truck bed.

*The night sky is clear, stars shining brightly, and the air
smells of fresh-cut grass. "Some of us have heels on,"* I reply
as I pull myself up on the tailgate to join him.

*"Well, some of us have a birthday present for our girlfriend
that we can't wait to give her."*

Cory hasn't forgotten one birthday or anniversary since we've been together, and I'm lucky, because he always puts thought behind his gifts.

He sits, patting the empty space between his legs. "Come here."

I crawl to him, stopping when I'm nestled safely between his legs. "You already bought me dinner."

He brushes my lower lip with his thumb before kissing me slowly. "That was just an appetizer," he whispers as he pulls back.

Reaching in his back pocket, he holds out a small black jewelry box. It's smaller than the one my bracelet came in a couple years before. My heart skips as I open it and see a small diamond ring shining back at me under the moonlight. "Cory!"

He pulls the ring out, visibly nervous as his eyes find mine. "That first night, when I asked you out, I didn't think it would lead us here. I didn't expect to find the girl I wanted to spend the rest of my life with so young, but I did. With this ring, I'm not asking for forever. It's a promise that someday I will, though. I can't imagine spending a single day without you."

My eyes gloss over as I search for words even half as meaningful as his. "The only thing I know I need in my future is you."

The words pale in comparison to his, but what does he expect when he leaves my brain a mangled mess.

"I love you," he whispers as he slides the gold band on my finger.

"I love you, too."

That night was unexpected, but I floated on a cloud for a long time afterward. And like everything else, I felt that promise fading when we entered college. We were out of our environment, and as we each started to find our own interests, we became less addicted to each other. For me, there was always hope, but now that he's gone, the hope and promise are both gone.

Digging another small hole, I drop the ring in next to the bracelet. In a perfect world, I would have left them inside his casket, so they could really be close to him, but this will have to do.

"I was wondering how long it would take you to come out here." I don't have to turn around to know who that voice belongs to. Cory's mom was never the easiest woman to get along with, but she loved her son. I could always see it in her eyes, in the little things she did for him. He was her pride and joy, and I took him away from her. "We didn't even get to see him after he died. It had to be a closed casket."

This is a small town, and it was inevitable that I'd run into her at some point, but I hadn't fully prepared myself for what I'd say. In fact, hearing her now, I'm scared to death. I took something invaluable from her, and if the roles were reversed, I'd be scared of me, too.

"I remember when he was a little boy. He used to run around in nothing but his diaper, a pair of cowboy boots, and a straw hat. He always had a huge smile on his face, especially when his daddy came home from work."

This isn't helping. I'm falling apart, piece by piece. I know Cory was loved. He had more friends than anyone else I know, and I didn't just lose him … I took him from them, too.

"A couple years ago, when he told me he thought you were the girl he was going to marry, I laughed. He was too young, had too much life to live, but he wouldn't hear it. I didn't think it would end like this."

Gathering up all the strength I have left in me, I turn to face her. She's a fraction of the woman she was before, thin and frail. Her long, dark hair is pulled back in a ponytail, and a trail of tears run down her pale cheeks. "I loved your son more than I loved anything else on this earth," I cry, covering my face with my hands. "This wasn't supposed to happen, and I'll never forgive myself because it did. I could say I'm sorry a million times over, but it won't bring him back."

I hear her shoes crunching against the dry grass as she steps closer. "Someday I hope I'll be able to forgive, but I can't do it with this much pain in my heart. It hurts too much right now."

I let my hands drop, looking up again. "If you never do, I'll understand, but I need you to know that I loved him. I wish … I wish I knew what happened that night. I wish I knew why I got behind the wheel of that car, but all I can do is say I'm sorry."

"I wish to God that was enough to bring him back," she cries, crossing her arms over her chest as if to chase away a chill.

"Me too."

She nods, swiping the back of her hand across her cheek. "I have a small box of things at home for you. I'll send them with your mom the next time I see her at church."

"You don't have to give me anything."

"I think it's all yours."

I'm imagining a box full of things I've given Cory over the years, another box full of memories that I'll have to go through and relive. "Thank you," I say softly, glancing behind my shoulder to read the words etched on his grave again.

"I'll let you finish what you came here to do," she says, walking away before I have a chance to reply.

I'm in shock. I figured she'd yell at me, and tell me what an awful person I am, but her subtle approach was worse. It makes my heart even heavier knowing how much I took from her. I can't replace him. There's nothing I can do to make it better.

I thought I could handle this, but it's too much at once. The cemetery. Goodbyes. Cory's Mom. Memories. I've had as much as I can take.

Looking at Sam, I wave my hand up in the air. He hops off his hood and quickly walks in my direction like he'd been holding himself back, waiting for my invitation. He's a protector, but he also knows how important it is for me to find my own strength. It's part of the healing process. It's what makes us come out of situations like this a better person than we were before. He knows it because he's been through his own trail of mud.

Turning back around, I press my palm to Cory's name and whisper, "I love you" one more time before Sam's feet appear beside me. His hands cradle my elbows, pulling me up from the ground, and when his face comes into view, I crumble into his arms. I don't know if it is minutes or hours, but we stay like that, his hands rubbing small circles against my back while I cry into his T-shirt.

"Are you going to be okay?" he finally asks.

"No." I want to say yes, but I'm not feeling it just yet. Time is all I really need right now.

CHAPTER *nine*

July 7, 2013

IT'S BEEN TWO WEEKS since I visited Cory's grave, and while I'm still having a hard time picturing myself living a normal life again, I haven't spent every single day crying. Little things I see or hear remind me of him. Memories are constantly being triggered. When that happens, I find a quiet place to think, to sort out the feelings that are whirling around inside me. For the rest of my life he'll always be a part of me. He'll always own some piece of me—one I can't get back or even want back.

For some reason, I'm here and he's gone, and instead of dwelling on the pain in my heart, I'm going to try to live a life that will make him proud. I'm going to figure it out … whatever it takes. Life doesn't always give you a second chance, so when it does, seize it. If you don't, you might always regret it.

After being stuck in this house with my mom, I'm realizing that the key to discovery doesn't lie inside here. I've never been much of a homebody, and if it weren't for books, I'd be going crazy with all the downtime. It merely gives me more time to think, and the more time I have to think, the more heartache I feel. I need to find a way to get out, or I'm going to find myself falling into a deeper dark hole. I don't think anyone would blame me, but I was saved to do more than that.

I'm hoping that a trip to the field today will begin to fill the emptiness inside me. It was once my happy place. Maybe it can cure me again.

"Rachel, I'm leaving!"

"Okay. I probably won't be here when you get back," I say, avoiding her steely blue eyes.

She stops, turning toward me. "Where are you going?"

"Sam's going to pick me up."

"You've been hanging out with him an awful lot lately. Do you really think that's a good idea?"

Sighing, I sit slowly, bracing my hands on the arm of the couch. "Give me one reason why it isn't a good idea." I stare into her eyes, daring her to deny me this little bit of freedom. Besides, I'm twenty, so there's not much she can say about what I do or who I hang out with.

"Maybe you should call up Madison and see if she has plans. You need to find a way to get back to your old life."

"Madison's been busy with work and summer classes. Besides, Sam is part of my past, too."

She rolls her eyes, but doesn't say anything else as she pulls her purse from the table by the door and disappears outside. She wanted to argue with me—it was written on her face—but she knows I'm not the girl I used to be. I'm not going to smile. I'm not going to put on some nice clothes and walk around town like nothing's wrong so she can brag about all the good things I've done when all I can think about is the bad.

Glancing up at the clock, I see I have a few minutes before Sam arrives. I haven't seen him since he took me to Cory's grave. For a couple of days after, I retreated inside myself, staying in my room and listening to slow, sad songs—turns out they're the kind that make tears fall faster. I swear the melodies and words—draped in a cloak of meaningful sadness—draw emotions out of me with magnetic force.

We've texted back and forth every evening, and when he mentioned last night that he wanted to take me out to the fields, I felt the workings of a smile on my lips. It's a place full of butterflies and tall grass, a place where a person can hide amongst the better things in life.

A place that feels more like home than any other place I've ever been.

He knew I wouldn't tell him no … I knew I couldn't tell him no. Maybe it was a cheap trick, but it doesn't matter to me.

When I hear the purr of Sam's engine coming toward my house, I slip on my flip-flops and tighten the bun at the top of my head. Wanting to surprise him, I get to my feet and walk to the old screen door just in time to see him coming up the sidewalk. As soon as he sees me, a smile lights up his face, and he takes the steps two at a time to get to me quicker.

"Looking good," he says, standing on the opposite side of the screen.

"Wait until you see my real tricks. This is nothing."

He laughs, running his fingers through his longish blond hair. It separates him from most of the other guys in town. He's not the clean-cut guy you bring home, but more like the guy you'd see behind the drums of a grunge rock band. But what really sets him apart is his eyes. Soulful. Chocolate brown. Luring. "Should I get an ambulance on standby?"

I shrug. "Probably not a bad idea since you're driving."

Opening the door, he steps a little closer, fingering one of my large hoop earrings. "You really do look good, like there's less weight on your shoulders."

"I've cried enough tears this week to last me ten lifetimes. I decided I could either sit in my room and work on my eleventh, or get out of this house for a couple hours. I choose the latter."

"Did you have dinner?" he asks, letting go of my earring.

"No. I haven't had much of an appetite."

"That's going to change tonight. You're too skinny the way it is." He stands back and holds the door open for me as I breeze on past. When I get to the stairs, I hold the railing tight and take them slowly knowing he's standing right behind me. "You've come a long way in a just a couple weeks."

"Give me a few more and I'll be ready to run a marathon."

"Maybe we should try a 5k first and see how that goes."

"Have a little faith," I say, patting my hand against his chest before climbing into the Camaro.

He shuts my door and runs in front of the car to the driver's side. I've never seen anyone move so quickly to get from one spot to another. "Ready?" he asks as he climbs in and rests his arm along the top of the seat to peer out the back window.

"I've been waiting all day," I say, crossing my arms over my chest. "I could probably walk, you know."

"Fuck that. Besides, I don't have to carry our dinner this way."

As he puts the car in reverse, I relax into my seat. Within a few months, they'll be harvesting the corn from the fields that surround my house, but for now, they turn the roads into a maze, making it almost impossible to see anywhere but straight ahead.

The grass field Sam and I go to is different. It's a serene, secluded place where the grass is never mowed. When the corn's not so high, it's easy to see from the road but this time of year, it's impossible.

Sam pulls onto a dirt drive and slowly eases his car around potholes that have developed from the spring rain. As the fields come into focus, it all comes back to me again. It's a sizeable lush green area, with a small grove of trees in the center and a creek that runs along one edge. It's a little piece of heaven smack dab in the middle of Iowa.

"Does it look like you remembered?" he asks, slowing to a stop.

"Almost exactly."

I look over to see him smiling. "That's the best part of nature," he says, "it doesn't change unless we change it. In one hundred years, it would still look the same."

"Maybe that's what makes it feel so special. It outlasts all of us. I wonder how many people have had this as *their* place?" I ask.

He shrugs, gripping the door handle. "Others may have been out here before, but it belongs to us now."

Mr. Bryant, a farmer who lives between Sam and me, has owned this land for as long as I can remember. He rarely uses it, but I think he's afraid of what might happen to it if he sells it. Maybe it has the same type of hold on him that it has on us. At least he doesn't seem to mind us being out here.

"Let's get out of this hot car. I heard the fields are even better when you can feel the grass against your feet," Sam says. The corners of his eyes crinkle from the huge smile that forms on his face.

I can't help the little dance that goes on inside me as I open my door and step outside. The air smells of wild grape blossoms and freshly baled hay with a hint of the horses that graze in the distance. The grass tickles my feet as I stretch my arms up in the air. It really is the best place on Earth … the best one I've been to anyway.

"Should we eat in the shade?"

The sun's already heating my skin after being outside for a matter of seconds. In July, Iowa's as hot as it is serene, but I don't mind the summer air. "Sounds good to me."

"Good girl. I didn't want to start our first argument in over five years."

A smile touches my lips. As much as Sam and I always enjoyed spending time together, we also had some pretty good arguments. I blamed it on the fact that we're both only children; we didn't have many options for petty arguments. "I kind of miss those."

"It's only a matter of time," he says, pulling a blue cooler from the backseat. "I hope you still like bologna."

"You better be kidding, Sam Shea."

"You know I don't make the same mistake twice."

As I follow him to the spot between the trees, I remember the summer I was eleven and Sam was fourteen. We'd gotten in the habit of taking turns bringing food out so we wouldn't have to hurry home when we got hungry. It was going well—a steady rotation of peanut butter and jelly, cheese and turkey sandwiches—but then one night Sam decided to surprise me with bologna. That was the last time I went out that summer without packing a snack, and he's held my bologna fear over my head since.

When we're under the trees, Sam lays out an old, blue fleece blanket, smoothing out the edges. "Where would you like to sit tonight?"

"Hmm, I think I'll take the spot closest to the water."

"I should have guessed. That's our most popular seat."

As I take my spot, a little part of me wonders if he's ever taken anyone out here … to our spot. I've never had any claim on him. Maybe it's just this place that makes me feel this way.

After we're both comfortably seated, he lifts the lid from the cooler and pulls out two water bottles, handing me one. I unscrew the cap and bring the cold plastic up to my lips as I watch Sam pull out two sandwiches and a container of strawberries. I can practically taste them on my tongue; there's nothing better than the red, sweet fruit this time of year.

"I picked them from the garden this morning."

I curl my hands into fists, doing everything I can to not pull the container from his fingers. If I wanted to, I could easily eat them all by myself.

"You're showing more self-control than I remember," he jokes, pulling one of the strawberries from the container. I watch as he takes most of it into his mouth and bites down, closing his eyes. He's a master at teasing.

"Shouldn't we eat our sandwiches first?" I ask.

He shrugs, using the back of his hand to wipe the sweet juice from his lips. "It's all a matter of preference."

"Pass those over here," I say, reaching my hand out.

"What do you say?"

"Hand them over."

He shakes his head, his lips pressing into a close-lipped smile.

"May I please have a strawberry?"

"Since you asked nicely." He grabs two more berries from the container and passes it to me, a smug look on his face.

"Thank you." I waste no time pulling my first berry out and sinking my teeth into it.

The only sounds I hear are the tall grass blowing in the wind, and the occasional crinkling of plastic bags as we eat every bit of food that Sam brought with him. There's nothing extravagant about it, but it's more than I've eaten in weeks, and it tastes like five-star cuisine. The turkey is flavored with maple, and the wheat bread is freshly made by our local bakery; I'd recognize it anywhere.

"You're quiet over there," Sam says, breaking through the tranquility.

Closing my eyes, I breathe in the air that blows off the creek. The smell has the same effect as the medicine they gave me in the hospital, to calm me but without the drowsiness. "It's nice just to be out here. Almost like the last five years never happened."

"But they did," he says softly, brushing the hair from my face.

"And up until that last day, they were all worth it. Even though I lost him."

I haven't talked about Cory much since that day in the cemetery. I think my parents believe that the sadness and misery will all go away if we don't talk about it. That may be true, for them, but some days I feel it all building up, weighing heavier on my chest. All I've really needed is to talk about it, bring it to the surface. That's what we all need when we're drowning.

"I'm here if you need me," he says, leaning back on his elbows. The position showcases the muscles in his arms and his strong chest. It would be so easy to fall against him and cry a puddle of tears on his blue T-shirt, but it doesn't feel right. For so long it was Cory's responsibility to catch me when I fell … I'm not ready to let go of that. Sometimes I wonder if I ever will be.

Sam's eyes never leave mine. He surveys me like one might an abstract painting, but I hide behind the lines. Sometimes it's easier that way, but I know it won't take Sam long to figure me out. He sees the shapes of my emotion and the color of my heart. He sees all of me.

I lie back on the blanket, tucking my hands under my head. A breeze blows overhead, but it feels good against my damp skin. "I miss him," I whisper, swallowing the lump in my throat.

"What do you miss most?"

Surprised, I turn my head, looking up at him. "You don't really want to hear this, do you? You weren't exactly his biggest fan."

"If it's going to help you, I do."

I look back up, getting an eyeful of the green leaves that grow on the mature trees that surround us. With Sam, I've always opened up. He's heard my thoughts and feelings and never judged me for anything.

Bringing my eyes back down, I see the sincerity in his eyes. He really wants to hear this … to help me through the fog I've been lost in. I swallow down the lump in my throat and let the words trickle out. "His smile. It always made things better, and now, things are as bad as they've ever been, and I don't have the one thing I need to fix it."

"Do you remember the day when we first ran into each other out here?"

I nod, waiting to hear what this has to do with Cory.

"Dad and I had just moved here, and I thought this place was hell. I never thought I'd be happy or any semblance of it … until we started meeting out here. Sometimes you just need someone to show you that there's more than one right way to live your life. More than one way to be content."

"I've been thinking about that a lot lately, and I don't think that can happen for me until I let go of my old life," I reply, pulling my hair between my fingers. "I feel like everything around me fell apart, and I have nothing to pick up the pieces with."

He uses his finger to lift my chin, allowing me to look nowhere but at him. "I promise you, it'll get better. I'll make it better."

"Don't make promises you can't keep, Sam."

His finger drops from my chin, and his thumb brushes against my cheek. The way he looks at me reminds me so much of that day out here before the start of my freshman year … when I thought he was going to kiss me. "I'm not. I plan on keeping this one."

He shifts his eyes between mine, but the only way I can respond is to cross my arms over my chest and look out onto the water. His intensity, the hint of lust in his stare, are too much for me right now. Besides that, I don't have the heart to tell him that it may not be him who doesn't follow through on his promise … I may not let him fix this because it's what I deserve.

"Do you remember when we used to get our feet wet by sticking them in the creek?" I ask, needing a change in subject.

"Yeah." His eyebrow shoots up like he thinks I've lost my mind, or I'm about to anyway.

"Let's do it."

He grins, nodding his head toward the water. "If we're going in, we're going all in."

A challenge is something I've never backed down from, and I feel like that's what he's doing right now. Standing, I kick off my flip-flops and walk to the bank of the creek. The water's not quite as clear as I remembered it, but I can still see the rocks along the shallow edges.

Glancing back, I see Sam standing a few feet behind me with his hands on his hips. He's probably thinking there's no way in hell I'm going to do this, but I'm going to enjoy every second of proving him wrong. After shooting him one last look, I take two small steps into the lukewarm water. It only goes up to my thighs, not quite touching the bottom of my cut-off shorts.

"You coming in, Shea?"

"My shorts aren't as short as yours."

"Afraid to get a little wet?" I tease, splashing a handful of water at him.

He pulls his bottom lip between his teeth and takes two quick steps to the edge of the creek. "There's only one thing I'm afraid of, and this little creek isn't it."

With one more step, he's standing in front of me. Close enough, I can feel him there, but far enough to give me space so it's not uncomfortable.

"What are you scared of then?"

His eyes burn into mine. "Something that happened once. Something that I'm not going to let happen again."

"And what's that?"

"When I'm not afraid anymore, I'll tell you," he says, brushing a piece of my wind-blown hair from my face.

"You've always been on the mysterious side."

"If I were any other way, you wouldn't want anything to do with me."

"Why's that?"

"What fun would I be if you had me all figured out? Besides, not saying everything I think keeps me one step below arrogance." That makes me laugh. Sam had a male meltdown one day when he started high school, all because some girl called him arrogant. He went on and on about how she had him mixed up with the jocks, or she didn't know the meaning of arrogance. Maybe he just comes off as too good because he's secretive about his life; he doesn't talk to a lot of people unless he has to. I don't necessarily think it's a bad thing but he's definitely not arrogant.

"I guess you're right."

"Of course I am." His hand comes down, lightly smacking my rear end. I jump, and he smiles—the kind that makes all the girls think he's the overly confident guy he's not. His expression reminds me of the old Sam who used to be the cure for any heart ailment.

"I can't believe you just did that," I squeal, stepping away from him.

"Woke you up, didn't I?" His lips quirk even higher. It's contagious, no matter how annoyed I am with him.

"I didn't realize I was sleeping."

His grips my wrist, tugging my arm. "Are we going to stand here and talk, or are you really going all in?"

Looking down at the water and my dry clothes, I decide against it. "This is it for tonight."

He steps up on the bank, holding my hands to help me out of the water. His skin is warm and clammy against mine, but I can't let go. He's the only piece of security I have left.

Being with him also makes me feel more like my old self. Like maybe everything my life revolved around the last several years wasn't taken away … just thinking like that makes the familiar guilt come back.

"I should probably get back home," I say, carefully pulling my hands out of his.

He glances back, his eyes trying to read mine. Sometimes when he does stuff like that, I feel things I don't know if I should be feeling. It's different than looking into anyone else's eyes, I guess, and with the way he's touched me today, I feel uneasy. Like this is all too much, too soon.

"Are you okay?" he asks.

"Yeah," I lie. "I just haven't been out much yet, and I'm getting tired."

He watches me a little while longer, then nods, walking back to the blanket. "Why don't you go sit in the car, and I'll grab this stuff."

"I can help," I reply, tossing the empty containers into the picnic basket.

He shakes his head. "You've always been stubborn."

"I wouldn't be any fun if I always did what I'm supposed to do."

Neither of us says another word as we finish cleaning up, or on the quick drive back to my house. I like the short moment of silence because it allows me to separate my thoughts into safe little compartments. Tonight, I feel more normal than I have in weeks, and the only thing holding me back from really, truly enjoying it is my guilt. And just like that, with too much time to think, my mind drifts away. Should I be out having fun when Cory can't do the same? Do I deserve a night like this?

I'm so lost in my own little world of thought that I don't realize we're in front of my house until I hear Sam shift into park. "Am I going to see you again soon?"

Shaking my head, I ask, "What are we doing, Sam?"

"I just want to be your friend." His voice is low, but sure, with absolutely no hesitation.

"Is that all this is?" I stare at him, but he looks straight ahead. I'd do just about anything to see his eyes, to receive some of the easy comfort they give me.

His face finally shows, the corner of his lips turned upward. If only I could believe it when I look up into his eyes. "It has to be, doesn't it?"

I nod, biting my lower lip. There's more I want to say, more I want to explain, but it's been a long day. "I'll call you."

"I'll be waiting."

As I shift to open the door, his fingers wrap around my forearm, halting me in place. "Take care of yourself."

"I will," I say, forcing out an artificial smile. "And thank you for tonight. It meant a lot."

He winks, letting me go. "Only for you."

CHAPTER ten

WHEN I WALK IN the house, there's a box waiting on the table, my name scribbled on the top in thick, black permanent marker. I slowly walk up to it, like it might explode if I make a single sound on the old hardwood floors. I just stare at it, unable to bring myself to actually look inside. For God knows how long, I stand there, lightly tracing my finger over each letter of my name. I know exactly where it came from; I've been waiting for it since I saw Cory's mom in the cemetery, but finally having it in front of me fills me with an incredible amount of angst.

Being this close, running my finger over every curve, I can practically hear Cory's voice saying my name in his low, husky way. Having something that came from him—his house— makes me feel close to him yet again. It's a feeling that can't last forever because time steals away the powerful emotions that arise from our memories.

When I come back to reality, I push against the cardboard to gauge how heavy it is. Realizing I can carry it, I pick it up and bring it to my room. Once it's there, beside my bed, I just stare at it again. From the interest I've taken in it, one might think it is something more than a plain box—a plain box that came from Cory's house with my name scribbled on top.

Maybe I should be more anxious to open it right away, but I'm too nervous about what's inside. Is it just a bunch of Cory's things his mom thought I should have, or is it something else?

Feeling tired and worn out, I decide to save it for the morning.

As I wake up, I stretch my arms up and the first thing that crosses my mind is the box. I fell asleep last night thinking about it. It only makes sense that it would be the first thing on my mind this morning.

I wait until my mom leaves to run her daily errands in order to avoid any interruptions. No matter what's inside, I'm going to feel it. It's going to bring memories to the forefront that I've slowly begun to bury ... there's no way around that.

Sitting on the floor, I pull the box in front of me and carefully rip the tape that holds the top together. I hesitate, knowing that what's inside is probably going to pour salt into a wound that's just begun to heal. Yesterday was the first time life felt like a shadow of normal, and I don't want to lose everything I've gained.

My fingers tremble as I reach inside, ready for whatever it holds for me ... ready as I'm ever going to be anyway.

The first thing I pull out is a stack of pictures carefully tied together by a rubber band. Quickly thumbing through, I notice most are copies of photos I already have. Ones I'd taken of the good times we shared in the four plus years we were together. The only one I don't recognize is one of Madison and myself in our caps and gowns on graduation day. Cory must have taken that one when I wasn't looking.

Reaching in again, I come up with a stack of old notes and cards. That was the way I preferred to communicate my feelings to him when we were in high school. Immaturity can cause a person to do some stupid stuff, and we both did our fair share.

I unfold a piece of notebook paper and read the bubbly script written in the purple pen that was my favorite.

> *Cory*
>
> *I'm sorry about last night. I didn't mean to upset you by taking a ride home from Sam, but you were drinking and wouldn't listen to me. I hope you'll talk to me soon because I can't stand it when you don't.*
>
> *I love you.*
> *Rachel*

I remember that day like it was yesterday. Cory drank a little too much at a party, and when I begged him to let me drive him home, he refused. I was tired and pissed off, so when Sam showed up and offered to give me a lift home, I jumped at the chance. It seemed innocent enough … I trusted Sam. He'd been one of my best friends for years.

And that was all it was. Sam took me home; it was the first and only time I'd been in Sam's Camaro during high school. I learned quickly how big of a deal that was for Cory, that I'd taken a ride in someone else's car—especially Sam Shea's. I never did it again. Looking back, I should have stood my ground. It was selfish of Cory to essentially make me cut him out of my life. It was pathetic of me to let him.

Next, I pull out a sweatshirt with our high school mascot, The Wildcat, on the front and Cory's basketball number on the back. He had it made for me with my last name scrolled across the back. I wore it all the time but must have forgotten it at his house at some point. It still smells just like him—a mixture of faint spice and citrus cologne and fabric softener. I used to bury my head in the crook of his neck and inhale it until the scent was permanently stuck in my nose. Thinking about it now brings tears to my eyes … those moments are when I felt the calmest. He was a familiarity. He was my home.

After wiping my eyes, I reach to the bottom of the box and find a lacy black bra that I don't recognize as mine. It's confirmed when I look at the size on the tag. My mind races in a bunch of different directions, but I tell myself it's nothing. It must belong to one of his sisters, or maybe it's his mom's way of getting even with me for killing her son. As much as I try to convince myself, I know that not even his mom is that callous. She's got too much going on inside her own head to do something like this. And his sisters—they're tinier than me, so the chance of this belonging to them is slim.

Still, I have to believe that this is some sort of mistake. I have to believe that because my sanity can't afford to take another blow. In my mind, Cory's always been on a pedestal … I want to keep him there. He's earned it after what I did.

For the second night in a row, Sam and I are spending time together out in the field. It's relaxing and serene in the daylight, but at night, it's even better. The cricket song is lulling, and while we can't see the black creatures in the darkness, they provide a sense of companionship. It's the most peaceful thing in the world if you stop to think about it.

"Are you okay? You're kind of quiet tonight." Sam's voice breaks through the beautiful song nature's creating.

"I just have a lot on my mind, trying to decide what's real and what's not. It's exhausting." I haven't stopped thinking about the last item I pulled from the box this morning. It might be nothing … it's probably nothing … but I can't stop thinking about it.

"Anything I can do to help?"

"No. This I just need to sort out on my own."

Everything goes still, neither of us moving. It's good until I start to think too much … that's when my heart turns a deep, cold shade of blue. It's when I wonder if I really had everything I thought I did or if I was just clinging onto something I should have let go of a long time ago. It's when a distraction is the only way to escape my thoughts.

"I love that sound," I whisper, scooting closer until our shoulders touch, just barely. It's how I know he's still here when we're lying quietly, listening to the sounds that surround us in the darkness.

"Me too," Sam says, resting the side of his head along the top of mine. "Do you see the fireflies up there?"

"Yeah." A few of them glow up above us. It makes me think back to when I was a little girl. I used to try to catch them in my hands to see them glow up close. Now, I'm content just to look from afar. They're amazing little creatures.

"The light they shine is supposed to bring us back to life, to give us hope."

Wrapping my fingers around his, I ask, "What makes you say that?"

"It's just something I read once. Their light illuminates from the inside out. It takes a lot of strength on their part."

"I'm trying to find the strength. I really am." All I've been thinking about since this morning are the contents of that box. For the most part, it contained what I expected, but it also reminded me that things weren't always perfect. Our relationship was filled with so many moments that made me smile, but there were also struggles. Ones I tried to bury under a big, heavy rug so no one would see them ... so I wouldn't see them. What if those struggles were bigger than I even realized?

"If anyone can do it, you can. I'm going to do whatever I have to in order to make sure you find it, even if I have to give it to you. I'd give you the whole fucking world if I could."

His words steal my breath away because I think he might be the only person left on Earth who wants to give me the world. "Thank you for being here. Everyone else treats me like I have a contagious disease or something. Madison doesn't even come around anymore."

Sam is surprisingly quiet. I expected him to tell me she'll come around, but he doesn't. Maybe he knows I'm fighting a battle with my old friends that I'll never be able to win. Maybe he knows some of the friendships I had in high school were as real as the many silk flowers that decorate the cemetery.

"Do you want something to drink?" he finally asks, sitting up next to the small cooler he'd brought out with him.

"What do you have?"

"Water and Bud Light."

"I'll take a water. Thank you." A couple months ago I would have enjoyed a cold beer on a warm summer night like tonight. I don't know if I'll ever touch alcohol again for as long as I live.

He hands me a cold water and holds up a can of beer. "You don't care if I have one of these, do you?"

"You're twenty-three years old. You can do whatever you want."

"I just don't want to upset you."

"As long as you don't drive home, you're fine."

He pops the tab off his beer, then everything goes quiet again. For some reason, his silence bothers me tonight.

"Sam, what did you do after high school? I mean … we lost touch, and I feel like there's a part of you I know nothing about." I hate myself for letting it happen, but it was either him or Cory. Neither of them was going to let me have the other.

He lies back beside me, one hand wrapped around his beer can and the other resting on his flat stomach. "I've been running the shop full-time, and when the opportunity comes, I meet up with a couple of guys at the bar." His warm breath tickles my cheek, sending a prickle down my spine. I'm not sure if it's because I've missed the closeness of someone else so much or if it's him. "Honestly, it fucking sucks. Everyone should have a purpose … I don't know what mine is yet."

"For what it's worth, I'm glad you're here."

His finger brushes my cheekbone, his eyes lifting to get a better look into mine. "I'm glad you're here, too. I just wish it were under different circumstances."

"Me too," I whisper, pulling my bottom lip between my teeth. The way he stares at me makes me uneasy. It's too much—too intimate for the place I'm at in life. If it weren't for the accident, Sam and I would still be living like strangers. It's sad to think about it.

Pushing up to a sitting position, I twist the cap off my water and take a long drink. Most girls would dream about this kind of night with a guy like Sam, but I don't deserve to be that girl. I wouldn't be ready to be that girl even if I felt like I deserved it. I'm too closed off inside to let anyone in, especially in the way Sam deserves.

"I should probably walk back home."

"I'll walk with you."

I shake my head, even though I know he can't see me well in the darkness. "I need some time to clear my head."

"Rachel—"

"I'll text you when I get home ... I promise."

He sighs deeply, running his fingers through his mussed-up blond hair. "If I don't hear from you in the next twenty minutes, I'm coming to check on you."

"I wouldn't expect anything less from you," I say, standing and stretching my arms up above my head. It was over ninety degrees today, but since the sun has gone down, it's been tolerable.

"Am I going to see you tomorrow?" he asks, standing beside me. His hand comes to rest on my hip, lightly brushing the exposed skin between my shorts and shirt. My skin is warm, but his touch still feels hot against it. It would be so easy for him to pull me to him. So easy.

"I'll call you," I reply, tucking loose strands of hair behind my ear.

Under the faint moonlight, I see a half-smile touch his lips. Relief ... I've seen it a few times before. "You better," he says, letting go of me.

Without another word, I turn and walk down the path that leads back to my house. The corn is getting higher by the day, but I'm still able to see over the top. I still hear the crickets, but other than that, the night is quiet.

It gives me time to think, to reflect on the last couple months ... tonight especially. Sam is literally everything I need, and everything I shouldn't have. The way he always finds a way to touch me—the way my body reacts to it—is confusing the hell out of me. It doesn't feel right, but it's not conscious. I don't want to like Sam in that way. Maybe it's just my loneliness begging me to let him in. Whatever it is, it's making me crazy.

Someday, I'm going to wake up with a clearer vision and conscience. It's just not happening today or tomorrow, but it has to happen sometime, or the rest of my life will be pointless. A life without hope is a life without purpose. I need hope.

As I approach the spot where my yard meets the cornfield, my eyes are drawn to the tall light next to the old red barn. It's been there all my life, but something about it stops me in my tracks tonight. A strange, yet terrifying scene plays out, almost like it's happening right in front of me.

Glancing around the unfamiliar field, I see the light of the fire up ahead. Instead of running to it, I run away. Fast, like I'm trying to get away from something or someone. My body is filled—no, more like consumed—with panic and sadness. I have no idea why, but I feel it deep within my bones. A painful ache.

I hear my name. I recognize the voice as Cory's, but instead of stopping, I run faster. My cheeks are wet, and my hands are shaking. My feet are scratched up from stepping on the short cornstalks with only flip-flops on my feet, but I want to get away.

What I don't understand is why I'm intent on getting away from Cory. Why would I run from the one person I want to run to?

Shaking my head, I try to chase the scene from my mind. I want to think it was nothing but a terrifying daydream, but I was wearing the same outfit I remember wearing the last day of school. And it felt so real, like I was reliving a memory. I just wish I knew what it all meant. I wish to God that I knew why I'd run from Cory.

I hope it's not real. I hope it's just my mind playing tricks on me.

CHAPTER *eleven*

August 3, 2013

THERE ARE TIMES IN life where I've felt like I'm standing above everything, watching it all go by, but then there are times when life has completely run me over. It's come at me too fast, not giving me time to think. Sometimes great things come from it, but sometimes, it comes through like a tornado, leaving a pile of rubble in its wake.

That's where I'm standing now, in the midst of the rubble that the accident has left behind. I need to figure out how I'm going to pick up the pieces, and where my life goes from here. All I know is I don't have the energy to rebuild just yet. It's something only time can put back together.

Until I get to that point, I'm going to do my best to step over anything that gets in my way. And it never hurts to have someone holding your hand when you have obstacles to cross ... that's what Sam's done for me. He's been there for me while others I thought I was close to left me behind. I guess the only way to know if you have a true friendship is to see if it still exists after it's been tested.

Sam has this idea that I should join him in his woodworking shop for a few hours to relax. My first thought was no way, but the more I thought about it, the more I realized that just being with him would make me feel better. He makes life somewhat normal for me.

When I woke up this morning, I felt excitement that I hadn't felt in days. Life's nothing but a dark hole when you don't have anything to look forward to, but today I see a little bit of light for the first time in a few weeks. Since the last night Sam and I spent in the fields, I've been feeling out of sorts. Mostly because of the vision I had on the way back to my house. Was it a piece of the truth I'd been working so hard to remember? Whatever it was, I haven't been able to let it go. I think about it first thing every morning and again every night before bed … I hate it.

I crawl out of bed and make my way to the closet, pulling out a pair of jeans and a navy blue tank top. I wash my face and layer on some moisturizer, deciding there's no point in putting on make-up, and tie my hair into a knot.

I quietly make my way down the stairs, hoping to make it out the door without a barrage of questions from my mom. I love the woman and everything she does for me, but her constant inquisition in regards to Sam pisses me off. I don't need anything to tarnish my lighter mood today. I carefully make my way into the kitchen to grab the muffins I made last night and slip onto the back porch to put on my shoes.

"Where are you off to so early?" It's not Mom this time. It's after eight, and for the first time since I can remember, Dad's still home, wearing jeans and a Southern Iowa T-shirt. Something is very wrong with this picture.

"I'm going to help a friend," I say, looking down at my tattered shoelaces. I just want to get outside … to Sam.

"And what exactly does that mean?"

This is going to be worse than Mom's interrogations. My dad has a hard time remembering when he's not in the courtroom. He forgets that we're not all part of a case he's trying in front of a judge and jury. "I need to get out of the house, so a friend offered to take me to work with him today, to help out."

Looking up, I plead with my eyes for him to just walk away. Dad never does anything other than what he wants to do, though, so it's not a surprise when he crosses his arms over his chest and takes another step toward me. "I'm moving things around in the office today so my new intern has room. Why don't you help?"

"Daddy, I can't. I've already committed to something else."

He nods and smiles softly. It's a rare occasion. "You've always been one to keep your word. I guess I have to respect that."

Just as he's about to walk away, a familiar, extremely loud engine starts up the driveway. Dad steps to the kitchen window and then looks back at me, his cheeks bright red. "What the hell are you doing, Rachel?"

I flinch, wondering why things can't be easy for just a day. Why couldn't they allow me a day tucked away without a worry in the world? I guess I'm not meant to make it anywhere without a struggle. "He's just a friend."

"I'm sure you can find someone better to hang out with than the Shea boy."

"There's nothing wrong with Sam. In fact, he's the only person who's not treating me like a virus."

"No one's treating you like a virus, Rachel!" His voice rises as he throws his arms up in the air. "We're just worried about you."

I stand, watching out the window as Sam opens his car door and starts up the narrow sidewalk. This isn't going to end well.

When I don't reply, he starts in on me again. I do my best to listen, to actually hear what he's saying, but I'm too lost in what's going to happen when my dad and Sam collide. "When you make decisions, you need to do it with your future in mind. I know you think I worry too much about what other people think, but when you live in a town as small as this, sometimes that's all that matters."

"And would you mind telling me what Sam did to end up on the town trash list? Because I must have missed it."

Dad opens his mouth but is interrupted by a knock at the front door. I'm half expecting him to turn and try to beat me to it, but he surprises me by pushing past me and walking out the back door. It's the last thing I expected out of him; he never backs away from a battle.

Taking a deep breath, I grab my muffins off the counter and head to the front door, opening it just as Sam's about to knock again.

"Hey," he says, looking at me warily. "Are you okay?"

"Just a little morning chat with my Dad. You know how that goes," I reply, waiting for him to step back so that I can close the door behind me. As soon as he does, I make my way down the steps as quickly as possible. We need to get out of here before anyone else pours vinegar on my morning ... the only thing that would make the start to this day worse is if my mom walked out the front door to finish what my dad started.

As my fingers curl against the handle of the passenger door, Sam's hand comes to rest along the top of the car, stopping me in my place. "The whole reason I'm taking you to work today is to have some fun, so whatever you have going on ... leave it here."

"Once we get there, I'll be fine. I just need to be anywhere but here."

He removes his hand from the car, running the back of his finger along my jawline. "What did he say that's got you so upset?"

"Let's just leave that one alone." It would probably be no surprise to him that my dad's not going to jump on the Sam train, but something about admitting it seems off to me.

"It was about me, wasn't it?" he asks, tilting his head to the side.

"Maybe," I say quietly, staring down at his brown work boots. He's still caressing my cheek; it's soothing yet distracting. I want him to stop, but then I don't.

His finger moves beneath my chin, bringing my eyes up to his bright brown ones. "Yeah, what did he say?"

Swallowing down the lump in my throat, I try my best to pull sugarcoated honesty out from within. Sam's heard this over and over since he moved to this town years ago, but I hate that the words have to come out of my lips. "I shouldn't be hanging out with that Shea boy."

To my surprise, his lips curl. "You should probably tell your daddy that I'm not a boy anymore."

I can't help but smile at that. "I think anyone under the age of thirty is a boy to him."

"I have almost seven years left until I reach manhood, huh?" He laughs, cupping my cheeks in his hands. I stare up at his eyes, unable to look anywhere else. His smile fades. My heart races. His breath whispers against my lips. Being with him would be so easy ... I feel it when he touches me, when he looks at me. I'm just not ready. Maybe I never will be.

Wrapping my hands around his wrists, I pull his hands from my face. There was more than one connection that needed to be broken. "Can we get out of here? I'm trying to avoid getting the same speech from my mom."

He reaches his hand up like he's going to touch me again but quickly pulls it back, smiling. This is too much for me, and I think he knows it. "Let's go before your mom catches you with the town bad boy."

He starts walking backward toward the front of the car, and all I can do is stare, wondering what just happened. Maybe it's my tired, worn out imagination playing tricks on me. That whole line between reality and fiction is blurred again. It's blurry a lot lately.

When he reaches the driver's side, I open my door and climb inside. Five minutes was all it took for Sam to turn my mood from upset to happy to confused. I need a distraction from this messed up state of mind.

"So what are we making today?" I ask as I buckle my seatbelt.

"Well, I think we're going to make the king of all toy boxes. Think you can handle that?"

"I almost had straight A's in high school. As long as I have a good teacher, anything is possible."

He laughs, the deep throaty kind that breathes honesty. "I've heard he's pretty good."

I lift the lid on the Tupperware container I've been holding, letting the smell of fresh muffins fill the old Camaro. "I wanted to make a good impression on my new boss so I brought him breakfast. Do you think he likes blueberries?"

"Hmm. I've heard that he does." He grins, glancing at me from the corner of his eye as we turn into his driveway.

As we drive down the long gravel driveway, I notice that not much has changed since the last time I was out here. An old, small farmhouse sits on one end of the property, and a large shop sits on the other side. There's nothing flashy about it, but I don't think it's a reflection of Mr. Shea's success. He was known around town for his beautiful cabinets and furniture pieces. My mom was one of his biggest customers, and still buys things from Sam from time to time. In fact, the table my family eats at every night was handcrafted by him a few years ago.

He pulls the car up next to the door and turns off the engine. I can't believe that in all the time I've known Sam, I've never been here. When we were younger, his dad didn't want us anywhere near it because he was afraid we'd get hurt. Then, as we got older, we just didn't care. There were the fields and nothing else mattered.

"Ready to get your hands dirty?"

"I'm yours today." The second the words escape from my lips, his smile falters. His lips remain parted as his eyes journey to my mouth then back up.

"Watch what you say. Don't make any promises you can't keep," he says. His eyes hold mine for several seconds before he climbs out of the car.

Thoughts of what happened earlier flood my mind, but I push them away and hurry to catch up to him. "I was referring to work, Shea."

He stops dead in his tracks, causing the Tupperware container to hit his back. Every muscle in his body is rigid, so much so that I don't even have to touch him to know. "What I said has nothing to do with work, and I think we both know it."

I let the words marinate as we walk inside. Before Cory and I started dating, I liked Sam in a way that was different than just friends, but I always felt like I was too young. And then, there was that day when he could have kissed me but he didn't. I know Sam, and if he wants something, he takes it. He made me feel like he didn't want me, like he didn't feel the way I did. Besides, I've known him to go on dates every now and then, but I've never known him to stay with one person long enough to have a relationship. In high school, that was all I wanted. I wanted to feel love—what I knew then to be a deep, euphoric feeling—but now, I know that most things that come with a sense of euphoria also come with risk.

No matter what happens, I'll never regret falling in love with Cory, but there have been times I've wondered what Sam was doing. Was he dating? Was he happy? Those thoughts faded quickly whenever Cory walked in the room, but now that he's gone, I wonder what could have been.

And just like everything else, I have no right to even think about these things.

CHAPTER twelve

"ARE YOU SURE YOU don't want me to take you home?" Sam asks after he puts the last bracket on the massive toy box he's making for the Burtons. Neither of us has said much this morning because we've been too busy sawing and sanding. It's been nice … to just be with him.

"I'm okay unless you want to get rid of me. That box is going to need some finish before you deliver it, right?"

He runs his fingers along the top, going over a few imperfections a second time. "Having you around isn't that bad," he teases, "but let me make you some lunch before we get started on phase two. You're too skinny."

"Did you say *make*?"

"Yeah, I have a small apartment upstairs, and I make a mean sandwich."

I laugh, standing to stretch my arms above my head. "Show me the way. If I don't like your cooking, I'll just eat the last muffin."

"I don't think you're going to have much choice since I ate the last one an hour ago." He stands, picking the Tupperware up off the floor. "See."

Shaking my head, I follow him to the back and wait for him to unlock the door. A steep staircase awaits, but I follow like a stalker behind his prey, anxious to see what Sam Shea's apartment looks like. There's something so personal about entering his home, especially when there's this steady hum of electricity between us. Since the stare down we had back at my house, and what he said when we got out of the car, I've been on constant alert. When he talks, I listen for the hidden meaning behind his words. When he looks at me, I search his eyes like they hold a secret code. I'm not ready for anything like a relationship just yet. Something about it feels so wrong.

It doesn't mean I don't think about it … I thought about it years ago before I even knew Cory existed. Obviously, the thought has crossed my mind a few times lately with all his touches and looks. It's hard to tell if what I'm feeling is residual thoughts or the beginning of new ones. Maybe it's all in my head because I'm going up to a guy's apartment. The nervous energy travels through every inch of my body, almost enough to make me want to forget about lunch and run back down the narrow staircase. But the rational part of me screams loudly … I've been friends with this guy for over eleven years, and this skittish bullshit is ridiculous. I trust Sam, and he would never hurt me.

At the top of the stairs is one more door, which he opens easily, giving us access to a studio-like apartment. A half-wall separates the bed from the living area, and in the corner opposite the door is a small kitchenette. It's not much, but the stained cement floors give it a modern design, and large windows give it an open, airy feeling. The whole place reminds me of Sam.

"What do you think?" he asks, watching my reaction carefully.

"I like it. It looks like you—contemporary yet simple."

"Are you calling me a simple man?"

I shrug, walking toward the kitchen area. "No, you're just not a flashy guy." I stop, running my hand on top of the metal countertops, feeling the coolness against my fingertips. "I thought only restaurants had these."

"Most people don't like the look of them," he says, standing on the other side of the counter.

"I do. They're different."

Looking up, I catch him watching me like I'm that scene in the movie that changes everything. The one the suspenseful music cues up to, leaving you breathless until the big reveal. It's just Sam, the guy I've known for years, but there's something different about this version of him. I hadn't even noticed his hand coming up until his fingers brush my cheek and slide into my hair.

My first instinct is to escape his touch, move far enough away that he can't reach me, but his fingers curl behind my neck, holding me in place. "You had a woodchip in your hair." He loosens his hold on me but doesn't break our stare.

I'm free to back away, but his eyes hold me in place like a belt fastened on the tightest notch. I'm pulled into something that's impossible to escape.

"Rachel," he breathes, closing the distance between us. The space around us is quiet. My mind's been stripped of the ability to think clearly, making this ten times more intense than what happened this morning. I have no control as his eyes leave mine, making the journey to my lips.

And then, everything comes through with clarity. One reason to panic is drained away to make room for another, and I turn away, afraid and ashamed of what almost happened. Life gives us moments to get lost in, but I'm not ready for this one. No matter how many times I've thought about it in the past, I'm not ready for it. Not only that, but I don't deserve it. Cory can't have this. His heart will never race from merely having someone look him in the eye … it won't beat at all.

A hand grips my shoulder, turning me back around. "Rachel, I know you felt it this morning," Sam whispers. His eyes are desperate for the one thing I can't give him. It's all hitting me too hard, the powerful cocktail of regret and misery.

"Felt what?" I swallow hard, knowing exactly what he's going to say.

"Us. We were never meant to just be friends."

I take one step back.

He takes one step toward me.

"Don't," I say, shaking my head.

"Don't what?" He comes a little closer. Another step and our toes would touch.

"Say stuff like that," I reply, waving my arms up in the air. His shoulders slump in defeat. Sam hasn't been on the losing side of many battles, but this is one he won't win. I won't let him.

"It's the truth. You're just too scared to admit it," he finally says. He's right, but he's wrong. I don't even know the difference anymore.

"I should probably go home," I say, closing my eyes to hold in the tears that threaten.

"Stay," he begs.

"I can't. What just happened … I can't," I whisper.

"I'm not sorry. I got lost in you for a minute, and I'd do it again if you let me."

A tear slips into my lashes. I can't stop it. I can't seem to stop him. "You deserve someone to get lost in. It just can't be me."

"Maybe you're the only person I've ever wanted to lose myself in."

I start toward the door, swiping tears away. "No. Please don't."

"It's true, Rachel. Every time I tried to be with someone else, I compared her to you. It was wrong, but when you know perfection exists, it's hard to settle for anything less."

I spin around, giving him a glimpse of what he's done. When pain's already hanging around the surface, it doesn't take much to pull it back up. "I'm not perfect. Not even close."

He steps closer. "But you're perfect for me. That's all that matters."

"Why are you doing this now?"

He grimaces, searching my features for a hint of what to say. "I've done my best to hold back the last few months. Years actually. Today there was nothing to hold me back, not after I saw that look in your eyes earlier."

Words rarely fail me, but nothing seems to be working right for me today. "I need to go home."

He shakes his head, staring at me with sad brown eyes. "Please stay. I know you're not ready, and I promise I'll back off, but I want you to stay."

"I can't do this. Not now." *Why won't he just listen to me?* Looking up at the ceiling, I blink away tears. Sam and I could have been something … in another time. Maybe even a different life … that's what makes this hurt so much. "Please just take me home."

When my eyes land on him again, he's pleading with me. I don't give in. I won't.

"Okay," he says, rubbing the back of his neck.

I start down the stairs, and he follows close behind. I can't see him, but I hear his boots hitting against the metal, a weightier sound than when we'd made on our way up. I wish things didn't have to be this way. I wish he'd just made lunch like we'd planned. Why do things always have to get so complicated?

When my hand grips the knob at the bottom of the stairs, his hand wraps around my elbow, holding me back. "You don't have to go."

"Yes, I do."

He lets go, allowing me to disappear through the door. I woke up with hope this morning, but all I got was a glimpse of it before reality hit again.

I don't stop until I'm outside, tucked into the old Camaro. A part of me wants to tell Sam that everything is okay. I know what happened upstairs didn't come with bad intentions. His timing sucks, that's all. If I could find a magic eraser to erase some of the past, maybe things could be different between us. Sam Shea is one of those forever guys. The kind you like a little more with each minute you spend with him. The kind that opens your heart slowly and crawls deep inside before you even realize what's happening. He's the guy with the power to do it all, but he can never be my forever guy.

The driver's door clicks open, and Sam slides into his seat. I hesitantly glance over, expecting him to at least look at me, but he keeps his attention on the windshield. His jaw is tense, so much so I see the tiny muscles pulsing. I've become a domino—the first one in a line of many; I fell and I'm taking everyone else with me.

Not able to watch him any longer, I stare out the passenger window. There's nothing out there but fields and pastures. Flat, green grass blowing in the direction of the wind ... I wish my life were that simple. As simple as the plains of Iowa.

The drive only takes minutes but seems like hours under the circumstances. Besides the sound of the engine, it's completely quiet. Not a song. Not a word. It might as well be the longest ride of my life.

The second his car comes to a stop in front of my house, I unbuckle my seatbelt and reach for the door handle. "Wait," Sam says, drawing me back in.

I can only look, all out of words for today.

"I don't want this to change things between us." He runs his hands through his hair, pulling it at the ends. "I just got you back, Rachel."

"It's too late for that." I sigh, trying hard to pull myself together. "I need a few days to clear my head. I'll call you when I'm ready to talk." Without another word or look, I leave him behind. It has to be this way; he weakens me, and I don't have the strength to fight against it right now.

He lets me go. I don't think he's giving up on me, at least I hope he's not.

God must know I needed a break because I make it to my bedroom without running into my mom. It's not a promise that she won't be up here any minute with a million questions, but it gives me time to breathe.

After avoiding Sam for a few days, I realize how much better he's made the days since Cory died.

Since that afternoon with Sam, I've been sulking around the house, trying to avoid my parents. It's not hard with my dad, but Mom has tried to rope me into shopping and even a movie. Luckily, I retained some of my high school tricks and was easily able to fake a stomach virus to get out of it. While I felt guilty, I was also tired of wearing a mask of normalcy. It's never worked for me.

My phone vibrates in my purse, but I hesitate before answering it. Sam hasn't tried to contact me, but I know that won't last forever. Sam's not the runner; I am.

Pulling the phone from my purse, I see the name on the screen isn't anyone I was expecting.

"Hello," I answer.

"Hey, how are you doing?" Kate asks, her voice soft and soothing.

"I've been better. How are you?"

"That was a stupid question, wasn't it?" she asks. I can tell she's chewing on her bottom lip. It's something she does often.

"I would've asked the same thing. Don't worry about it."

"Yeah, I know better, though." I can hear her breathing on the other end, the only sound covering the silence. "I'm sorry I haven't called in a while. This summer has been really busy, but I know that's no excuse."

"No need to apologize. I haven't been that much fun to be around anyway." Sam could tell her … I've been a freaking yo-yo. Fun. Sad. Fun. Sad.

She hesitates, and then asks, "How are you feeling? I mean, really feeling."

"I've been good for the most part. I'm almost at one hundred percent physically, but I can't remember anything about that night. I don't even know if I want to remember."

"It will be hard for a while, but it will get easier. I promise. I know it would help to understand how it happened, but you need a plan in case that never happens."

If a stranger said that to me, I'd be pissed, but I get what she's saying, and she's one hundred percent right. That has been the hardest part—not knowing why I did what I did. Why would I get behind the wheel of my car after I'd been drinking? Why did Cory let me? And in all honesty, I might never know.

"I know things will get better. It's just going to take some time," I say quietly, my mind drifting off to the what-ifs. The land of the what-ifs is pretty miserable these days.

"Time is your best friend. Don't forget that." Kate should know after losing her boyfriend, Asher, last year. She's such an amazing person, a testament that sometimes pushing through the pain only makes us stronger.

"I'll try not to."

"Look, I was wondering if I can come visit on Saturday? I miss you, and I'm sure you could use a little girl time."

The thought of seeing Kate almost makes me cry. I know some of my old friends are back for the summer, but no one's made much effort to see me. Not even Madison other than that day in the hospital. They're probably all mad at me. They probably always will be.

"That would be great," I say, trying to make my voice sound as normal as possible.

"Okay, I'll be there around ten to pick you up. What do you want to do?"

"Swimming?"

"That sounds fabulous, because I think it's supposed to be over ninety tomorrow. Can you text me your address? I think it's about a two hour drive from my house, but I need to know where to go when I get there."

"I'll do it as soon as I hang up."

"Great. I'm excited to see you."

"Me too. I'll talk to you later," I say, squeezing the phone tightly in my fingers.

"Later," she says right before the phone goes dead.

Every time I think the sun is never going to come out again, it shines through the clouds, giving me a sliver of hope.

CHAPTER thirteen

August 11, 2013

SADLY, THIS IS THE first time I've put on a swimsuit all summer. My body is thinner than usual, leaving the top a little looser than I'd like, but after adjusting the strings a few times, it works. I pull on a pair of faded cutoff shorts and a white tank top before throwing my hair into a ponytail.

This is the second time in a week I've had something to look forward to, and I don't see any reason why it would turn out like the first. Dad left a couple hours ago; I heard his car speeding down the gravel driveway. Mom's home, but she's been tolerable the last few days. I think she got tired of babysitting me and decided to give me time to work through the fog in my head. We've just never had the type of relationship where I've felt like I can be open and honest with her. I've convinced myself she prefers I only tell her what makes her proud or gives her something to brag about to her friends. Maybe it's all in my head, but she hasn't done anything to disprove it.

I grab my beach bag off the bed and head downstairs to find something to eat before Kate gets here. The lake I want to go to is out in the middle of nowhere so my plan is to pack us each a light lunch for later. I haven't felt much like eating lately, but this isn't just about me.

As I'm pulling the toaster out of the cupboard, the doorbell rings. Looking up at the clock, I notice it's only nine thirty. After wiping my hands on the towel, I walk out of the kitchen and see Kate through the front window. I quicken my steps, excited to see her for the first time in a few months. When the door opens, her arms wrap tightly around me. "It's so good to see you," she says, squeezing me even tighter.

"It's good to see you, too." I wrap my arms around the center of her back.

After a few seconds, she lets go, stepping back far enough that she can see me. She spends more time than usual scanning me over, but it doesn't take long for her familiar, friendly smile to form. Besides being down a couple pounds, I look the same as I did a few months ago. "You look good," she remarks.

"Some days I don't feel that way, but I'm getting there. How was your drive?"

"It was relaxing actually … just me and Lifehouse." Her smile changes, a layer of sadness darkening it. She'd told me it was Asher's favorite band. They listened to them all the time before he died. Music can be the key to memories, good and bad. "Are you ready?"

"Actually, I was just making us some lunch. The lake's kind of out in the middle of nowhere."

"This whole state is pretty much the middle of nowhere," she replies, glancing around our overdone house. It isn't one of those you can walk into and feel at home. Most people don't even feel like they can sit down and end up doing exactly what Kate's doing right now—looking around in awe of the museum-like entryway. It's a mixture of expensive furniture in fine fabrics and antiques in mint condition, all kept impeccably clean.

"Follow me to the kitchen. I'll finish making our lunch and then we can hit the road."

She nods, her eyes scanning the room again as she takes a few small steps forward. "Your house is really nice."

I shrug, staring at a kitchen, so clean you could eat off any surface. "It's not really me, but my mom's put a lot of work into it. It has to look good in case anyone comes over."

"The house I grew up in was definitely more lived in."

While I finish packing a small cooler, Kate leans on the island and fills me in on her summer with Beau. While she speaks, it's obvious she's holding back, afraid her happiness will bring me more misery. Hearing about the fun things they've done together does make me think of Cory and all the things we would be doing right now. Swimming. Taking his parents' boat out on the lake. Bonfires with friends. Even simple things like holding his hand or breathing in his scent. I miss it all.

"Ready?" I ask.

"You better believe it."

On the way to the lake, we roll down the windows in Kate's car and let the wind mess up our perfect ponytails. Everything is easy with Kate—we have a lot of the same interests—two girls who like simplicity, who live for the loves in our lives.

"So what have you been up to? You said you were feeling better." Kate's hands grip the steering wheel, perfectly at ten and two, and she only takes her eyes off the road for a second to gauge my response.

"I didn't do much until just a few weeks ago. I've been hanging out with an old friend when I feel up to it." My heart rate picks up just thinking about Sam and what happened the last time I saw him. I still see that look on his face, the pain in his eyes. If I were a stronger girl, I'd have called him by now. I just can't do it yet.

"Yeah? Is it that Madison girl you talk about all the time?"

I shake my head, nervously looking out the passenger side window. I've never talked about Sam with her, but if anyone is going to understand, it's Kate. "His name is Sam. We've been friends since I was eight." When I think about what a best friend should be, it's Sam. He's more than just another friend. He's the person I tell the most to, the one I want to spend the most time with.

Her eyes widen, but she quickly recovers, focusing in on the road again. "You've never mentioned him before."

"We lost touch for a while. He's the only person besides you who's been around at all."

"It's weird how it takes something bad to point out who's really there for you. When it comes down to it, true friends are as rare as true love."

"Do you think it's possible to find a true love and true friend in the same person?"

She looks at me again, her mouth opening then closing. "That's Beau. Sometimes true friends make the best true loves."

She's right. With true friendship comes trust, and trust makes it easier to give your heart away ... it gives you confidence that the person who holds it won't break it. "How long after Asher died did you start seeing Beau?"

"Umm, it was seven or eight months. If it had been anyone else but Beau, I wouldn't have been able to move on so soon, but I'd felt things for him for a long time. It was easy because it was what my heart wanted."

I point her north, down the long dirt road that leads to the lake I like to go to when I don't feel like being around my old high school classmates.

After she's on the right path, I ask her what I've really been wondering. "How did you know it was the right time to move on?"

Without warning, she pulls over to the side of the road, putting the car in park. Her whole body turns toward me, looking at me like she's going to tell me the most important thing I'll ever hear.

"I think my heart knew it long before I convinced my head. Mine was a different situation, though. I knew death was coming, and by the time it did, I'd already gone through some stages of grief. I had time to process it way before it became reality. I'm not saying that it will take longer for you; I think it all depends on how much of you Cory took with him. How much do you have to get back before you can feel whole enough to give a part of yourself to someone else?"

I blow out the air I was holding the whole time she spoke, looking away to try to escape her knowing eyes. I swear she was born with a special ability to read people. Sometimes I think she knows what I'm thinking before I even say it. "I feel things for him. Things I felt before I started dating Cory. Things I felt with Cory … it's so confusing, and if I didn't already feel guilty enough about what happened, it's making it worse. When I want to be close to him, when he makes my heart race, all I can think about is how it wouldn't even be happening if Cory were still here."

"If Asher were still here, I probably wouldn't be with Beau. And if Asher hadn't gotten sick, he probably wouldn't have come to Carrington. If I really think about it, I wouldn't be with Beau if it weren't for Asher. He saved me."

"What are you saying?" I hear everything she's saying, but I'm not sure what it means for me.

"Quit thinking about the what-ifs and live with what you have. If you're ready to move on today, then by all means do it, but don't let anything but what you feel in here guide you," she says, placing her hand over her heart.

I lean back against the headrest and let her words sink in. Just because I think Sam might be the guy I move on with doesn't mean it has to happen now. If the things he's said to me are true, he'll wait … he's been waiting.

"Thank you," I say, tears filling my eyes.

"I'm here for you. No matter what."

Without hesitation, I pull her in for a hug. She's given me a clearer picture of the future than I've had in a long time. It may not be right in front of me, but it's definitely something I'm walking toward. There's a whole lot of living to do along the way.

All I've been doing since Kate left yesterday is thinking about what I'm supposed to do with the rest of my life. The talk we had on the way to the lake opened my eyes in a way they hadn't been in months. Our situations aren't exactly the same, but she still understands better than anybody. An afternoon with her was exactly what I needed, and by the time she dropped me off at home last night, I had a new resolve to figure out why I'm still here. For whatever reason, I survived that crash, and it wasn't to sit here and do absolutely nothing.

At one point, I had my whole life mapped out, a path from birth until the day I die. Something came along and flooded it, making it impossible to stay on course. I guess that's what happens when things are too perfect. Actually, the more I look at it, the less perfect it all seems. It's beginning to look more like a façade of perfection.

Tonight, I just want to forget about my crazy life and escape to the fields to watch the fireflies and stare at the night sky. They're two things that make me think of happier times and forget everything else.

I grab an old flannel blanket from the closet and head outside, carefully closing the door behind me to not rouse my parents. I've considered getting my own place since I'm not returning to school this semester, but in order to do that, I need a job. That, I don't know if I can handle yet.

My flip-flops make a rhythmic sound as I walk across our property toward the fields, the grass brushing against my feet. The air smells of the horses my neighbor raises mixed with fresh cut grass. It's quite possibly the best combination ever.

I find my usual spot where the grass is so long that it's impossible to see me, and lay the blanket down. The minute I'm comfortably seated, I kick my sandals off and cross my arms over my legs. There's a light breeze tonight, which blows my long blond hair behind my back. When the crickets begin their song, I lay back and close my eyes. I breathe in, holding it for five seconds before slowly letting it out again. I repeat it, over and over, until I feel so calm it would be easy to drift off to sleep. It's in these moments that I get to know myself. Often times, I think we get caught up in getting to know everyone around us and forget that we may not know ourselves well enough to know anyone else. I've been working hard at this because I think it's the only way for me to rewrite my life in a way that will give me some semblance of happiness. I'd do anything to get a peek at it every now and then.

As I file my thoughts away, the cricket song fades, and I know he's here.

Keeping my eyes closed, I listen for his footsteps in the grass. Soon they come, each a little louder than the one before. My heart rate increases just thinking about him being near. I know what he means to me, but I'm trying to forget. Someone should have warned me that it's impossible to forget Sam Shea.

The footsteps stop above me, and I feel him lowering himself to the blanket. He never asks for permission.

Even when I feel the warmth of his body next to mine, my eyes stay closed. When his fingers wrap around mine, I take a deep breath through my nose but don't give anything away. His bare arm brushes against mine, and I feel him looking at me. His eyes set fire to my cheek.

"I've been out here every night since that day in the shop," he says, so low it takes all the concentration I have in the stillness of the night air to hear him. "I've been waiting for you."

"I've had time to put things into perspective."

"Yeah? And what did perspective show you?"

I open my eyes and turn toward him. It's hard to make out the expression on his face, but I've known him long enough that my imagination is just as good. "That I have two choices."

He waits patiently for me to go on. "I can either swim in this pool of regret for the rest of my life, or I can take the steps necessary to move forward."

"What did you decide?" he asks. Sam Shea, one of the surest people I've ever met, sounds so unsure.

"Life's too short, and we all deserve a second chance."

"So you're moving forward?"

I've thought about this for hours over the last week, and if the tables were turned and Cory was still here, I'd want him to be happy. I wouldn't want him to walk around with guilt on his shoulders.

"It's not going to happen overnight, but eventually I'll find a way to live normally again. I like you, Sam, but I don't know what that means for us. I mean, it feels wrong to act on it right now."

The space around us is quiet, only the sound of the crickets filling the air. "So you're not saying no?"

"I'm saying not right now. I need some more time to think about what I want. Where it's going to bring me. Until just a few months ago, I thought I had it all figured out. Starting all over isn't that easy."

"Even if we're not together, I don't want to lose what we have. The last few weeks have felt so good ... I didn't think I'd ever have you back in my life again."

I stare up at the stars in the sky, trying to find the words that will show Sam that he means more. "I'm here. I just haven't decided what version you get."

"I'll take whatever version I can get." His warm hand covers mine, his thumb brushing over the top of my hand.

Simple. Uncomplicated. That's what I want my life to go back to.

"Sometime, I'd like to sleep out here under the stars," I announce out of the blue.

"We can make that happen."

"So, you'll go camping with me, Sam Shea?"

He sits up on his elbow, staring down at me with only the moonlight above us. "I'll go camping. Sweetheart, I'll even share my sleeping bag with you ... whatever you want me to do as long as I'm with you."

Smiling, I bite down on my lower lip. "I kind of like that idea." I kind of just like the idea of Sam.

CHA*fourteen*

September 15, 2013

IT'S BEEN FOUR MONTHS since Cory died. Every day I feel a little less sadness and have a slightly better view into normalcy. He lives inside me, and he'll always have a piece of my heart; but I'm realizing little by little that I can't let my guilt control me.

If I could just remember everything that led up to the tragedy, I'd feel better about moving forward, but that may never come. The more time that passes, the less hope I have that I'll ever regain any recollection of that day. I'm just going to have to deal with it the best way I can.

Unfortunately, the better I start to feel the more life with my parents is starting to bother me. Before I left for college, I was too busy with Cory and normal high school things, but now, I notice how distant the two of them are with each other and me. I think you have to feel true loneliness to recognize it. You can have all the people in the world around you but that doesn't mean you have anybody.

Since I decided not to go back to school this semester, I've been applying for jobs. There's not much for the taking in a small town, and given that I'm not really the town prize right now, I've been struggling. Until yesterday, however, when Ms. Peters, who owns the town's only flower shop, called me and said she needed someone to help with deliveries in the afternoons. It's not much, and it doesn't pay more than minimum wage, but I lost my right to be picky a long time ago.

I dress in a nice pair of jeans and a black T-shirt, remembering that I'd have to wear an apron while I worked. I actually take the time to straighten my hair and put on make-up, wanting to be prepared in case she has any deliveries for me on my first day. If I'm going to face the town, I'm going to put my best foot forward.

When it's finally time to leave, doubt consumes me. What if I'm not ready for this? For years, I hid behind Cory. Not intentionally. It happened gradually. I liked him so much I wanted to make him happy. I did what he wanted to do, and after a while, his hobbies became mine. I saw his friends more than my own. I lived in Cory's shadow, and now, it's time to step out from under it.

When I walk into the kitchen, Mom's standing in front of the sink, rinsing the dishes from breakfast. She's not too excited about me starting this job. I think she's told me over ten times that I don't need to work, but that's not what this is about.

"Do you want something to eat before you go?" she asks, wiping her hands.

"I had a big breakfast. I'll just bring a snack for later." Someone might as well staple my mouth shut when I'm nervous. I couldn't eat if I tried because I'm worried about how today will go. I've never had a real job before.

"Are you sure you don't want me to drive you?"

"I might need my car for deliveries."

She nods, folding her arms over her chest. "I know. I just worry about you."

The hardest thing about people who aren't always genuine is deciding when they are. I know she loves me. I know she worries about me, but there's this little voice in the back of my head that's always telling me she's more concerned about the social damage it would cause if it happened again … if I disappointed her in some way. I hate that I even think like that.

I pick a red apple from the bowl on the counter and a cold bottle of water from the fridge before taking one last look at her. "I'll try not to get into any more accidents."

"I didn't mean it like that."

"I know," I say softly as I walk out the door. The air is humid, and the sun instantly heats my black T-shirt. With any luck, there will only be a couple more weeks of this weather before fall rolls in. I quickly make my way to the new "safe" car my dad bought me a few weeks ago. It's white, small, and made in the USA. Most importantly, it gets me from one place to another.

Climbing into the driver's seat, I wrap my fingers around the hot steering wheel and take several deep, cleansing breaths. Driving sucks. Every time I do it, I have a tiny seed of fear buried within me. I imagine it would be even worse if I could remember anything about the accident.

After turning the key, I make sure my seatbelt is fastened and slowly make my way down the driveway. I think the country roads are the worst. Speeds are higher than what is allowed in town. The blacktop is narrow with gravel lining the sides, and this time of year, the tractors are starting to come out and slow traffic along the usually quiet roads.

It's only three miles to town. One hundred and eighty seconds. Less than one song on the radio. The first time I drove it, I was in full-on panic attack mode by the time I got to town. The therapist said it would be best if I did it over and over again until I felt very little anxiety so I drove it every day, even when I didn't have a purpose.

I do okay now, but I still hate it. Thank God for The Civil Wars, and the killer speakers in this thing. At least they keep my mind occupied.

Today, as I drive through downtown, I have something new to worry about ... my first day of work. I've known Ms. Peters since I was a little girl so this shouldn't be that hard. She's nice but quiet; I'm hoping that's how she runs her shop, too.

After parking my car, I take a few seconds to straighten my hair in the rearview mirror, more out of nerves than the desire to look perfect. A few deep breaths and a quick application of lip gloss later, and I'm ready. *I can do this,* I tell myself over and over again. *This is nothing.*

The storefront is adorned with a black and white striped canopy that reads *Simple Elegance.* I've seen Ms. Peter's work many times over the years and that pretty much sums it up. She has a talent and a reputation for being the best; it's an honor to be given this opportunity, even if it's just deliveries.

The door dings when I pull it open, alerting anyone inside to my presence. I slowly walk up to the counter, taking in the scent of fresh flowers that fill the room. Walking in here every day, greeted by that smell, is going to make working here worth it.

"Hello!" a voice calls from the backroom.

"It's me, Rachel." I fidget with my purse strap, waiting for instruction on what to do next.

Less than a minute later, Ms. Peters walks up front wearing a black *Simple Elegance* apron. She smiles—the warm welcome kind that eases some of the tension in my neck and shoulders—and reaches her hand out to me. "Nice to see you again, Rachel. Are you ready to get started?"

I place my hand in hers, noticing how small and cold it is. "Of course. Just tell me where you need me."

"We're going to start with some paperwork, and then I'll show you the computer system we use to take orders. If we have any time left, I'll give you a mini-lesson on flowers in case someone stops into the store and I'm not around."

"I think I can handle that," I say, glancing around at the floor-to-ceiling coolers full of fresh fall bouquets. I love the rich reds, oranges, and yellows, so bright and beautiful.

"I know you can. That's why I hired you." She smiles again … it makes me feel more comfortable. If nothing else, I'll have someone nice to work with. "Follow me," she says, letting my hand fall from hers.

We spend the afternoon doing new employee paperwork and a general orientation on how to answer the phone and record an order, as well as tracking the number of deliveries for each day.

Just as she's about to take me into the cooler at the back of the shop to get a lesson on the types of flowers she carries in shop, the door dings. On instinct, we both turn to see who walked in, and to my surprise, it's Sam, standing there with his hands tucked in his jean pockets. Part of me is thrilled to see him and the other is a little embarrassed that he came in on my first day. I told him I was starting here so it's no coincidence.

"How can I help you?" Ms. Peters asks while I stay frozen in place.

"Hi," he says, sneaking a quick look in my direction. "I was wondering if you carry daffodils. I just need one."

To say I'm surprised by his request would be an understatement, but when the corner of his mouth turns up, I know he's up to something.

"I have a few out here, but let me get you a fresh one from the back cooler," Ms. Peters offers.

"Perfect," he replies, never taking his eyes off me.

Ms. Peters turns to me, speaking just loud enough that I can hear. "I'm going to run to the back. Why don't you try using the computer to ring it up?"

My eyes double in size; she literally showed me the system about ten minutes ago.

"Don't worry," she adds, "You can't mess it up too much." And with that, she disappears to the back, leaving me to take my first order by myself … at least it's just Sam.

Before I have time to collect myself, Sam's beside me, his hand resting gently under my elbow. "The computer is over there."

"What are you doing here?"

"Buying a flower." He slowly walks us to the register, his hand never leaving my arm.

"Since when are you into flowers, Shea?" I ask, walking around the counter, out of his grasp.

He shrugs. "Since you started working here."

I roll my eyes, yet inside I'm laughing a little. This was his way of checking up on me. I see that now. "So one daffodil. Do you need anything else with that?"

He leans his arms on the counter while I pretend to look for daffodil in the computer system. I find it right away, but keeping my eyes on the screen is giving me an excuse not to look directly at him. He unnerves me in the best and worst ways. "Well, I was wondering if you wanted to come out to the lake with me tonight. We could watch the sunset."

"I don't know. After work I have therapy—"

"You're usually done with that by seven. I'll meet you at eight."

I hesitate, not because I don't want to watch the sunset with Sam, but because things feel different since he told me how he feels about me. He's been respectful, giving me my space, but it's always in the back of my mind. If I knew I didn't want him, it wouldn't be a big deal. But I do. I do kind of want him. "I don't know," I finally answer.

"Please," he begs, sticking out his lower lip. *How am I supposed to say no to that?*

I smile, mostly because of how ridiculous he looks. "I'll try, but no promises."

"If that's as close to yes as I'm going to get, I'll take it," he says, pulling his wallet out of his back pocket. Ms. Peters chooses that moment to come out with a single daffodil wrapped in light green floral paper. She makes a simple flower look amazing.

"Did you find it?" she asks, handing the flower to Sam.

"Yep, that will be four dollars and fifty cents. Please."

Sam hands me a five, and as I reach back out to place his change in his hand, his fingers brush mine. I feel it deeper than just my skin. Way deeper. Like scary deep.

"Thank you." He winks. He starts toward the door, but before he opens it, he turns back around. "And that thing tonight … it's on the dock."

And just like that, he's gone, leaving me feeling a little unsettled. I'm excited about the prospect of spending more time with him but nervous about it, too. I'm not ready for anything in the relationship department, or at least I never think I am until I lay eyes on him. He messes with everything I think I know. Everything I've tried to convince myself of.

Glancing over at Ms. Peters, I notice her eyes haven't left the door either. It's the Sam Shea effect. I guess it doesn't discriminate against age.

I clock out a little before six and head to see Dr. Schultz at his office a few blocks away. It took my parents almost three months to convince me to go, but now I look forward to it. He's helping me work through my grief and to see through the fog in my head, even if it hasn't triggered any memories of that night.

I'm always his last appointment of the day, but he's still eager to see me, or at least he acts that way. How someone can still smile after listening to other people's problems for hours is beyond me. "Rachel," he greets me, briefly shaking my hand. He's almost old enough to be my grandfather, but he's good at what he does.

"Dr. Schultz."

"Have a seat and let's get started," he instructs, gesturing to my usual chair. "I hear today was your first day of work? How did that go for you?"

I clear my throat, trying to switch gears from the flower shop to this. Keeping things locked in to now letting them all spill out. "Yes. It went much better than I expected."

"I'm happy to hear that. I've known Gretchen Peters for years. I had a feeling she'd take good care of you."

"It's going to be good to get out of the house for something other than this. No offense."

He smiles. "None taken."

I thought therapy would be a place for me to sit and have someone else tell me everything that's wrong with me and how to fix it. Up 'til this point, it's been anything but. It's a ship I drive with Dr. Schultz giving me a few pointers on which direction to turn. It's amazing how much a therapist helps just by asking the right series of questions.

"Sam came in while I was working," I blurt, jumping immediately to the one thing I'm dying to talk about. The one thing, besides the accident, that I've talked to Dr. Schultz about quite often.

"Oh," he says, watching me curiously.

"I think he was checking on me, but he also invited me out to the dock tonight to watch the sunset."

"Are you going to go?"

I glance down at my folded hands, noticing the chips in my purple polish. There's no point in wearing it anymore if I'm going to be working at the flower shop. "I don't know."

"What's holding you back? You've spent a lot of time with Sam, so why is this any different?"

I know after almost six weeks of working with the doctor that he's not going to tell me what I should do ... he's simply going to lead me to my own conclusion. I love how he does that ... most days. "It's a sunset, and I've always thought them to be romantic. I feel like it's too soon for that. I mean, I feel things for Sam, and it's becoming harder and harder to be around him and not act on them. It just doesn't feel right."

"Tell me why it doesn't feel right."

I hesitate, trying to pull together the words to describe it. It's harder than one might think. "If I start a relationship—something more than a friendship—with Sam, I feel as if I'll forget about Cory, and I don't want to."

"Do you really think that's possible?"

"What?" I ask, drawing in my brows.

"Forgetting him. From everything you've told me, he was a big part of your life."

I let his words roll around for a little bit. If my life is the series of short stories I think it to be, Cory had his own. Maybe even two. He was a whole phase of my life. "No, I could never forget him."

"Then what are you really afraid of?"

Shaking my head, I feel the truth coming to the surface. It's not new to me, but I tried to bury it away. It's become too easy to blame all fears and hesitancies on Cory's death. "Losing the one person who has been there for me."

"I see," he says, pulling his glasses from his eyes. "Do you feel enough for him to think your life could be better if you let him in ... in the way he wants in?"

"There's no doubt he can make me happy."

"Then you have some thinking to do, but Rachel I'll tell you, I don't think this is really about if you're ready or not."

At least once a session, he leads me to a truth. Sometimes I hate how easy it is, but I also appreciate it. He gets me places a lot quicker than I would on my own.

CHAPTER fifteen

MY FLIP-FLOPS HIT against the old wood dock as I make my way to where Sam sits. When I'm just a few feet away, he turns to me with a devilishly handsome smirk on his face. I can't see his eyes because they're hidden behind his aviators, but I know he's thinking he somehow won the battle. In a way, he has.

"I was hoping you'd come," he says as I slide down next to him.

"I've never turned down a front seat to a perfect sunset."

"You make it sound like you've been invited to quite a few."

I laugh nervously, gripping the end of the old wooden platform. "This is actually my first."

"I was hoping it would be something different, not just another recycled idea." He looks up to the clear blue sky where a flight of birds moves from one end of the lake to the other. "Do you ever wonder what the world looks like from up there?"

If he only knew how much I think about seeing the world from a different angle. "They get to pick where they land and when things get in their way, they can just take flight again. I wish it were that easy for us to disappear."

"Why would you want to disappear?" he asks.

"Maybe disappear wasn't the right word," I reply, pulling my legs up and wrapping my arms around them. "Don't you ever wish you could go somewhere else and forget everything? Just pick up and leave like the past never happened."

He pulls his sunglasses from his eyes, letting the true depths of his emotions show. "There's no need to run when everything you want is right in front of you."

The way he's looking at me, eyes locked onto mine so tightly, I couldn't turn away if I wanted to. He has always looked at me like he's interested in what I have to say, like I'm the only thing that matters, but now, I'm getting something even more, which makes it hard to fill my lungs. His dark brown irises warm me to my core, taking me in like a man who's been given the ability to see for the first time ... who only wants to see me.

He's got a hold on my heart. I feel it ... he's using his pull on it to bring me closer to him, my lips closer to his. It's a moment that's been coming for a long time. Two souls, once lonely, brought together in the fields but joined on the edge of the lake. When one story doesn't have a happy ending, there's always a chance to start another one. I don't want to stand alone for the rest of my life and wonder what could have been if I'd been given my happy ending. I'm going to go after it.

His lips lightly brush against mine, so quickly that I could debate on whether or not it qualifies as a kiss. The intensity of it is almost more than I can handle. Everything inside me warms. I've never experienced anything quite like it. Even when he backs away a few inches to stare into my eyes, I can feel his lips imprinted on mine. He's branded me. His lips own mine. His heart owns me.

One kiss is all it takes to make me an addict, and I crave a second. I focus in on his perfect lips, hinting for more. This time, Sam doesn't give; he takes, pressing his mouth to mine. His hand cradles the back of my head, like he's afraid I might pull away if he lets me go. He may not realize it yet, but he has me ... I've given him little pieces of myself over all these years. He just had to claim the last piece.

His fingers curl around the back of my neck as his lips continue to work against mine. His lips warm, much more eager than the first time. He sucks my lower lip between his, then presses his tongue into my mouth. It tastes of peppermint as it tangles with mine. He's methodical, making me feel and want more. Grabbing his shirt, I pull him closer until I can literally feel his heart beating against me. There's more emotion behind this kiss than I've ever felt before. He's telling me so much without words, and it feels like he's been holding it in forever. He gently caresses my tongue with his, like he has wanted to do it for a long time and needs to savor it. I wish this moment could last forever ... maybe it can. He cups my cheek in his calloused hand, running his thumb along my jawline as he slows his movements.

His lips linger for a minute longer before he presses his forehead to mine. "Do you know how long I've wanted to do that?"

I shake my head, pulling my bottom lip between my teeth in a bid to keep them off him. His eyes burn into mine, igniting a fire deep inside of me. I want to taste those lips on mine again.

"That night you disappeared with Cory at the party ... I wanted you even back then. I'd wanted you for a long time. I knew if he asked you to, you'd be his. I didn't think he deserved you, but I didn't think I did either," he says, skimming his fingers across my cheek to brush the hair from my face.

I'd always felt like Sam was trying to play the big brother role. Of course, I thought he was cute ... he keeps getting cuter with age ... but I never thought he saw me that way. Not then. Things might have been different if he had said something before that night, but we can't dwell on the things we cannot change, and I'm grateful for the time I spent with Cory. I wouldn't be the same person I am today without him. Thinking about him now is dampening this moment like rain in the middle of a perfectly sunny day. I hate that this keeps happening to me, but I know it's inevitable.

When I don't say anything, he continues, "Do you remember the last day we spent out in the fields before your freshman year?" I nod, holding my breath. He responds by closing his eyes and running his thumb along my lower lip. "I almost kissed you that day. I wanted to, but I was afraid that you didn't feel the same, and I didn't want to ruin what we had."

My heart jumps. I've thought about that day so many times over the years. Now, everything I thought I felt that day has been justified. "I think everything happens for a reason," I whisper. I regret the way I said that as soon as the words leave my mouth. "I don't mean that I think there's a reason Cory died, but I do think there's a reason we couldn't be together back then. We were both too young."

He stares at me curiously with a hint of pain in his eyes that hadn't been there before. He closes them, curling his fingers against my face. "I still regret not telling you how I felt. I could have saved you so much pain ... sometimes I feel like part of what you're going through is my fault."

"What do you mean?"

"At least if you were with me, I could have controlled what you went through. I never would have hurt you, or done anything that could hurt you," he says, opening his eyes.

I sit back, pulling my face from his as defensiveness takes over. "He didn't hurt me. *I* hurt me."

His face turns in the other direction until all I see is the squint of his eyes and the pensive line his lips have taken. "I'm sorry. I shouldn't have brought it up. I always have shitty timing."

I grab his hand in mine, bringing his attention back to me. "The only way this is going to work is if you accept my past, every part of it, and leave it there. I loved Cory. I still love Cory, and you need to know that." I rest our joined hands on my thigh, feeling the brush of his arm against my chest. "Love doesn't fade completely. In a way, I'll always love Cory.. I need to know that you understand."

He nods. "Are you sure you're ready for this?"

"No," I answer, honestly, "but I want to try. Something about this feels right, and I'm tired of living the way I've been living. Besides, I like you, Sam. I want to explore that, but I need us to go slow."

He smiles, the cocky one I like so much. "Slow is the only way to go when you like something and want to savor it. Once you're mine, I'm not going to let you leave for anyone else.

I've waited way too long for this." He places our hands over his chest. "There are things in here I've held onto forever just to give them to you. They belong only to you because you're the one who made me feel them."

I lean into him, kissing him sweetly, the way he kissed me the first time. "I didn't know you were such a romantic."

"It's just for you. You're the only person who ever has or ever will bring it out of me."

It feels like my heart just blended itself into the lake water, but yet I still feel it beating in my chest. Never in my life did I see this coming, but I realize I've wanted it. Subconsciously, I think I've wanted it for a long time.

I realize this could all end badly. Another short story that leaves me lying on a pillow soaked in tears, but Sam's worth it. He's more than a constant for me. "So, what did you have planned for tonight?'

"I thought we'd put our feet in the water. See how it feels."

"I think we already got that covered," I reply, resting my head against his shoulder.

He leans in to kiss my forehead. "I guess all that's left to do is watch the sunset. You in?"

"We might as well." I smile, feeling as content as I have in a long time. Life is a journey, and very few come without wrong turns and speed bumps. For the first time in months, I'm finally on the straight and narrow.

"Hey, Sam?"

"Yeah," he replies, wrapping his arm around my shoulders.

I snuggle in closer. "Why did you buy the daffodil?"

"I almost forgot," he says, reaching to his other side. "I bought it for you. To congratulate you on your first day of work."

"Thanks, but isn't that like buying a shake for someone who works in an ice cream shop?"

He laughs. "I wanted to toast to new beginnings and since you don't drink, I got the next best thing."

"I'm not following."

"All flowers have meanings. Didn't you learn that at work?"

I shake my head, waiting for him to continue. I've only spent five hours in that shop. What does he expect?

"The daffodil symbolizes a new beginning."

"How do you know that?" I ask, crinkling my nose up a bit.

"I Googled it."

"You Googled flower meanings?" I ask, looking up at his moonlit face. A beautiful crease forms around his lips. I kind of like that I put it there.

"You should know by now that I'll do just about anything for you," he says.

He turns my heart into a vibrant rainbow when the last few months it's been a raging thunderstorm.

CHAPTER sixteen

September 22, 2013

THE SUMMER BREEZE BLOWS through my hair as I drive to work with my car window down. I've been at the flower shop for a week now, and it's starting to feel more and more like something normal. Like just another place I go without even thinking about it.

And Sam, I see him everyday, too. Sometimes we meet at the lake and other times we meet in the fields. Being with him has given me hope, but it's also made me feel conflicted.

Things aren't serious, by any means, but he says stuff that alludes to something deeper, more meaningful. It's not that I don't think it's a possibility; it just scares the shit out of me. When you open your heart to someone, you also open it to the possibility of heartbreak. That's what I'm most afraid of now; I lived through it once, and I'm not willing to open myself to it again. Not yet.

There hasn't been a single day that I haven't thought about Cory, but as time goes on, the weight on my heart lessens. The pain eases. The guilt still lives inside me, and the thought of him often brings sadness, but I'm able to look back at some memories and smile. And every single day, I find that I'm forgiving myself a little more.

Pulling in front of the flower shop, I glance up at the black and white striped canopy. Taking this job has been the best decision. It's given me a purpose. It was never my life's ambition to work with flowers on a daily basis, but I love it. For the most part, my job is to make people happy, and it's more fulfilling than any other job I could have gotten in this small town.

When I walk in, the shop is empty, which usually means that Ms. Peters is busy working in the back. She's always swamped, especially on Fridays and Saturdays, because of weddings. Sometimes, when I have a few minutes of downtime between deliveries and helping her prep flowers, I watch her arrange flowers into beautiful bouquets. She mixes colors that I'd never think to put together, but they always looks amazing. She has a talent for seeing things that other people can't.

The other day she had some flowers she was going to throw out because they were starting to wilt. I stepped in and asked if I could play with them instead. It took me a couple hours, but I created an arrangement of lavender and burnt yellow roses. Those are the colors I imagined using for my wedding … they remind me of the flowers that grow in the fields.

Opening the door to the backroom, I see Ms. Peters assembling flower wreaths. The colors are deep and rich, very much like what you'd expect in autumn.

"Hey, Rachel. How was your weekend?"

"Good," I say, tucking my hands into my jean pockets. "What's on the list for today?"

She cuts the stem off a red rose, carefully filling in a gap on the wreath. "This is the last wreath I have to finish, and then I need these taken out to the cemetery."

"The cemetery?" She's never asked me to go there before. It's usually the hospital, offices, or churches … but never there.

"Yeah, a woman called from out of town and wants me to put fresh wreaths on her parents' graves before the weather turns cold."

"Okay," I say quietly, leaning forward on the counter. It's not as easy to breathe as it was just a couple minutes ago. I haven't been back there since the first time, and I'm not sure how I feel about that.

She drops her scissors, coming to stand next to me. "Are you okay?"

I nod. "I will be."

"If you're not feeling good, I can manage."

"No," I say, straightening myself up. "I'm fine."

She walks back to her place at the counter, cutting the stem of another rose—a white one this time. "I wondered if you would be up to going out there."

I didn't realize she'd drawn the line between her request and my reaction. I don't hold anything against her … it's been months. I should be able to handle this, to be close to Cory.

"I've been out there, but it's hard, you know?"

"I can only imagine." She doesn't talk about her personal life, but there's no Mr. Peters. Mom told me after I took the job that this little shop has always been her life. To an outsider, it might sound sad, lonely, but when I watch her work, I understand it. This is her passion, her peace … she doesn't need anything else.

The room is quiet for the most part, with only the occasional snip of scissors filling the space. I catch Ms. Peters looking at me every now and then, but she doesn't say a word. That's very unlike her. She usually has directions to give, or little tidbits on history and flowers to speak about.

After she finishes the last wreath, she holds it up, making sure everything is perfect and symmetrical. I can always tell if she likes it by the look on her face … she must like what she's done because a bright smile forms. "All ready to go," she announces.

"I'll start bringing them out to my car. Do you have instructions on where they need to go at the cemetery?"

"Of course. Take this one first, and I'll get the delivery slip for you."

The smell of fresh roses fills my nose as I step back out into the sun. Having a car that permanently smells of fresh flowers isn't bad either.

When I walk back into the shop, she has the other wreath tucked away in a box with a delivery slip attached. On top is a bouquet of Gerbera daisies in a variety of colors. I look up at her, confused.

"You said they're your favorite. Take as much time as you need."

My eyes tear up. I'm speechless. I've experienced more kindness the last few months than I did in all the years before combined. "You didn't have to."

"There are lots of things people don't have to do. The ones who do them anyway are the ones who can make a difference. Always remember that." She squeezes my shoulder and disappears behind the cooler door. I wish there was something I could give back to her. A way to repay her for all the good things she does, even though I know she doesn't expect it.

I tuck the second wreath and the daisy bouquet into my backseat before climbing into my car and making my way to the edge of town. I'm so caught off guard by today's assignment that my hands grip the steering wheel tighter than necessary. I planned to come out here again at some point, but not today. Maybe it was meant to be.

I pull my car along the curb and put it in park, scanning the cemetery to see if anyone else is around. It's quiet today, with the exception of one landscaper in the distance. After taking a deep breath, I step out of the car and pull the first wreath out of the backseat.

The cemetery isn't large, which makes it easy to find the gravesite for the couple. I lay the first flower arrangement down and walk back to my car to get the second one along with the flowers Ms. Peters sent just for me. The whole time I'm thinking about what I want to say to Cory that I didn't get to say last time. That time had been about leaving a piece of us with him, but this time, I feel like I have to take a piece of myself back. I was the one given a second chance, and I can't let it waste away. It's not fair to either of us.

By the time I reach Cory's grave, my body's wound so tightly I feel sick. I'm nervous about what to say. I'm worried that his mom, or someone else, is going to pick this time to come visit him. For this, I just need it to be him and me. I need him to hear me … only me.

Kneeling in from of the large stone that bears his name, I run my fingertips over each letter. "I know it's been a few months since I've been out here, but I had some stuff to sort out, mostly because I've been missing you so much."

My fingertips trail the date next. "I don't know if you can see me, but if you can, I need you to know that just because I've started living my life again, doesn't mean I've forgotten about you. You'll always be a part of me, no matter where this life takes me."

A gust of wind blows through, spreading leaves across the grass. I sit back, letting my hands fall into my lap. "Anyway, I needed you to know that. If I had a choice, it would always be you."

Not able to help myself, I run my fingers across the cool stone one more time, branding the pattern to my skin. "I love you, Cory Connors. Don't you ever forget that, no matter what."

Closing my eyes, I say a silent prayer, begging for more forgiveness and for God to look over him. It's the first time I've asked for anything as a true believer; I hope that counts for something.

"I have to move on, Cory. I thought about it a lot, and if it were you in my place, I'd want you to be happy. I hope you understand … it doesn't mean I love you any less." I probably don't need to explain my feelings for Sam, but it makes me feel better about it.

Before I get up to leave, I pick up the daisies from the ground and set them carefully in front of his grave. It's a piece of me I'm leaving here while I take a bigger piece of me back, a part I want to be able to give someone else someday. I always thought I'd find that one person I love and love them all my life. Not all stories are meant to be fairytales—I get that now—but it's been a hard pill to swallow.

As I walk back to my car, I look at the dates on the tombstones I pass, noting that many of the people buried here lived a long life. Cory's will always stand out. He'll always be among the youngest, and I'll always be the reason for that.

Sam and I made plans to meet tonight after dinner, but I couldn't bring myself to do it—not right away. I had too much on my mind from my trip to the cemetery this afternoon, and I was back in a place where I felt guilty about moving forward. The whole reason for going there was to let go, but instead I poured antiseptic over an open wound. I'll heal faster because I did it, but right now, it burns worse than it has in months.

I was supposed to meet Sam at eight.

My eyes didn't sway from the clock until 8:20 when my cell phone buzzed. It's him, asking if I'm coming. I begin to type a reply but toss my phone back on the bed. There's a tiny voice in my head that's still begging me to go out there, to let the guilt go. But it's not that easy.

I become my own therapist, going through the reasons why and why not. In the end, there are more reasons why I should. Most of them revolve around Sam. He makes me feel like there's still something worth living for. He's my firefly, my ray of hope.

At exactly 8:35, I slide out of my bed and grab a sweatshirt from my closet. Something tells me tonight's going to be a long night. I have a lot of things to explain, bridges to mend.

I manage to slip through the living room without alerting my mom who's curled up with a book. I half expect her to come running out the door after me to ask where I'm off to, but I make it through my yard without question.

I venture through the path I have carved in the cornfields, not stopping until I'm standing at the edge of the grassy area that Sam and I frequented as kids. The sun is just starting to set so it's not hard to spot him sitting along the edge of the creek. A vision of a Midwestern boy in a red and blue flannel and faded blue jeans. My heart lurches at the sight of him, and while part of me wishes I hadn't come out here tonight, the other screams because I didn't come sooner.

Most see him as a tough, hard-nosed guy who will never go anywhere in life, but I see something else. He's broken, withdrawn from most of the world. He's afraid of letting others see his weaknesses so he tucks them away. I'm a master at hide and seek … I see them and most of the time; he doesn't even try to hide them from me.

He sits on the bank of the water, one arm wrapped around his folded knees and the other by his side, a beer bottle resting firmly between his fingers.

Seeing him like this is pure agony, but I know it's thoughts of me he's running from tonight. I want to catch him, to assure him that everything is going to be all right, that I'm going to try my best not to let him down again.

I take quick steps toward him, waiting for him to hear my footsteps. He either doesn't hear me, or he doesn't care. When I'm standing right next to him, I get my answer. His eyes don't leave the water, and I know I've poked holes in the foundation of the relationship we'd just started to build. He's had enough pain to last the rest of his life so I hate that I did this. I hate that my own selfish need to deal with my feelings alone brought him here.

"Sam," I whisper, sliding down next to him. His silence is deafening, saying more than his words ever could. I glance over at him, but he looks in the opposite direction, doing everything he can to avoid my eyes.

Without any choice, I continue to do all the talking. "I'm sorry I'm late. Something happened today, and it didn't feel right to come out here, not before working through the stuff in my head first."

"Was your cell phone broken?" he asks, still not looking at me.

"Don't push me away," I plead, hesitantly placing my hand on his shoulder. He doesn't waste a second before shoving it away like an insect. I feel the rejection deep down in the pit of my stomach, a pain and sickness mixed into one.

"I'm not," he answers, his head snapping to face me.

"What is this then?" My voice is timid, a mirror of the uncertainty I feel inside.

"This is you pushing me away. This is you trying to convince yourself that you never deserve another good thing in your life. You've punished yourself enough, don't you think?"

I nod, wrapping the long, green grass around my fingers to keep them entertained ... to keep them off him. "I went to the cemetery today."

"I know." He swallows hard. I easily follow the path of his Adam's apple, up and down, giving me somewhere to focus besides his disappointed eyes.

"How?" I ask, unconsciously narrowing my eyes at him. He's not the stalking type, not that I know of anyway. That's the thing about small towns. Things travel like the telephone game from one neighbor to another. Eventually, it would get to him.

"I called the shop to see if you wanted to meet me for dinner before coming out here. Ms. Peters told me she'd sent you on a delivery to the cemetery." He watches me, but I remain still, terrified about where this is going, not so much because of where I was or what I was doing but because I don't know why this is such a big deal to him. I was late getting out here, and I'll admit to my doubts, but now that I'm here, he's it. He's my whole reason for being here.

He shakes his head, momentarily breaking eye contact, before finding me again. "I thought you were ready to put your feet in the water. I feel like you're pulling back on me again."

I can't look away. His eyes translate so much of what's going on inside him—sadness and hopefulness wrapped in a heavy coating of fear. The latter is something I've never really seen in him.

"What do you want from me?" I ask, my voice a hair above a whisper.

He closes the space between us until only inches separate our mouths, his brown eyes all I see. "You. I'm only going to get one chance to make you mine, and I want it to count. I need your heart to be in it so I can make it count. I need to know I have all of you."

"I thought we already agreed to this. Slow, right?"

"I'm going slow, but I need to know you're moving right along with me."

"That's what I was doing at the cemetery today … moving. I took a part of myself back because I want to be able to give it to you. I want you to be the next phase of my life. You have to remember, even if the past is behind me, I'm still going to think about it from time to time. People will trigger it. Places will trigger it … he was a big part of my life. He'll always be a part of who I am."

"I want to be who you're with. I'm not a guy who needs a lot of reassurance, but I need to know that I'm not pushing you. I don't want this to end because of a stupid mistake." His words trail off at the end, his hand reaching to cup the side of my face.

Tears well in my eyes, taking mere seconds to fall over the edge. "I'm with you now, aren't I? If you push me, I'll push back, and for the record, nothing about you has ever been a mistake."

"I hope you always think that way."

"Ball's in your court, Shea."

The sun is setting, but I see a smile forming on his face under the orange glow. "I like having some control."

"I've known you long enough. You don't have to tell me … just don't let me down."

"Never," he says, right before his lips brush across mine. "But I think I should get one kiss for every minute you left me waiting. That's not pushing it, is it?"

"No," I whisper, biting down on my lower lip. "I'll even let you add one for good measure."

"This is already the best relationship I've ever been in."

I laugh, quickly brushing the last of my tears away. "That's not saying much."

His fingers clasp my chin, his face as serious as I've ever seen it. "It's says everything."

"Show me," I mouth, my eyes zeroed in on his lips. And he does … once for every minute I left him waiting out in the fields. By the time he pressed his lips to mine for the bonus, I never wanted to leave … not him anyway.

CHAPTER seventeen

September 23, 2013

THINGS AREN'T ALWAYS EASY when a Clark dates a Shea, but it was never easy when I was just friends with Sam either. We agreed to give this thing between us a shot, and I'm hoping that my parents give him one, too. I've lived on this earth for too many years to have to hide something that isn't wrong. Sam isn't wrong ... he's just something they don't like—or understand.

Last night, I saw his vulnerability. I saw the side of him that he doesn't really let other people see ... the one that shows the size of his heart, a window to his beautiful soul. It wasn't guilt that made me want throw out my misgivings and give us a chance ... the burn was in my heart, a small concentrated part of my chest where I only feel him.

I'm scared—scared because this is a whole new arena for me. When Cory and I started dating, I didn't have a friendship with him. There wasn't anything to ruin if things didn't work out between us. With Sam, there's so much to lose. For many years, he was my only—the only person who I could tell everything to and escape judgment. The only person who really listened to what I had to say and asked me questions to try to dissect my words. He was the only person I felt genuinely cared.

Now, I'm back in that same place ... he's my only.

My phone buzzes on my dresser, forcing me to finally get out of my warm, comfy bed. Pulling my pink cami down to cover my bare stomach, I stumble across the room and grab my phone from the dresser.

"Hello," I yawn, tucking it under my chin to stretch my arms up in the air.

"Just waking up?" It's Sam. I should have known since he and Kate are the only ones who ever call me anymore.

"I've been up for a while ... just been laying in bed thinking." I smile, brushing my thumb against my lips as memories of last night flood my mind.

"About me, I hope." The amusement is evident in his voice. I wish he were here so I could kiss the grin off his face.

"Hmm. It could have been you. Things are a little foggy at," I stop, looking over at my digital alarm clock. "Ten in the morning."

"I'll give you a pass since it's Saturday. Don't you work today?"

"No, there was only one wedding, and it was out of town so Ms. Peters is going to take care of it." I offered, but she said everything had to be perfect with this one. High maintenance customer, I guess.

"Sounds like you're mine today. Get dressed. I'm picking you up in thirty minutes." He sounds like a little kid who can't wait to show me some big surprise. Like he's been waiting for this moment forever. Besides that, he has a newfound hold on me, and I kind of like it.

"Are you going to tell me what we're doing so I know what to wear?"

"Jeans, boots, and preferably a jacket. Might get a little cold."

"We're not going fishing, are we?" Sam loves fishing. It's the one thing his dad did with him when he was a kid, besides feeding him and putting a roof over his head. I'll go, if I'm with him, but it's not my favorite thing in the world.

"No, I've got something better than that."

"I didn't know there was anything better, in your eyes."

There's a long pause, then he clears his throat. "I can name two things better than fishing." His voice is not teasing like it was before. He's nervous; this can't be good.

"Yeah? You know you have to tell me what they are now."

"Well, there's that thing I'm going to show you as soon as your ass gets dressed."

"And?"

Another pause. This one punctuated by a deep breath. Sam's not shy when he has something to say. Ever. "You."

Now it's my turn to stay silent for longer than is normally acceptable over the phone. It suddenly feels like I jumped on a train that is moving just a little too fast. I want to go where it's taking me, but I'm hesitant about the ride.

"I'm going to get ready. I'll be ready in a half hour."

"Hey," he says, "That wasn't meant to scare you. I was just being honest."

"I know. Slow, right?"

"Snail's pace," he whispers.

I close my eyes tightly, inhaling a deep breath to keep my racing heart under control. "I'll see you in a little bit then."

"Bye, Rachel."

As soon as the phone clicks off, I jump into action, pulling a pair of jeans and a white T-shirt from my dresser drawer. The whole time I'm doing it, the way he says my name plays over and over in my head. I love the way he says it, like he's not just saying it but feeling it, too. I don't think I really even liked my name until just a couple minutes ago.

I tie my hair up in a ponytail and take a quick shower, letting the hot water warm my goose-bumped skin. The mornings are much cooler now than they were just weeks ago, but not to the point where it makes sense to turn on the furnace. Hot water and a cup of coffee work just as well.

After stepping out of the shower, I dress quickly in order to keep the chill from my skin. I skip most of my morning make-up routine, choosing only to apply moisturizer, lip gloss, and mascara. When I'm done, I throw on my brown leather bomber jacket and a pair of matching brown booties. With one last look in the full-length mirror, I smile at my reflection, feeling more like myself than I have in a long time.

Like most Saturday mornings, Mom is in the kitchen baking. She bakes so much that there's no way our family of three could ever eat it all, but she brings it to church on Sunday. She says it relaxes her after a long week. I don't really get what that means since she doesn't work.

"You were out late last night," she remarks, grabbing a carton of eggs from the refrigerator.

"I was in before midnight." I breeze past her, grabbing an apple from the fruit bowl. When I was in high school, as long as I was with Cory, she didn't care much about what I was doing or what time I came home. I think she just assumed there was no way I'd ever get in trouble with him. It's like reading all the ingredients on a package and deciding something's going to taste good without ever taking a bite. I hate when people make assumptions.

"You just haven't been out that late in a long time." She cracks an egg into the steel bowl, but her eyes are on me.

"I'm just trying to live my life. He would want me to be happy."

Her head tilts as her eyes warm. "I want that for you too."

We stare at each other, two women with souls that the other really hasn't taken the time to see. I've been too stubborn to put my glasses on, and she's been too busy running from this meeting to that one. She cares, but she shows it differently than the moms I grew up seeing on TV, or even some of the moms of my old friends. It doesn't mean she doesn't love me ... she just has a hard time with the warm and fuzzies. She's more into show-and-tell.

"I know, but I don't want you to be disappointed in me. I'm not going to college right now. I'm running deliveries for a flower shop."

She shakes her head, bracing her hands on the counter as she moves around it to where I stand. "What are you talking about? I'm not disappointed in you."

"Are you sure?" My chests heaves, my emotions brewing ... they're either going to turn into anger or tears as they slide over the edge.

She grips my shoulders, forcing her eyes on mine. "I'm just glad you're here, Rachel. I spent days in the hospital wondering if you'd even make it through, and every day I thank God that you're in this house. Walking. Talking. Trying to get on with your life. The last thing I'm worried about right now is your education or career. You have years ahead of you to think about that stuff."

The teeter-totter of emotions weighs heavier on the side of a weird feeling of happy sadness. A tear slips from my eye, but it's because something I perceived for so long has been proven wrong. Sometimes, like now, it's better to be wrong. Maybe I've been wrong all along.

As I wipe the tear from my eye, all I can manage is a nod because opening my eyes would be like taking the lid off an upside down container.

"Everything's going to be okay," she says, pulling me into a tight embrace. I wonder where this version of my mom has been all my life. There's no use in asking because we can never get those years back.

"I just didn't want you to think I was going to live here forever and be content to make flower deliveries."

She pulls back, quietly laughing. "As much as you don't get along with your father, you have some of his fire inside of you. I know you'd never be happy doing that for the rest of your life."

I can't help but laugh right along with her. Dad's the shark, but he passed a little bit of his bite on to me.

A loud engine sounds outside, bringing our attention to the window that faces the drive in front of our house. My mouth hangs open ... Sam's long legs are wrapped around a black bike—motorcycle to be exact.

"What on earth is he doing?" Mom asks, her eyes trained to the same spot as mine.

"He's picking me up."

"On that?" Never in my life have I had a desire to get on a motorcycle. I'd pretty much tagged them as death traps, especially after a guy I went to high school with crashed one coming around a corner and banged his body up pretty good. God knows I'm not going to be able to resist getting on the back of one with Sam, though. He could tell me there's an invisible rope from here to the clouds above, and I'd try to climb it.

"I guess so."

Before I head out to him, I take one last look at Mom who stands with her mouth hanging wide open. "Thank you for this morning ... I really needed that."

I'm not sure if the words even registered with her, but I can't wait much longer to find out because Sam's walking up the front steps. As I walk to the front door, a mixture of nerves and excitement consume every part of me. I can't believe I'm really going to get on one of those things.

In a matter of seconds, I'm standing in front of him. I don't remember opening the door or even walking across the front porch. This sight of him in jeans that fit snugly in all the right places, a black leather jacket, and black riding boots have me in full zombie mode.

"My name's Sam."

I blink, my eyes scanning his body until they land on his. "What?"

He laughs; I kind of want to wipe that sexy, cocky grin off his face, but I like it too much. "You're looking at me like you have no idea who I am. Thought I'd help you out a little."

"I thought you were going to pick me up in your car. You know, one of those things with four wheels ... I wasn't expecting this," I say, circling my finger in the direction where his bike is parked.

"You never asked for specifics."

I can't help but examine every inch of it. The seat is narrower than I'd thought it would be, heightening my anxiety. And, it's not very long ... how are we both going to fit? "That doesn't look safe. Maybe you should go trade it out for your car ... I can wait for you to come back."

"I'm sorry, but that's not happening," he says lightly, tugging on my ponytail.

I want to beg, but other than the whole is-this-thing-going-to-kill-me argument, I have nothing. My mind is a dictionary of blank pages.

"Besides you," he says, "this is the one thing that's better than fishing. We're going to get on here and just ride with no destination in sight." His voice is low yet resonant ... I swear it could come out of a two-faced monster and still be sexy.

"What if it rains?"

He shoves his hands in his pockets, looking up to the sky. "It's clear blue with a hundred percent chance of being sunny for the rest of the day. I think we're good."

Damn him. He's so good that he doesn't leave me any room to argue, and that says a lot because I always have room to argue.

"You ready?" He passes me a helmet, running his fingers through his wind-blown blond hair.

"Where's yours?" I ask.

He shrugs. "I only have one."

"Isn't it dangerous to be on a bike without a helmet?"

"No, if something happens, the helmet's not going to help much ... not on the highway anyway."

He's not helping to ease my nerves ... at all. "Then why do I have to wear one?"

Grabbing the helmet from my hands, he pulls the straps out and gently places it over my head. His hands stay there a little longer than they probably need to. "Because it makes me feel better."

I'm really going to do this, I think as I peer through the tinted visor. I'm going to get on this little machine with nothing over my head, going God knows how fast. This can't really be anyone's idea of fun ... can it?

He climbs on the motorcycle, leaving just enough space on the back for me. "I promise to go five miles under the speed limit since this is your first time. Now hop on."

Someone must have encased my feet in cement while I've been standing here because I can't move. Fear is a crazy little thing, but the only way to get over it is to face it. My mind wants to, but my body isn't on the same program yet.

"Lift one leg over the cycle and hold on to me tight." He smirks like he finds this amusing. I kind of love-hate him right now.

I take one more deep breath and hoist my leg over the top, centering myself on the seat. I wrap my arms around his waist, burying my face in his leather jacket. "Is this too tight?"

"No, you're good."

"Then let's get out of here before I change my mind."

CHAPTER eighteen

As the motorcycle pulls out of my driveway, I'm worried that I won't feel balanced, but it's different than I expected. The seat I'm on is only inches wide, yet I feel comfortable, and the farther we go, the more relaxed I become. Sam starts out slow, but as my arms loosen around him, he gives the bike more gas.

There's something freeing about this—traveling down miles of open road with fresh air hitting every part of me. We move at a comfortable, steady pace as if nothing else matters. The engine screams loudly, but it keeps the unwanted thoughts away. It's just us now. It couldn't be more perfect. We pass cars and houses as we go, but to me, it feels like we're the only two people who exist.

I rest my cheek against his leather jacket feeling the smooth, cool material against my skin. It smells like the perfect combination of leather and his usual cologne.

We pass miles and miles of country land—fields waiting to be harvested, farm animals such as cows and horses, as well as a few lakes and rivers. People who live in the mountains wouldn't think it's much, but it's always been home to me. Peaceful. Flat. Safe.

After two hours or so of riding, we pull into one of the many small towns that exist in the area. It's not big enough for stoplights; in fact, we only encounter one stop sign near the town center. Sam stops behind it and takes the opportunity to rest his hand on top of mine, lightly rubbing my exposed skin with his palm. "You doing okay back there?"

"Perfect," I reply, squeezing his waist once.

"I knew you'd like it."

And just like that, it's time to ride again. His hand leaves mine, and I immediately ache to have it back again. Being with him on the open road is intimate in a way I'd never imagined. His warm touch is the only thing that's missing.

We pass through three more small towns before driving into one slightly larger one. It's not a city by any means but its downtown is filled with tiny shops and restaurants—the specialized type you won't find anywhere else.

Sam pulls the bike into one of the only open parking spots and braces his feet on the ground, looking back at me with sexy as hell aviators shading his eyes. I need to convince him to wear those a little more often. "You hungry?"

I nod, feeling the hollowness in my stomach. I was enjoying the ride so much I didn't realize how much time had passed.

"Hop off, but be careful. Your legs might be a little shaky."

I do as he asks, carefully lowering myself to the ground. He was right about my legs; they vibrate like they're still wrapped around the moving bike. To be safe, I stay where I am, watching him put the kickstand down and lift his leg off the bike.

He stands right in front of me, a vision of the gorgeous bad boy types that always get me in the movies. I know better, though … when it comes to Sam. He might look badass, but there's a huge heart inside that broad chest. One that cared about me enough to help me through a lot of shit, even when he wasn't getting much from me in return.

His large hands grip either side of the helmet, gently pulling it from my head. "That's better," he says, placing it on top of the handlebars. When he turns back around, his fingers reach up and brush the hair away from my face. "You're sexy as hell in that helmet, but I like looking at your beautiful face more."

140

My cheeks heat instantly. Sam's always been honest, but our new status as a sort-of couple has completely unfiltered him. "I like your glasses," I say, momentarily taking the filter off my own thoughts.

He slides them down just enough so I can see his eyes. "Are you flirting with me?"

"Maybe," I answer, consciously biting my lower lip in a way I know will drive him crazy.

He pushes his sunglasses back up his nose and cups my jaw in his hand, tipping my face to his. "I spent so much time talking you into getting on this bike this morning that I forgot something."

The fire in his eyes tells me exactly what he's talking about … what he's about to do. I want him to kiss me. No … I *need* him to kiss me. When I said I wanted to take things slowly, I didn't mean we had to stop kissing. That part of our relationship just feels right.

His thumb brushes across my lower lip, sending shivers down my spine. "Are you going to kiss me? Because if you're not, I think it's time to go eat." My voice is low. I'm baiting him, and by the creases at the side of his eyes, he knows it. He likes this game as much as I do.

"I can't decide," he teases. "Why don't you tell me what you'd rather do."

"Kiss me, then feed me. Please."

His mouth forms a small smile as his tongue darts out to lick his lower lip. Slowly, he moves closer. I shut my eyes, and an anticipatory song starts playing in my mind. It gets louder and louder, until his warm breath tickles my lips. And when we finally touch, everything goes still again. The music stops and the only sense that's still in use is touch. I feel him on my skin and deep inside my heart. The one empty place he reserved a long time ago has now been checked out. A part of me has always been there for him.

Our lips brush, the tip of his nose lightly nuzzling mine. It's a perfect mix of sexy and sweet that he repeats, his body moving closer so our chests touch. There's a part of me that wants more when we're like this, but I also know that for now, it's enough.

He breaks contact only to reinstate it seconds later, pressing his forehead to mine. "That's just the start of what I'm going to show you later," he whispers.

My body tenses. I don't know what he's promising, but it might be too much for where I am right now. Cory left a hollow space inside of me, part of which I know can only be filled with time, but there's also a space left by pure loneliness. It's one that will never go away unless I patch it up with something else ... not that I really consider Sam to be a patch.

"Hey," Sam says. "Come back to me, baby."

I blink a couple times, clearing the fog from my head. "Sorry. I'm just—"

"Hey, all I was referring to is another kiss. A better kiss." His hand grips the back of my neck as he kisses my temple, allowing his lips to linger there a few seconds. "Let's eat."

Without another word, he entwines his fingers with mine and leads us toward a little diner across the street—Bonnie's. It doesn't look like much on the outside, but when we step inside, it's packed. It's decorated in retro fashion with red leather seats and black-and-white décor on the walls, mostly pictures of old movie stars and musicians. It's the kind of place you step into and immediately want to order a burger, fries, and shake. Maybe even put on a big, pink poodle skirt.

"Does this look okay?" he asks.

"More than." I smile when I see a waitress carrying a huge piece of apple pie with a pile of vanilla ice cream on top. It's one of my favorites.

A waitress in a red Bonnie's T-shirt comes up to us. Her brown hair is pulled up on top of her head in a neat, round bun, and a warm smile lights her face. "Welcome to Bonnie's. It should only be a few minutes, and we'll have a table cleared off for you."

"Thanks," Sam says, wrapping his arm around my waist.

My nose is filled with the aroma of fries and onion rings. I'm not usually a junk food eater, but those two things are hard for me to resist. Deep-fried deliciousness.

"Rachel?" I look to the right and spot Kate walking toward me. What the heck is she doing here? We're practically in the middle of nowhere.

"Hey," I say, stepping out of Sam's grasp. I wrap my arms around Kate and hug her tightly. It's been a while since I've seen her.

She steps back, keeping her hands wrapped around my forearms. "What are you doing all the way out here?"

I grin, glancing over my shoulder at Sam. He's standing by himself with his hands tucked into his pockets. When he sees me looking, he winks and takes one hand out to brush his thumb along the corner of his lips. All I can think about is the feel of them on my lips from just a few minutes ago. Looking back to Kate, I notice her smiling, too.

"So?"

I clear my throat, nodding back to where Sam stands. "We were on a motorcycle ride and stopped to grab something to eat. I didn't realize what town we were in."

"Welcome to Carrington," she says, waving her hands up in the air.

"Shouldn't you be back at school?"

"We had a three-day weekend so Beau and I came back home to work."

"Is he here now?" I ask, glancing around for my old roommate.

"He's working with his dad, but he is going to stop in after. Should be here in thirty minutes or so."

"I haven't talked to him in a long time." I didn't realize how much I missed Beau until now. Always wise. Always doing what's right. Kate's a lucky girl.

"Just admit that you miss seeing him in his towel." She laughs, trying her best to stifle the sound by covering her mouth. I absolutely love this girl and the sound of happiness that emanates from her; it's not something I heard often when I first met her the beginning of freshmen year.

A hand comes to rest against the small of my back, and I look over to see Sam standing beside me. "Who do you miss seeing in their towel?"

His eyes are narrowed in on me, and I still hear Kate laughing. She's about to get me in a whole lot of trouble.

"My boyfriend," Kate blurts.

Sam looks lost as he glances between the two of us. "I didn't have any sisters growing up so someone's going to have to explain what's so funny about this."

"Kate!" an older man yells from the small opening to the kitchen. "Order up!"

She rests her hand on mine. "Gotta go. I'll catch up with you guys later. Don't you dare leave without saying goodbye."

With her gone, Sam steps in front of me, looking like we completely lost him somewhere along the way. "Who was that?"

"Kate. She's a friend from college."

He nods, doing that thing where his thumb brushes his lips again. Every time he does it, I want to kiss his hand away … I'm pretty sure he knows it, too. "So, tell me, how do you know so much about how her boyfriend looks in a towel?"

I bite down on my lower lip, remembering the handful of times I saw Beau come out of the bathroom in his favorite post-shower outfit. After the first time, I thought he'd get smarter about it and bring clothes in with him. He never got the hint, or he didn't care.

"He was Cory's and my roommate all of last year." I've noticed that saying his name is getting easier over the last few months, but saying it to Sam feels weird. It's like talking to a waiter about another restaurant you love across town.

"Hmm," he says, wrapping his fingers around mine again. "We're going to have to work on erasing that vision from your mind with something better."

All I can do is shake my head. Boys are born with this competitive gene, which grows right along with them as they become men. Sometimes when it comes out as jealousy it's annoying, but this is kind of cute. I like that he wants to be the only one I think about in that way.

"You can try," I say, reaching up to kiss his cheek.

He groans, bringing our entwined hands up to his lips. "I'll do more than try."

Before I can respond, the waitress from before walks up with two menus in hand. "Follow me," she instructs.

She leads us to a booth along the window and lays the menus on the table. I sit down on one side and instead of taking the booth across from me, Sam slides in next to me.

The waitress has a hard time hiding her amusement, but it's probably not the first time she's seen it. If fact, she smiles at us like we're the cutest things she's ever seen. "Can I get you two something to drink?"

"Can I get a chocolate milkshake and a glass of water?"

She nods, turning her attention to Sam. "And you?"

"I'll have the same."

"Okay, I'll let you look over the menus while I grab those. Be right back."

As I glance over the menu, I realize it's everything a junk food junkie could ever dream of. Fried food. Frozen treats. Bacon is an option on just about everything. It's going to be difficult to narrow this down to the amount of food I can actually eat.

"What are you going to get?" Sam asks, folding his menu back up.

"That's the question of the century. I want a hamburger and french fries, but the onion rings and cheese curds sound good, too."

A grin spreads across his face. "What if we each get a hamburger and then get a sampler platter to share. It has all that fried crap in it."

"Okay, you twisted my arm." I close my menu, signaling to the waitress that we're ready. The longer I sit in this place, the hungrier I become. "So, where are we going after this?"

"You're not ready to go back home?" He leans in close, his hand resting on top of my thigh.

I cover his hand with mine and rub my thumb along his knuckles. "Being on the bike is actually one of the most relaxing things I've ever done in my life."

"I'm glad you feel the same way I do. I don't think this thing between us would work if you didn't," he teases. "We'll head back home, but we're taking a different route this time. Might make a couple stops along the way."

"Take your time. I don't have anything to get home to."

He leans in to kiss me just as the waitress arrives at our table with our drinks in hand. "Are you two ready to order?"

Sam takes the lead, ordering for both of us. My mouth waters just thinking about all the sinful treats that will soon be in front of me.

When he's done, his attention is on me again. "I wonder what else we can get you to try since you took to the motorcycle so easily."

"Don't get too carried away. I have limits, you know."

The space between his lips and my ear is a mere whisper. "Limits are made to be tested. That's how we grow as individuals ... by pushing ourselves to do things we wouldn't normally do."

Closing my eyes, I feel him even though he's not actually touching me, not right now anyway. I don't answer, not because I don't want to, but because I'm mentally checking off all the limits I set for myself. Some of them are less daunting than others, but they're all on that list for a reason.

"Name three things that scare you. I want to know so I can help you through them, because nothing should stand in your way. You're too good for that."

"This is too deep of a conversation to be having in a little diner, don't you think?" I ask.

My eyes follow his as he glances around the room. This place is packed with people, but they're all deep in their own conversations. Not one person is paying any attention to what we're doing. "Looks safe to me," he says, focusing back on me.

I exhale, seeing no way to escape this. He literally has me trapped on this old red leather seat. "I'm afraid of being alone. It's actually the worst thing to be."

"Why do you say that?"

I think back to the last several months. To my time in the hospital when I couldn't wake up. To the hours I spent in my bedroom with too much time to think about everything that went wrong in my life. To all the nights I've spent talking to Cory but not hearing anything back from him. These are moments that created so much sadness within me, my heart so weighted that I'm lucky I didn't completely drown from it all.

"Because I've been there."

"I hope you're not feeling that way right now … or ever again." His eyes are pained, like I've rejected him in some way. Like I said he wasn't enough.

I lean my head against his shoulder, feeling the smooth leather against my cheek once again. "You make me feel like I have everything."

"You don't know how fucking happy that makes me," he whispers, kissing my temple. "What else are you afraid of?"

"Heights. I remember one time my parents took me to the mountains, and there was a point when we stood at the edge looking down with nothing as a barrier. It was as if I didn't have any control. All of a sudden my feet and legs didn't feel like steady platforms. I left to go sit in the car and stayed there for the rest of our ride through Rocky Mountain National Park."

Saying it now makes me feel silly. Deep down I know nothing is going to happen to me unless someone pushes me, but it doesn't take my fear away.

"So what's the last thing?"

Honesty is an open window to the soul … this admission might be me opening that window just a little too far. I open my mouth, but before I get a chance to speak, the waitress sets our plates down on the table. This was definitely not the type of conversation we should be having here, because the heaping piles of fries and onion rings no longer look that good to me. The hollow, hungry feeling in my stomach has been filled with uneasiness.

"Can I get you two anything else?"

Sam looks at me, but all I can do is shake my head and flash a fake smile.

"I think we're good," Sam replies, gently squeezing my leg.

"Okay, I'll check back with you in a few minutes." I watch her walk away, almost wishing she'd come back and take all this food with her, or better yet, just stand at the end of our table so this whole conversation didn't have to continue.

"Are you going to eat?" Sam asks, pulling my attention back.

"Umm, yeah. I was just thinking. Sorry."

His finger brushes against the side of my jaw. It's light and calming. "Eat. We can continue this later. I won't forget."

I hope he does, because I don't think I can lie to him, yet I don't want to tell him the truth. I haven't told him my biggest fear. The one that consumes me most of my days.

Our table is quiet as I force a piping hot fry into my mouth. At first, my body wants to reject it, but the salty goodness overwhelms me, making me crave more. My stomach begins to warm up to the notion of being full, so I take my first bite of my cheeseburger, immediately noticing the buttery flavor of the bun. It practically melts on my tongue.

"That good, huh?"

Grabbing a napkin, I wipe the corners of my mouth before looking up at Sam. He's got a little bit of ketchup at the corner of his lips, but I'm not going to say anything. "What?"

"You're making these little moaning sounds after each bite. It's cute."

My eyes go wide. "No, I'm not."

"Yes, you are." He laughs. "By the way, you missed some on your chin."

Horrified, I quickly pick the napkin back up and dab my face. "Did I get it?"

"Here," he says, wiping his thumb along the center of my chin. Then he does something I never expected, sucking the end of his thumb between his lips. It's shocking but a little sexy.

"I can't believe you just did that."

"What? It tastes even better coming from your skin."

Shaking my head, I pop another fry in my mouth, then chase it down with a long drink of ice water. "You make crazy look cute," I finally say.

"As long as you find me cute, I don't care how I got there."

I'm about to respond, but I'm interrupted by a new voice. "Rachel."

Looking to the end of the table, I see Beau in faded blue jeans and a white T-shirt, his hair mussed up but stylish all the same. He hasn't changed one bit.

"Beau. Long time no see. How you been?"

He shrugs. "I'm adjusting. School's different this year without you and…" He trails off.

I've been so caught up in trying to pull myself together that I never thought about what this is like for Beau. He probably knew me even better than Kate did, just from being around me so much. He definitely saw more of my relationship with Cory.

"I'm sorry. I never even thought about that." I stop, taking a second to glance at Sam whose eyes are firmly fixed on Beau. "Do you want to sit?"

He watches Sam, who finally nods his approval. "Yeah, as long as I'm not interrupting anything."

"Of course not. I actually wanted to ask you a couple questions anyway."

He slides into the booth across from us, folding his hands on top of the table. "Shoot," he says.

"I'm just going to come right out and ask this because there's really no easy way." I pause, looking over at Sam who's finally giving me his full attention. "The last day of school ... did you see us before we left for home? I still can't remember anything past mid-morning." Sam's arm wraps around my shoulders, but I keep my eyes on Beau.

"I came home right as you were leaving to drive home. You'd just finished packing everything into the car."

I instantly feel some hope. "Did anything seem off to you?"

He shakes his head. "No, Cory was helping you out with the last of your things. We made plans to meet up a couple times over the summer and said our goodbyes."

"Did either of us mention a party?"

"I don't think ... wait, right before you left, Cory got a call. When he got off, he mentioned the lake, and you didn't seem too enthused. I think you said something like, 'We'll talk about it when we get home.'"

The parties at the lake were nothing but tests on who can drink the most. It wasn't a game I liked to play, but Cory didn't agree. I always ended up watching him so he didn't take it too far; he never knew when to stop.

"Do you remember who it was that called?" Maybe if he can give me that, I'll be able to put together more of the pieces.

He scrubs his hands over his face. "I do, only because I thought it was strange that she called him instead of you."

"Who?" I ask, my heart beating fast.

Sam pulls my hand in his, gently squeezing. "Do you really want to do this?" he asks quietly.

I look him straight in the eye. "I need to. Nothing's ever going to be over until I remember everything that happened that night."

Sam closes his eyes and nods.

"Who?" I ask Beau again.

"Madison." I don't know if I heard the word or read it off his lips, but it stuns me. She swore that she didn't come home until the following day, so why would she have called Cory to tell him about a party? Had she tried to call me first? It's times like these that make me wish I had my old phone with calls and text messages on it. Maybe there was something on there I could have used to help clarify all this.

"Are you sure?" I finally ask, swallowing down the quiver in my voice.

"I'm sure."

I nod, feeling the world spin around me. Sometimes learning more just messes the whole situation to a greater degree. That's how I feel right now. Nothing about that day or night makes sense, but I'm going to keep trying to figure it out until it does.

"How are you doing, Rachel?"

"It's getting better." I look at Sam and manage a sad smile. For his part, Sam is quiet. I don't miss how uneasy he looks. Maybe it's because he's staring at Beau, the infamous towel boy.

"How are y'all doing?" the waitress asks as she reappears at our table.

"Good," I answer, eyeing my mostly untouched plate.

"Are you going to need a couple boxes?"

"No, thank you," Sam answers. "Just leave it here. We might eat a little more."

"Okay. I'll bring your check."

As soon as she disappears, Kate slides in next to Beau. "I have a fifteen-minute break. Let's make it count." Beau wraps his arm around her and kisses the center of her forehead like I've seen him do countless times before. They're one of those couples you only have to be around for a few minutes to know they're forever.

We spend Kate's break telling stories about our freshman year of college. I never doubted Sam would get along with my new friends, but they mesh even better than I expected. Kate approves; I can tell by the way she smiles at the two of us.

At one point, when we're all laughing, Sam gets a serious look on his face and leans across the table. Beau and Kate both look at me, wondering what the heck he's doing, but Sam's eyes are fixated on Beau.

He motions for Beau to lean in. He complies. "You're a cool dude, but you need to keep your clothes on when you're around my girl."

"What?" Beau asks, his eyebrows pulling in.

"Towels are not clothes."

Understanding washes over Beau's features as Kate sits beside him, her hand covering her mouth. "I'll remember that."

Laughter echoes from our table again. It feels nice—being here with new and old friends.

"You guys should be proud of Rachel. I got her here on my motorcycle."

"No way," Kate says, her mouth hanging open in disbelief. "I thought you hated those things."

I laugh. "I did until a few hours ago. Sam convinced me otherwise."

"Can I see it?" Beau asks. When Kate shoots him an inquisitive look, he continues, "I'm thinking about buying one … when we're done with college."

"Let's do it," Sam says. "It'll give the girls a few minutes to talk." Sam winks at me as if he knows something I don't and throws a couple twenty-dollar bills on the table. "I'm buying."

Kate stands to let Beau out while Sam leans in to my ear. "I'll wait for you outside. Take as long as you need."

"Thank you," I say, kissing his cheek.

CHAPTER nineteen

"ARE YOU DOING OKAY?" Kate asks as soon as the guys are out of earshot.

I shake my head. "No. Beau just told me something, and I'm having trouble reconciling it in my head."

"What did he say?"

"Do you remember me mentioning my best friend from high school, Madison?"

She nods.

"Well, Beau told me that she called Cory the day of the accident to invite us to the party I can't remember. It doesn't make sense because she told me she wasn't in town that night."

"Maybe he mixed her up with someone else. It was a hard night for everyone."

At this point, I hope that's what happened, but he seemed so sure of himself. There was no hesitation or confusion. I wish there had been because I'd be holding that doubt tightly in my hand. Every part of me wants to believe that he was mistaken.

"I don't think so. I'm going to try to call her when I get home," I say softly, ripping the edges from a napkin.

"Can I see that napkin for a minute?"

I lift a brow at her as I hand her the thin, white paper. There are at least ten other ones on this table so why does she want mine? I watch as she grabs the pen from the top of our bill and begins to scribble on the napkin.

"What are you writing?" I ask.

"You'll see."

While I wait, I glance at the bill. I feel horrible for making Sam pay for something I barely touched. Looking at his plate, I notice he didn't touch much of his either.

"Here," Kate says, handing me a folded napkin. "But don't read it until you get home."

I roll the material between my fingers so tempted to defy her. "Why can't I read it now?"

Her eyes lock onto mine in warning, like my mother's would. "Because I said so. Trust me."

I tuck it deep in the pocket of my jacket, but the thought of sneaking off to the bathroom to read it crosses my mind. I'm not good about surprises.

"Look, I have to get back to work before they start yelling at me. We'll talk again soon, okay?"

I nod, standing to give her a hug before she gets too far away. "I miss you."

"I'm only a phone call away," she says, folding her arms tightly behind my back.

"I'll try to remember that."

"Take care, Rachel." She lets go, taking a few steps back.

"You too." I miss her as I watch her walk away. It sucks that we live a couple hours apart.

As I step outside, I notice how much cooler it's gotten since we jumped on the bike this morning, and despite Sam's forecast, the skies have clouded over. When the motorcycle comes into view, Sam's leaning against it with his hands tucked into the pockets of his jeans. His hair is sticking up in all directions, but it just makes him look even better than usual, and that's hard to do.

"Ready?" I ask, stepping off the curb.

The corner of his mouth turns up, his eyes scanning the entire length of my body. "Did I tell you how fucking sexy you look in that coat and boots?"

"You may have mentioned it."

His fingers loop into my belt loops, using the leverage to pull me forward until my body is flush against him. "In case I didn't, I'm going to say it again. You're so fucking sexy, Rachel, and I can't believe that after all these years ... all this time, you're finally mine."

Wrapping my arms around his neck, I step up on my tippy toes and kiss the cleft of his chin. "I'm the lucky one."

He kisses me back, but on the lips. He tastes me slowly, like one might let a smooth piece of milk chocolate melt on their tongue. When he pulls away, I crave him. I want his skin back on mine.

"Since our relationship is new, I'm not going to argue with you about that, but it's not always going to be this way." He goes in for one more kiss, leaving me nearly breathless by the time he's done. "We should probably get going," he says, looking up to the sky. "It looks like the weather man may have lied."

"Okay. Maybe we can go back to my house and watch a movie or something."

His head tilts. I know what he's thinking ... my parents will have a heart attack if they see Sam Shea walk through my front door.

"Or your place," I add, making that smile of his reappear.

"Now, that sounds like a plan."

He slides the helmet off the handlebars and places it firmly on my head, making sure it's fastened in place. "Ready?" he asks.

"I'm actually looking forward to it."

"Why are we still standing here then? Climb on."

With my arms tightly around him, we make our way out of town, taking the same route we used to get in. From there, we turn onto a winding country road that's completely different. The path is lined with mature trees, which are just starting to change color with autumn moving in. Even under the cloudy sky, I have to admit it's beautiful.

With the sound of the loud engine once again in the background, I think about what Beau said back at the diner. About Madison being the one who called about the party that day. Something about Madison hasn't sat right with me since that day in the hospital. There's something she's not telling me.

Maybe she called but wasn't able to make it back in time for the party. Maybe she's protecting me by not telling me something she knows would break me. Whatever it is, I just want to know, to try to put the pieces together.

As we continue to make our way toward home, the sky becomes darker. It's a different feeling—being out here in the dead of night. It's harder to see where we're going. My control starts to slip, and that's when the old feelings come back. The hopeless sorrow I've been fighting. Visions of Cory's smiling face flood my mind. It's hard to imagine one event affecting a person this much, but it has. I freaking hate it.

Soon, I recognize some of the houses we pass ... not too much farther to go, I tell myself. As we come around a big curve, panic fills my chest. There's no reason, no thought behind it, but all the sudden it's extremely hard to breathe. My hold on Sam is tight, yet it's like I'm not holding on at all. My arms feel like rubber, and my jaw tingles. Then, as we round the last quarter of the curve, I hear them ... the voices. Mine and Cory's.

"What are you talking about, Rachel? I'm not the one who fucked up." It's Cory. He's sitting in the passenger seat of my car.

"Me!" I scream. My fingers ache from how tightly I'm gripping the steering wheel. "I didn't do anything wrong. You're the one who fucked up. I know exactly what I saw!" I yell.

"Pull this car over right now! We're going to find somewhere to talk until I get it through your fucking head ... I didn't fucking touch her."

Anger. Just thinking about this is making my blood boil. I saw something that night. Something I wished I could un-see. What was it? God, I wish I could remember.

"So putting your fucking lips on her neck isn't touching? What the fuck, Cory? I'm not an idiot!"

"So what now? Hmm? You going to make me suffer for a week or two while you work through the shit in your head? What if I don't wait for you?"

I laugh, but sad tears run down my cheeks. It's maniacal—like I'm going insane. "No, I'm going to take you home and spend the next weeks and months convincing myself you never existed, because right now, I wish you didn't."

"Damnit, Rachel!" His hand covers mine on the steering wheel. "Pull. This. Car. Over. Now!"

"No," I say, the tears spilling over at a quicker rate.

Then it happens: his hand tightens over mine, and as I try to free myself, he pulls against the steering wheel. Looking up through the windshield, I start to panic. My car veers off the curve and down a deep embankment. It's falling fast, and there's nothing I can do about it.

"Shit! Shit!" Cory screams, but then there's silence. Everything goes black.

My body trembles as I remember what it was like in those last seconds. How helpless I felt. It's why I always feel like I've lost control. I knew what was coming the minute the car rolled into the grass, but there was absolutely nothing I could do to stop it.

I'm so lost that I don't realize Sam's pulled along the side of the road. I don't realize my eyes are closed until I notice the overwhelming darkness. I feel dizzy, as though someone slapped me hard across the face, and I'm trying to regain my footing.

"Rachel, what's wrong, baby? Talk to me please." Not only has the motorcycle come to a complete stop, but Sam's standing over me with my face in his cold hands. I want to say something, but I'm too numb. Insensible. Unfeeling. I see him. I feel his worry, but I'm unable to respond to it.

"Rachel, please. Please, baby." He cradles me in his strong arms, holding me close to his body. In the distance, I see a wooden cross, surrounded by faded silk flowers and a stuffed teddy bear. This is exactly where it happened … where Cory's life ended.

My breathing becomes more labored as tears cloud my eyes. It's not long before I feel nothing. My body goes limp then I see nothing.

CHAPTER twenty

I OPEN MY EYES to an unfamiliar, dark space. The only light in the room is a street lamp that shines through the window showing the outline of a dresser on the other side of the room. There's a door along the same wall, but I don't make any move toward it, even though I know this room isn't mine.

Stretching my arms above my head, I realize I'm in a warm bed with a blanket pulled up to my neck. It takes me a minute to adjust—to remember where I was before this—and as soon as I do, the tears immediately start up again. Something really bad happened the night of the accident before we even got in the car. What did Cory think he saw? What did I see? My head hurts trying to recall what it was and after a while, I give up completely. I have enough to wrap my head around.

If the memory is accurate, the last thing I said to Cory is something about wishing he didn't exist. I don't even want to imagine what was going on in his head as the car went toward the tree. Was he replaying my words? If he's in a place like heaven, is that what he remembers? Can you even remember things like that in heaven?

Rolling to my side, I fold one of the pillows in half and let it soak up my tears. Burying my nose into the soft cotton, I realize it smells just like Sam—the mix of his cologne and soap. I inhale it, wishing he were still here and slowly drift back to the darkness. Days like this, I like it better there anyway.

I try to turn over, but a strong arm holds me in place, a large chest pressed against my back. I don't have to look to see who it is. I recognize the safe feeling. The warmth. The mixture of firm and gentle in his touch. Pushing back, I align my whole body with his; it fits perfectly.

"Are you awake?" he whispers, sounding half asleep.

"Yeah," I answer, rubbing my hand over his forearm.

He loosens his grip. "Look at me, baby."

Feeling the weight of this situation in the center of my chest, I follow his request. I'm too tired and weak to do otherwise, and I've put him through enough as it is.

Even in the dim light, I recognize the pain and worry in his eyes. Creases exist at the corner of each, ones I couldn't see as easily before now. If there were room in my heart or mind for anything besides my sadness and contemplation, I'd feel guilty for what I put him through.

His fingers curl into my hair as his thumb brushes along my cheekbone. "How are you feeling?" His words come out quickly as if he's worried I'll drift off again before he gets an answer.

I open my mouth, noticing how painfully dry my lips are. It's like the hospital all over again. "Confused and tired."

"You scared the shit out of me last night."

"I'm sorry. I remembered something about the accident as we came around the corner, and I lost it."

"Talk to me." His hand trails down my jawline before combing through my hair yet again. It feels good to fall into his touch.

"I can't put it into words, not yet. Besides, I feel like I haven't slept in days, and my mouth is so dry."

His large hands come down, cupping my jaw. "Baby, please let me help you."

"I need time. Please … just be patient with me."

His fingers slide to the back of my neck as he kisses my temple. With that simple touch, some of the built up tension in my body fades away, like footprints washed away in the sand by a coming wave.

"I'll grab you some water. Sit tight."

He rolls out of bed before I have time to protest the loss of his warm body against mine. His form quickly disappears through the door, giving me just enough time to realize he's only wearing a pair of gym shorts … no shirt. If this had happened yesterday, I would have jumped out of bed to get a better glimpse at his tight, toned abs, but today's a top ten worst days ever type of day.

"Here you go," he says, reappearing.

I prop myself up, grabbing the bottle from between his fingers. "Thank you." I gulp the cold water down until the inside of my mouth doesn't feel like it was scraped with sandpaper.

"What time is it?" I ask, realizing just how dark it is outside.

"Almost three in the morning."

"Oh my God," I screech, sitting straight up. "My mom's going to freak out."

"Hey," Sam says, crawling up next to me on the bed. "I called her earlier. She knows you're here and that you're safe."

"You didn't tell her about what happened, did you?" I see hours and hours of therapy in my future. Hundreds of questions I can't necessarily answer. Just when things started to feel normal again, they had to fall apart.

"Of course, I didn't. She thinks you fell asleep on my couch, and I didn't want to wake you."

"Ugh … I bet that went over well. Sorry."

He wraps his strong arm around me and kisses the top of my head. "Having you here next to me makes it all worth it. Besides, she took it better than I expected."

"Hmm, that sounds unlike her," I mumble, lying my cheek on his chest. It's not as comfortable as a pillow, but it's more comforting. It's the equivalent of having a warm fleece blanket. I want to wrap myself around him and never let go.

"Go back to sleep. We can talk in the morning," he soothes, his hands slowly brushing over my hair. It's not long before my worries start to fade. Sleep really is the only true escape … the place where thoughts of nothingness take over.

CHAPTER
twenty-one

September 24, 2013

THE RECOLLECTION I HAD on the motorcycle last night came to me again in a dream. It was much the same, no more, no less, but it was like I was seeing it in a different way. It hurt more. Instead of being someone who lived in it, I saw it as an outsider.

I hated how I talked to him.

I hated the anger I felt toward him.

I hated the physical pain I felt in my sleep even though it was months ago.

I hated it all, and I'm holding onto the hope that it didn't really happen that way. That it's all made up in my mind. I know better, though. It's all too vivid, too real. Besides, it can't be a coincidence that it came to me in the exact place my car veered off the road. It was a trigger I wish hadn't been pulled.

Glancing back, I see Sam sleeping behind me, his long dark eyelashes highlighted by closed eyes. His full, slightly puckered lips parted. It's so tempting to reach for him, to bring his lips to mine, to beg him to make me forget. But I don't deserve a guy like Sam. The more my actions with Cory replay, the more I feel like I don't deserve anything remotely like this.

As if he knows I'm staring, his eyes flutter open, immediately focusing in on me. Those eyes are the most beautiful, soulful shade of brown. I wish I could completely lose myself in them and let them lull me like a lullaby, but that's not even possible.

"How did you sleep?" he whispers.

"Okay," I lie, swallowing down the emotions that have been tugging at my heart all morning.

He sits up, placing all his weight on one arm. "Are you crying?"

"I'm just adjusting to the light," I quickly answer. I made myself stop a while ago knowing he'd wake soon, but it wasn't soon enough.

"I hate to see you cry," he says, cradling the side of my face in his hand. "Talk to me. Let me help you."

I shut my eyes to him and the light. "I'm so tired, Sam."

"Of what?"

"Of everything. Of feeling better about how things are going one minute, then having the world come down on me the next."

He slides his fingers along my cheek. "I want to make it better. What can I do to make it better?"

"You can't."

With one quick motion, I'm enveloped in his arms, his soft lips touching my forehead. He's everything I should need right now, yet he's not enough. Being here like this makes me want to cry, and that's not how this should be.

What I really need is time to work through this, and I can't think with him this close. I want to scream. I want to cry into my pillow. I just want to disappear to where no one can find me—to be alone.

"Can you bring me home?" I ask, pressing my hand against his chest. It's a half-hearted effort. I want to be here, but I don't. Actually, who am I kidding ... I don't freaking know what I want or need anymore.

"Let me make you breakfast first." He tries to pull me back into his body, but I fight it, pushing harder against his chest.

"Please, Sam. I'm not feeling well."

"Rachel—"

"Please," I interrupt. I break from his hold, scooting up against the old wood headboard.

He throws the sheet off his body and stands up next to the bed, running his fingers through his tousled hair. "I'd feel better about this if I didn't feel like you were running away."

"I'm not running. I just need to go home, okay? I need to work through this shit that's piled in my freaking head. It has nothing to do with you ... nothing to do with us!" My voice rises to levels I didn't expect it to, but I can't help it. I'm going through more than I can handle right now.

"Give me a few minutes. I'm going to throw some clothes on, and then I'll get you home." He doesn't wait for me to say anything. He's behind the bathroom door before he even gets the last word out.

Pulling the sheets off myself, I realize I'm in all the same clothes as yesterday, with exception to my leather jacket. There's not much I can do to myself here. I'm sure my hair and face are a mess, but it doesn't matter because as soon as I'm home, I'm going to jump in the shower and try to wash away the memories of last night.

I wrap my arms tightly around my folded legs and rest my cheek against my knees. The area of the loft where Sam's bed is has muted gray walls and a few colorful abstract art pieces on the wall. It's not really how I pictured his room to be, but it's still him. Bold yet simple.

The bathroom door clicks open, and Sam steps out in a fresh pair of khaki shorts and a Bob Marley T-shirt. His hair is still a mess, but it's more expertly done.

"Ready?" he asks, slipping on a pair of brown flip-flops.

"I just need to use the restroom. Give me two minutes."

"Want a clean T-shirt or something to change into?"

"I'll be okay," I reply, rolling off the bed. "I'm going to shower as soon as I get home anyway."

He nods, scrubbing his hand over his handsome, unshaven face. He's frustrated with me and maybe a little disappointed. It's obvious because he won't look directly at me. "I'm going to put my bike away. Come outside when you're ready."

"Okay."

Like a small piece of debris picked up by a tornado, he disappears. I instantly wish I could take back some of the coldness in my demeanor, but I can't. The past is something we live with because it can't be erased. For some things, there's no do-overs or second chances.

Sam's bathroom consists of a small shower, toilet, and pedestal sink. Nothing fancy, but it's very modern. After straightening my clothes from their crumpled state, I squeeze a line of toothpaste on my finger and attempt to freshen up.

When I feel like I've done all I can, I look at my reflection in the mirror. Most of the make-up from yesterday has faded, leaving nothing but a smudge of mascara under each of my eyes. I look worn like a mother with a newborn child or a college student after cramming all night for an exam. It doesn't suit me.

After splashing a few handfuls of cold water over my face, I go looking for Sam. There's a part of me that wants to smooth everything over, to leave us on good, solid footing, but the selfish part of me wants to leave it like this. The only way to get the time I need to get over the turmoil this most recent flashback created is to push him back enough to give it to me.

I move through the living area, picking up my jacket from the back of the couch along the way. As I come down the stairs, I hear the soft purr of the Camaro outside. The drive between his place and mine is roughly four minutes. That's four minutes I'm not looking forward to because I don't know what to say. Four minutes of what's probably going to be uncomfortable silence.

Walking out, I see his car right outside the front door. Even through the light tinting on the windows, I can make out his whole profile. He sits with his wrist propped up on the steering wheel, staring straight out the windshield. His forehead is wrinkled, and it's evident that he's biting down on the inside of his cheek. He's so deep in the ocean of thought that he doesn't see me coming until I open the door. Only then does he look up—the worried, contemplative expression on his face not changing.

"You okay?" he asks.

I nod, pulling the seatbelt over my shoulder. I only consider it a half lie; I'm physically all right. My head's just not in the right place.

He shifts the car into drive and lays his right hand on the seat between us. I think he's hoping I'll reach for it. He wants assurance that I can't give him right now. I can't even convince myself that everything is going to be okay.

"I'm still going to be here when you're ready to talk," he says quietly as we pull onto the road that connects his driveway to mine. A part of me wishes I'd gotten out of bed and walked home instead of watching him sleep. It would have been childish but easier.

"I know."

"And I'm not going to let you hold it in forever." As we turn onto my driveway, I keep my eyes on the house at the end. A pit forms in my stomach when I see Mom's car parked out front. I'd been hoping to get in and up to my room without having to talk to anyone else.

When the Camaro comes to a stop, I undo my belt and reach for the handle, anxious to avoid any more awkwardness.

A large hand wraps around my elbow before I get the chance to see that through. "Rachel."

He feels me slipping … I feel myself slipping.

"Yeah?"

"Can I see you tonight?"

I don't look back. I can't. "Call me later. Okay?"

"Look at me." His voice shakes like a glass pane during a minor earthquake. I hate myself for it, for giving him hope then pulling it all back.

My stomach tenses even more as I turn around to where the most beautiful, fragile man sits staring at me with a pained expression. *I hate myself.*

"Everything in me is saying not to let you get out of this car. Tell me you're going to pick up the phone later when I call."

I try to carve a smile on my face, but my lip quivers instead. The truth always has a way of coming to the surface. "If you call, I'll answer."

"Rachel—"

"No, you have to believe me. I just need a few hours to myself."

"Okay," he says, loosening his grip on my arm. "I just got you, and I'm not going to let you go."

"I don't want you to." I lean across the seat and press my lips to his cheek. It's quick, and when I'm free of his hold, I open the door and step out before he can pull me back. "Bye."

He waves but still looks unsure. "Bye."

After closing the door, I hurriedly make my way up the stairs and disappear inside. The door is barely closed when my mom appears in the entryway with an apron wrapped around her waist.

"Looks like you had a rough night."

I shrug, crossing my arms over my chest. "This is just how a person looks after sleeping in their clothes."

"I wasn't really talking about your clothes. You look like you just ran through an emotional gauntlet," she says, taking two steps toward me. "Sorry, I didn't mean to sound so harsh. I'm just worried about you."

"I'll be fine. I'm tired, that's all."

I start toward the steps, but her voice stops me in my tracks. "Did something happen with Sam?"

She's probably waiting for me to say yes so she can go on and on about how wrong it is for me to be hanging out with the likes of Sam Shea. If only she knew how right it is being with Sam. He's too good for me.

"No, Mom, nothing happened with Sam."

She nods, running her hand along her chin. "Do you want me to call Dr. Schultz?"

My first thought is to say no, but then I hesitate. Maybe he'll tell me it was all a fictional tale that snuck into my mind. My biggest fear spun into reality. "Yeah, you can do that."

Without another word, I make my way up the rest of the stairs and disappear into my bedroom. I peel off all my clothes and haphazardly throw them on the floor before shutting myself in my bathroom. It was a long night, but I'm hoping hot water will wash it away.

After turning the shower to the hottest setting I know my skin can bear, I climb in, letting it run down my face, much like how the tears had a short time earlier. It's almost scalding, but I like the pain. It gives me something to concentrate on besides the excruciating push and pull in my heart.

Where did my life go so wrong? In one night, I went from the girl who had it all to the girl who'd lost it all. It doesn't seem fair, but then I guess life isn't fair. And just when I think I've fallen into a better place, I'm uprooted again. I wonder if it will always be like this … if that one night will always chase after me.

"Rachel!"

"I'm in the shower."

"Dr. Schultz said he could see you later today. Does six work?" Mom yells from the other side of the door. I'm kind of surprised the doctor wants to see me on a Sunday, but I'm not going to argue.

"That'll work!" I brace my hands against the wall, silently begging her to go, to give me the time I need.

"Are you doing okay in there?"

"I'm fine! I just want to finish my shower. Please!"

"Okay, okay. I'm running to town. I'll see you a little later."

With newly gained silence, I go back to my place under the hot water, letting it run off my skin until my fingers look like wrinkled prunes. I turn it off and wrap a towel around my body, taking a moment to stop in front of the mirror and look at my deep pink skin. It doesn't hurt nearly as bad as it looks.

After toweling myself off, I pull on a pair of black yoga pants and a tank top, and run a comb through my hair. Then, out of pure exhaustion, I fall onto my bed and drift to sleep, knowing no better way to let it all go.

CHAPTER
twenty-two

WHEN I FINALLY WAKE up, it feels as if I only slept for a few minutes, but, looking at the clock, I realize it's been hours. I panic, thinking I'm late for work, then I remember it's Sunday; the shop isn't open on Sunday.

Stretching my arms above my head, I feel a little better than I did before. My heart still aches, but it's more of a dull ache. A minor annoyance. It's usually my own thoughts that puncture it, but when I'm able to turn them off, the bleeding slows. If only there were a permanent Band-Aid.

As I roll out of bed, I hear my phone vibrating from on top of my dresser. I pick it up, noticing I have one missed call from Kate, six from Sam, and fourteen unread texts, not to mention six voicemails.

I lie back in bed, deciding to listen to the voicemails first.

"Hey, Rachel, it's Kate. I just want to tell you it was nice seeing you yesterday and make sure you got home safely. Talk to you soon."

I delete it, making a mental note to give her a call later. Putting the phone back to my ear, I wait for the next one.

"Rachel, it's Sam. I thought you were going to answer when I called." He laughs quietly. "Anyway, call me when you get this. I really just need to hear your voice."

I think I really like this guy, but hearing the sweetness in his voice reminds me that he probably belongs with someone better than me. Someone who doesn't have all this crap going on in her life.

"Hey, I called you over an hour ago and haven't heard back. I'll understand if you don't feel like talking today, but at least text me and let me know you're all right."

I hit delete again and move on to the next. "Please, call me. I think I've said everything else I want to say."

With each one, his voice is more desperate. I hate that I do this to him.

"If I don't hear back from you within the next thirty minutes, I'm going to call your mom. Fuck. You're making me sound like a little kid now. Please, just call me."

Frustration is still there, but now anger is laced in with it. It makes my chest hurt. So much so, I don't even want to listen to the last one, but I do. I've obviously become a fan of self-torture.

"Hey, Rachel. I talked to your mom, and she said you're sleeping. Can you give me a call when you wake up? Give me a few seconds with that voice of yours."

The last message is calmer, which in turn calms me, but the little voice in the back of my head starts talking again. That stupid little voice never gives me a break anymore. What if Sam talked to Mom? What did he tell her? Does she know everything that happened last night? Deep down, I know Sam wouldn't do that to me, but rationality isn't winning right now.

Thumbing through my texts, I notice they carry the same tone as the voicemails Sam left. A string of increasingly more panicked messages followed by a levelheaded one.

I think about calling him, even placing my finger over his number, but it moves away when I realize I don't have anything to say. The fire in my heart was partially extinguished by a few hours of restful sleep, but I can already feel the flames igniting again. If the guilt would only fade away and never come back.

Sitting up on my bed, I grab my old pink notebook from my nightstand and find the first blank page. It's always taken me a few minutes of mindless staring before the words begin to form. I need to pull myself into the right place, the deepest place in the soul, and pull out what's hidden within.

When you're lost, the only thing left to be is found.
You can be lost in sadness and found in happiness.
Lost in regret but found in forgiveness.
The key to being found comes from within …
No one is going to hand it to you.
…Life isn't meant to be that easy.

When I look back up at the clock, it's a little past five. I fold the page over and hop out of bed to find some clean clothes before I head out to visit Dr. Schultz.

"Rachel, are you awake?"

"Yes!" I yell back, thumbing through the sweaters that line one side of my closet. Fall has always been my favorite season because it's perfect sweater weather. Not warm. Not cold. Just right. Even that's been tainted. Nothing is as good as it seemed before.

For the sake of time, I choose a thin black turtleneck that I haven't worn in almost a year. It's wrinkled, but that doesn't even faze me. Black is suitable for every mood, or that's what they say. To me, it's just a simple choice. One that doesn't require a thought. I pair it with faded blue jeans and run to the bathroom to splash cool water over my face to wake up. I could have easily slept through the rest of the day, but that only delays the inevitable.

I do a quick-once over in the mirror, and I'm ready. A brush never touched my hair. My face is bare, dark circles surrounding my blue eyes. Several months ago I would have cared, but not now.

"Rachel!" Mom must sense how much I need this because she's not letting up. She really has nothing to worry about because even I know how much I need to talk to someone.

"Coming!" I pick up the simple black booties that are haphazardly scattered across my floor and quickly pull them on.

I hurry, because if she yells my name one more time, I swear I'm going to lose it. My nerves are already about to explode.

It's not a big surprise that she waits at the bottom of the staircase. "Do you want me to take you?"

"No," I reply, walking right past her.

"I wish you would tell me what's bothering you. I haven't seen you like this since…"

I stop, my hand pressed against the cold windowpane that's set in the center of the front door. "Don't say it, okay? I'm not dealing with it very well right now."

"I'm sorry. I didn't realize…"

I shake my head. Maybe in some way, I'm hoping it will shake the pain away. "It's okay. I remembered something when Sam and I were riding last night, and I don't know what's real anymore."

When she's quiet for longer than I expect, I glance over my shoulder. She looks sad, her eyes glossy. She's not my usual confident and bright-eyed mother. "I hate that you're going through this."

"At least it can't get much worse," I say, smiling sadly.

She tries to match my expression but fails. "Things will get better. I promise."

I nod. I'm not convinced of that, especially right now. "I need to get going, or I'm going to be late."

"Call me if you need anything." She waves, and I head out the door, breathing in the cool autumn air. It must have rained earlier because the ground is wet, and it smells of musky leaves. Days like these, I wish I lived in town so I could walk to clear my head, but I'll have to settle for the short car ride with the radio on blast.

Once I'm heading down the deserted blacktop, I roll down my window a crack to get more of that rain smell. I inhale it while listening to "You" by Keaton Henson. I try to focus just on the lyrics, but every simple word and phrase leads to a deeper thought. Everything is much clearer than it has been the last twenty-four hours. The accident didn't happen because I'd been drinking. I didn't take a moment of pure innocence and turn it into the worst type of tragedy. We both had a hand in it. Cory and I battled over something that night … neither of us should have been in that car, at least not in the shape we were in.

As my car slows at the first stop sign in town, I see a motorcycle in the distance. My car could have made it across the street with plenty of time to spare, but I wait, watching Sam pass by. I never did call or text him and, up until now, when his eyes connect with mine, he probably assumed I was still sleeping. There's no way I'm going to be able to hide now.

I expect him to turn back around, but he cruises down the street without another glance back. His figure becomes smaller and smaller until he disappears altogether.

I know I need to call him later to work this out. To tell him the reason behind my silence. I think he'll understand, or I hope he will.

A horn sounds from behind my car, startling me. I carefully look in each direction then put my foot on the gas. A few seconds later, I'm parking on the vacant downtown street. If it were dark, this would be eerie. No people. No cars. The rainy weather.

I push my bangs from my face and run my fingertips below my tired eyes. God, I hope the doctor can make me feel better. I can't keep doing this.

With one foot out the door, my cell rings. Looking down at the display, I see Sam's name. My stomach rolls when I think about what must be going through his head, but I'm already a few minutes late for my appointment, so I hit ignore and toss it back in my purse. Dr. Schultz isn't going to wait for me forever, especially when he took time out of his Sunday to meet me.

Walking into his small office building, I'm surprised to see the doctor sitting behind the reception desk. "Hi Rachel, I didn't know if you were still coming."

"Sorry, I got a little distracted along the way."

He smiles warmly. "It's okay. I'm glad you came. Should we head back to my office?"

I'm about to say yes, but then I remember how dark and drab his office is. Black leather furniture, a dark wood desk, and a small window to the alleyway. It's professional, but I'd rather stay out here, with the rain hitting against the large window.

"Can we sit in here? I like watching the rain."

"Normally, no, but since it's just you and me, I'll make an exception," he answers, steepling his hands in front of him. "Take a seat and tell me what brings you in today."

I glance around the empty waiting room, ultimately choosing a chair across from the window. Sitting back, I cross my legs then uncross them. Nothing makes me feel comfortable enough.

"I had a flashback last night. At least I think that's what it was."

He comes around the desk, taking a seat kitty corner from me. "Do you want to talk about what happened in your flashback?"

My eyes well with tears. "I remembered what led up to the accident. Cory and I were fighting, and his hand ended up on my steering wheel." Tears slip from my eyes. "If the memory is correct, I said some things I wish I hadn't."

He makes a quick note on his notepad. "Do you remember what you were fighting about?"

"Not really," I say, shaking my head. "I mean, I mentioned something, he mentioned something, but there wasn't enough to it for me to draw a clear conclusion."

"Did how it happened make you feel worse about the accident?"

"I learned that it wasn't all my fault. If he hadn't grabbed the steering wheel, I think we would have been okay. But on the other hand, I can't believe the things I said to him. I basically told him I wished he didn't exist."

A lump forms in my throat as I stare down at my folded hands. When I glance back up, he's watching me carefully. "You didn't really mean it, though, did you?"

"No!" I shout, blinking back tears as I look up at the ceiling tiles. "I can't think of a single person in this world I think that of."

"So why do you think you said it?" His tone is lower than it had been. It's what he always does when he thinks I'm close to some sort of revelation. He's brought me to quite a few.

"I was angry," I say, focusing back on him. "I was so angry."

The tip of his pen rolls along his lip. "Why were you angry?"

"I don't know ... that's what's so frustrating." And the fact that I may never remember is eating away at me.

He nods, pulling his glasses from his eyes. "Is that what's bothering you most about this?"

Is it? I don't freaking know. It hit me too hard and fast last night to even really think about it. The anger bothers me. The things I remember saying bother me. But they aren't the worst part ... not to me.

"That things weren't as perfect as I'd thought them to be. I always had my blinders on with Cory, and I think if I'd taken them off a long time ago, he might still be here." I swipe the back of my hands across my cheeks, wiping away saltwater streams. Maybe it would have been better if I'd never remembered anything at all. I was doing so well ... with Sam.

Dr. Schultz leans forward, placing his glasses back on his nose. "What do you need to move past this?"

That's what I came here for. "I guess I need to accept what I cannot change. I was actually doing pretty good until yesterday ... it's something new to process."

He nods again. "And how are you going to do that?"

I glance down at the coffee table in front of me. Right on top is one of those celebrity magazines, the ones filled with half-truths. On the cover is a young couple: he's the nation's pop super star, and she's an up-and-coming actress. They look so disgustingly happy with her hoisted up in his arms. That's not even the thing that gets me most ... it's the squint of his eyes when he looks at her. The way his lips turn up. The way his hands splay against her lower back.

Love can't be faked.

"Sam's been helping me," I say, taking one more look at the happy couple. "He makes my worries fade away."

"Is he going to be able to help you through this?"

I shrug. "If I let him."

He stands from his chair and walks to the picture window, hands resting on his chino-covered hips. "The sun's out now," he says simply.

Since I've been in here, the rain has stopped and a rainbow has formed toward the edge of town. It's the most beautiful thing I've seen in a long time. "That it is."

"Sometimes the only thing that's going to make the rain go away is time, but look what can happen afterward." He turns back around. "Life is much the same."

I hope he's right.

CHAPTER
twenty-three

THE WORLD IS A beautiful place if you open your eyes to it. Sometimes ugliness steps in front of you, though, and you have to walk around it for the color and light to come into view again. Those who say it doesn't exist simply don't believe enough to go after it. It's there. Even I see it.

Tonight, beauty sits across from the fire with a flannel blanket pulled over his shoulders. I've ignored him all day. Convinced myself that I didn't need him, that he didn't want me. It didn't work … all signs pointed me back to him. When I try not to think about him, I do anyway. He's buried deep within my skin, into my heart and soul. He's the constant in my life … the one who has been there for me no matter what. The more times he saves me, the more I believe he'll always be here.

For a long while, I stand back and simply stare at his still figure in the distance. The whole time I've been out here, his eyes have been fixed on the high flames of the fire. His lack of movement says a lot about his emotions. He's broken up, so much so that he looks like he doesn't care anymore. Like he's been left at a point where staring at a raging fire is the only way to burn away the agony inside him.

Taking slow, hesitant steps in his direction, I get a better glimpse at the scene around him. There's a small dark tent, a cooler, and the single lawn chair he occupies.

As I approach, my stomach flutters. With every step, my boots make a crumpling sound in the long grass. It's so quiet out here, I'd hear a whisper from feet away. He has to hear me coming, even with the gray stocking hat covering his ears. What if he doesn't want me out here? What if I burned the last bit of trust he had in me?

"Sam," I say softly, afraid that if I speak too loudly, he'll reply back in the same way.

For the briefest of moments, he looks up at me with no emotion written on his face, but just as quickly as he looked, he looks away.

"If you don't want me out here, just say it. Please." I can't hide anything anymore. The veil that covered my face is gone. My emotions don't show only on my sleeve; they're written all over my stupid designer sweater. My lip quivers. My voice shakes. I need him so freaking bad, and all I can do is silently pray that he hasn't given up on me.

His full face comes into my view again, but he doesn't say a single word. His mouth opens, but as his eyes take in the distraught expression I wear, he closes it. He's fighting a battle—one that's probably similar to the one raging between my heart and my head.

"I only have one chair," he finally says, looking down at the beer bottle in his fingers.

"If you'll listen to me, I can stand."

He shakes his head. "You've always been stubborn."

I quietly wait for him to say something else, to let me know that being here is okay. He's still struggling, but I can feel the power shifting to my side. *Please let it stay there.*

I watch him take a long swig of his beer, moving it around in his mouth a couple times before swallowing. "Talk. I'm listening."

"I'm sorry that I didn't answer your calls."

He takes another long swig before locking his eyes with mine. "I was worried about you."

"I should have texted you, but I didn't know what to say."

"All I wanted to know was that you were okay. I'm not asking for the world here, Rachel."

Anger boils inside my chest. I wanted to disappear for one day. One freaking day to work through my guilt and resentment, and this is where it got me. The worst part is I feel like no one ever understands. Sam might be the closest to getting it, but even he doesn't get it all the time. It puts me in a different world—a lonely world. I can't do this anymore. I just can't.

"I'm okay," I whisper, turning toward my house. I take long, confident steps, and no matter how much I want to look back, I don't. I'm not a strong enough person right now.

Most decisions we make in life have consequences, but the result of this may be more than I'm willing to accept. Strength comes from the ability to face those things.

"Rachel!"

Feeling my stubbornness surface, I keep walking. I don't want to lose this one, not in his eyes anyway. I know I've already lost.

"Rachel, stop!"

His voice is closer … it reels me in. His presence is my weakness. I stop, turning my head in his direction. His tall form hovers over me, placing me in his shadow.

"It's been a long day. If you can't forgive me for wanting some space, then maybe this isn't going to work." My heart beats quickly as I try to get a read on his eyes under the moonlight.

His fingertips rest beneath my chin. It's a touch so light, but it holds me in place like a chain. "I want you to talk to me. If what we have really means something to you, I need you to let me in so I can help you."

Talking about Cory with Sam doesn't seem normal. But I want Sam more than I want something resembling normal.

"I needed time to think about what happened last night. It wasn't something anyone would ever want to remember, Sam. It hurt so fucking much to know what happened in those last minutes."

He shifts to one side, stroking his fingers lightly against my jawline. "Come sit with me."

I nod against his touch and let his cool hand envelop mine. He leads us back to the fire. It can't be more than fifty degrees out here tonight, and the hot air that comes from it is welcome against my skin.

He sits down in the lone chair and pulls me onto his lap. "That's better," he says, nuzzling his nose in my hair.

"We've never had a fire out here before."

"I was hoping my first fire out here would be with you, but I gave in a couple years back."

I lay my head back on his shoulder, feeling his warm breath against my neck. "This is the most relaxing place on Earth. It's better than the lake."

"That's because the rest of the world hasn't discovered it yet."

"And hopefully they never will."

His hands come down to rest on the top of my thighs. "Talk to me."

"Are you sure you want to hear this?"

"I always want to hear what you have to say," he says, kissing the skin below my ear.

I close my eyes and inhale. The cool wind is starting to pick up. I feel it against my cheeks. "When we went around that curve last night, I remembered part of the car ride with Cory from the night of the accident. We were arguing about something, and I said some things ... things that I wish I could take back. Things that should never be the last thing to play in a person's mind before they die."

His arms tighten around my body. "Do you remember what you were fighting about?"

"No," I answer, fixing my eyes on the bright orange flames. His arms relax. "But I told him I wished he'd never existed. Those were my last words to him before he died, Sam."

"I'm sure you both said things you wish you could take back."

Tears well in my eyes. "But I'm the only one who can even think about that. He's not here because of a stupid argument, and I can't remember what it was even about."

His lips brush against my earlobe. "Do you remember what caused the accident?"

"Yeah," I cry, leaning closer to him.

"That's one thing the police never figured out … how your car came off the road."

"We were fighting, and his hand came up to cover mine on the steering wheel. I tried to pull mine away, and his came down hard on the wheel and the car swerved. It happened too fast, and I couldn't react, not in the right way."

"It's not your fault, baby. It's not his fault. It was just a night of bad circumstance." His fingers slide up, clasping on my stomach.

"People would hate me if they knew what I said to him."

"No one has to know."

"Do you think I should tell my dad how the accident happened?" I ask.

He kisses my cheek. Cool lips. Cold skin. "It's not going to change anything. You did nothing wrong."

"Do you think I'll ever remember everything that happened that night?" I ask.

"Do you want to?"

"I think I have to in order for the rest of it to make sense. Right now, it's just a bunch of scattered pieces with no glue."

The air around us is quiet again. All I can do is stare ahead and try to forget everything. I want a reprieve from the trouble that stirs inside me.

Sam didn't run in the other direction. He didn't judge. I think the mind magnifies things, making them seem much worse. Being with Sam in our favorite place makes everything okay, even if it's really not.

"Hey, Sam, why didn't you stop when you saw me in town earlier?" I finally ask.

"I wanted you to come to me when you were ready," he replies, kissing the side of my head.

"But you called—"

"I know," he interrupts. "On my way home, I got to thinking, or maybe hoping, that you'd come to town to look for me."

"I'm sorry," I say, leaning my head back on his shoulder. I feel like all I do is let people down these days. It's a big change for a girl who spent most of her life trying to make everyone happy. "Do you remember when we were at the diner, and you asked me the three things I was most scared of?"

"Yes," he whispers.

"I never told you the last one." I pause, inhaling a deep breath. "The thought of losing someone I care about again scares me to death. I care about you, Sam. Don't let me push you away. I can't lose you too."

He brushes my hair behind my shoulder, nuzzling his nose in the side of my neck. "I'm not going anywhere."

We both remain silent as he holds me close, his face nestled in the crook of my neck. All I can do is close my eyes and take everything in. Sam. The smell of wood burning. Crickets chirping. Moments like these are why people risk heartbreak … falling in love is worth it.

"Stay with me tonight," he finally says, gripping me a little tighter.

"I don't—"

"Please. You said you wanted to go camping. Here's your chance."

I'd almost forgotten about the night I told him I wanted to go camping; a lot has happened since then. And honestly, I want to be out here with him, because if I go back inside, all those unwanted feelings are going to rise back to the surface. How can I say no to him?

I'm tired of not touching him, of not seeing his eyes. "How steady is this chair?"

"It's holding us, isn't it?"

If this chair can hold us both with my back against his chest, it can hold us with me facing him. Wrapping my fingers around his, I lift his hands from my body and scoot off his lap. I feel his arms reaching for me, but I'm too quick.

His hooded eyes study my face. "Please stay with me." His voice is low, sexy, and demanding with a small serving of whine. It's the only push I need.

"Okay," I reply, carefully straddling his lap. My hands wrap around the back of his neck, bringing our bodies together like glue. The fire burns in the center of his eyes, but I feel it most in his hands—the way they grip my ass like their one and only job is to protect it. Our chests touch, two hearts dancing a beat against each other.

"Is it okay if I kiss you?" he asks. His fingers move up my back, tangling in my hair.

"Since when do you ask?"

"Since I don't know if this is the right time."

I move in, my lips a hair above his. "It's the best time. Kissing is the best medicine."

"Yeah," he says, wrapping his hands around the back of my head. "How many doses is it going to take?"

"Why don't you start over here," I whisper, touching my finger to the left corner of my mouth. "And I'll tell you when it feels better."

He smiles. "Anything you want, you got it."

My skin is still warm from the fire, but when his lips touch to mine, they're a cool contrast. It elevates everything as he travels from one corner to the other, leaving a trail of electric tingles in his wake. When his lips fully press to mine, the world stops spinning. My heart melts. Not even Cory could make everything better like this. This is Sam's own form of magic. His lips like his magic wand. My heart's rapid beat his trick.

When he pulls away, I hate it. I hate the loss of him. "Should we go inside for the night? It might be more comfortable than this chair."

"I don't know. I was actually feeling pretty good."

He smiles, running the backs of his fingers along my cheek. "What if I promise I can make you feel even better?"

That's a promise I'm going to let him keep. Sam's the rainbow at the end of the storm. I see the bright, changing colors clearly now.

As I slide off him, I can barely feel my legs.

"Here," he says, rising to his feet. With one quick motion, I'm in his arms being carried to the tent. "I've always wanted to do that."

"I could get used to it."

He leans in to kiss my cheek. "I'll allow that."

He sets me back on the ground and kneels down to unzip the small door. This is going to be a first for me—sleeping in a tent—but the simplicity and solitude of it excites me.

"Have you slept out here before?" I ask.

"Sometimes, when I just need to escape everything, I do." He holds the door open and motions for me to enter while he holds the canvas material back.

"You have your own apartment," I say as I duck inside.

"That's part of my life. If I'm there, I can't escape everything like I can here."

When we're both inside, he zips it back up and crouches down at the end of the air mattress. The space is much larger on the inside than it looks on the outside. The mattress is the size of a double bed and takes up most of the room. There's also a lantern that leaves a soft glow.

"I have an extra pair of sweatpants and a sweatshirt if you want them."

"Are you trying to get a free show, Shea?" I joke, feeling my cheeks turn red from the innuendo.

"No," he says, reaching into his duffle bag. "The first time I try that, or anything more, is going to be in my bed."

"Oh," escapes my lips as I haphazardly catch the clothes he tosses to me. "What's wrong with this bed?"

I don't know where the question came from. It's not what I came out here for ... it's not something I even feel ready for.

"Because I've been saving my bed for a special girl. A certain girl. I didn't wait all this time to take her on an air mattress."

My mouth hangs wide open. He's always so freaking candid. He laughs, crawling over to kiss me. "I'm going to go put the fire out. Change your clothes, and I'll be back in a few minutes."

As he heads out of the tent, I can't take my eyes off his perfect ass and the way his jeans fit against it. I've never known him to be the type to hit the gym every day, but all the work he does in the shop looks like it's paying off.

When he's out of sight, I quickly take off my clothes and pull on the warm, soft sweats he'd handed me. They have that worn feel, the cotton hitting against me like a second skin. The best part is they smell exactly like him, clean yet sexy.

While I wait, I lie on top of the air mattress and stare up through the mesh ceiling. It gives a perfect view to the stars above; it's better than any five-star hotel I've stayed at with my parents.

"Looks like you made yourself comfortable." I'm so lost in the pattern of the stars above that I didn't hear him come in.

"I didn't realize these things came with a star roof."

"It's one of the many amenities, and to think I got it all for less than $200."

I slide over, giving him room to crawl in next to me. "If it came with a bathroom and kitchen, you could almost live in one."

"Until winter comes," he says, pulling his side of the sleeping bag over both of us. "Zip it up."

"Why? This is fine."

"I said I'd share my sleeping bag with you, and I meant it. Now zip it." He says it like it's an order rather than a request. This is one time I'm okay with him being bossy. Being this close to him will probably give me the best night's sleep I've had in a long time. I do as he asks, settling my body up next to his. He lies on his side. I'm on my back.

"Are you feeling better?" he asks, his arm wrapping around my stomach.

"Much, but do you know what would help?"

"Hmm."

"A few more of those kisses you gave me outside." I try not to stare at his lips, but I can't help it. Anything that perfect deserves to be stared at.

"If that's all it's going to take, lift your head." I do as he asks, allowing his arms to snake beneath me. His fingers run through the strands of my long blond hair, and his generous lips come down on mine. It feels so good, so right. Nothing's better than a kiss under the stars, especially when you're with someone who makes you feel like part of a new pattern. With Sam, I'm forming the most meaningful, brightest of constellations.

CHAPTER
twenty-four

September 29, 2013

AS I STEP OUTSIDE, rain pelts my face. It's been a long day of deliveries with weather like this, and luckily, this is my last. This being my first job, I'm finally starting to appreciate the concept of Friday and why everyone looks forward to it. It's not that I don't like my job, because I do, but it's just nice to have days to do whatever I want. More than anything, it's nice to have more time to spend with Sam.

It's been five nights since I slept under the stars with Sam. It was a cool night, but being wrapped in his arms under a large sleeping bag left me with the best night's sleep I've had in a really long time. His warm, sweet kisses helped too.

We've made it a point to see each other every day, whether that means meeting for lunch or watching a movie at his place after work. It's getting too cold to stay out in the fields, but after last weekend, I'm looking forward to doing that again this summer.

I've spent every night in my own bed, drifting to sleep with thoughts of Cory and the argument we had. I try to bury them down with thoughts of Sam, but it doesn't work as well when Sam isn't with me. Sam makes me forget.

When I finally reach the hospital doors, my shirt is soaked through, and my hair is a ratted mess. That's another thing about this job—it's virtually impossible to carry a vase full of flowers and an umbrella at the same time. It leaves no way to open the door.

The hospital greets me with the smell I hate and institutional colors I loathe.

"Rachel, is that you?" I look over to the waiting area, seeing Cory's mom and sister occupying two chairs.

I hesitantly walk over, my hand gripped tightly around the glass vase. "Hi," I answer, managing something that feels sort of like a smile.

"I thought you'd be back at school," his mom says, her eyes roaming my disheveled appearance. Everyone in this small town knows everything about who is coming and going. There's little possibility that she didn't know, but she's probably waiting for me to admit that I didn't just ruin Cory's life … I ruined mine, too.

"I'm taking the year off, helping Ms. Peters at the shop," I reply, nervously shifting on my feet.

"I see." Awkward silence follows. Maybe I should have just kept walking, told her I had to be going to make my deliveries on time.

I feel mindless, grasping at straws for something to say. "What are you guys doing here?"

"Oh, Craig had to have some tests done. We're just waiting." Cory's dad had some heart problems a couple years back. It required a surgery to clear a blockage.

"I hope everything is okay."

She throws her hand out like it's nothing. "It's just routine stuff. That's what happens when you get older."

The more I stand here, the more relaxed I feel, but I'm waiting for the other shoe to drop. The one they're probably holding to kick me in the teeth with.

"Well, it was nice to see you. I better get these delivered before someone calls and wonders where they are."

I start walking away, ready to get out of here before my luck runs out, but Mrs. Connors stops me before I get too far. "Rachel, can I speak with you for a second?"

I stop, but I can't bring myself to turn around. My whole body stiffens. "I just wanted to tell you I'm sorry for the way I acted in the cemetery. I know this can't be easy for you, so I hope you can at least understand where I was coming from."

Only then do I dare face her. She's given me a small, soft pillow to fall back on. "I understand, and I hope you know that I'm so sorry. I wish things had turned out differently, but I can't go back."

"I know," she says, her bottom lip quivering. "I just miss him, you know?"

I nod. Every day I see something or hear something that makes me miss him, too. Fifty years from now I'll still think about him. I can't forget my firsts.

"Thank you for the box, by the way. Not everything in it was mine, but I doubt you want that item back," I say hesitantly, watching for any indication of malice in her eyes. That whole thing has bothered me since I opened it, no matter how much I try to forget.

Her eyebrows draw in, and I take a deep breath. She has absolutely no idea what I'm talking about. "Whatever it is, keep it. I'm sure he'd want you to have it."

After all this time, talking about him still makes her face twist. She's so close to crying, and it automatically stirs those same emotions up in me. "Anyway, I should probably get going."

She nods. "Okay, don't be a stranger. Please."

"I'll try not to."

The interaction between us feels too uncomfortable to become something more common, but at least I won't be as scared to run into her around town.

I make my way to the receptionist desk to drop off the flowers, then quickly exit. Anywhere but here is where I want to be. It's not just the people inside who scare me away; it's the bad memories this place holds. Bad things didn't happen here, but I learned of them within these walls. The smell, the color, everything makes me think of things I'd rather forget.

When I come out from under the awning, the rain is falling harder, drenching any part of me that wasn't already wet. At least this time I can run since I have nothing to carry. I push the unlock button as soon as my car is in view and climb in so fast, only a few drops fall on the inside of my door.

For several minutes, I just listen to the rain against the car windows. The sound soothes me as I rest my head back on the seat. I don't know what wound me up more—the fact that I ran into Cory's family or that it went better than I'd expected. Preparing myself for the worst was almost as bad as actually facing it.

That's something I've learned lately. Things are rarely as bad as I think they're going to be. I'm resilient ... much stronger than I ever thought I could be.

Just as I'm about to head back to the shop to clock out for the day, my phone buzzes. Picking it up, I realize it's Sam. He must be off work already.

Sam: Can I cook you dinner tonight?

Rachel: I thought you didn't cook.

Sam: I order a mean pizza.

This will be the third time this week that Sam has "cooked" for me. Not that I mind it. It's better than an awkward meal at home with Mom staring at Dad's empty chair.

Rachel: That you do. Getting off work. Be there around 6:30?

Sam: Or sooner.

Sam is all I need to motivate myself out of this parking lot. Spending the night cuddled on the couch with him, listening to the rain. He's one of the best things to ever come into my life. I'll always be grateful that my mom had the church ladies over that day almost twelve years ago.

The first couple times I came up to Sam's apartment, it didn't feel quite right. Now I walk right in like the place is mine. No knocking. No soft footsteps. When I reach the door at the top of the steps, my knuckles brush against the door, not for him to answer, but to let him know I'm coming in.

He's always in the kitchen … that's no different tonight. Blue jeans. A white muscle-hugging, long sleeve T-shirt. No shoes or socks. He's truly a vision of pure, uncensored human sexuality. I'm relieved they didn't teach us about the little tingles in the stomach that come with attraction back in Sex Ed because it's so much better when it just hits you without warning.

"Hey," he says, stalking over to where I stand frozen inside the door. The best part of his greeting is the kiss. He'll grip my chin with his calloused fingers and bring his lips down to mine with his eyes open. Up until a few days ago, I always kissed with my eyes closed. I thought it was better that way, but Sam showed me how much more you can feel when you do it with your eyes and lips. I see deep inside him and feel him even more when I take in the warmth of his brown eyes.

Sam makes hours feel like seconds. He has this ability to make me get lost in him.

When he pulls back, a grin spreads across his face. "It's kind of rude of me to kiss you before I give you a chance to say hi."

"I'm okay with it. I like the way you say hello," I say, biting down on my lower lip.

"Well, did I tell you how sexy you look? I know I screwed that up."

"Don't sweat it. I forgot to mention it, too."

He grips my hips, pulling me closer. "Your eyes said it all."

"Am I that obvious?"

"Yeah," he says, pressing his lips to mine. "But I'm okay with that. If I can't see that sparkle someday, I'll worry."

This time, when our mouths meet, he wastes no time tangling his tongue with mine. He moves with expert motion, every bit of it felt in places besides my mouth. We stand hip to hip, as close as two people can be with their clothes still on. I feel everything, especially the way he hardens against my stomach. It's not the first time I've felt it, and I'd be lying if I said it didn't make me crave more of him.

He slows his motions, ending with a soft peck on my lips. "Dinner is ready."

"We could just skip it."

"I didn't slave away for nothing." He winks, grabbing my hand to lead me to the kitchen. There's nothing fancy about our dinners together; they're usually spent sitting Indian-style on the couch. "I ordered a veggie this time since you mentioned the pepperoni was greasy."

"What if I don't like vegetables?"

He cocks his head to the side. "Seriously, baby? If that's how it's going to be, we're moving to cereal."

"If you do, I prefer whole grain."

He rolls his eyes, opening the door of his tiny refrigerator. "What do you want to drink?"

"Water."

"If you grab the plates, I'll bring over the drinks."

In a short time, we've settled into this easy, almost domesticated, rhythm. There's not much I've found that irritates him, which makes it easier for him to accept my quirks … and I have a lot of them.

"What are we watching tonight?" he asks, setting two bottles of water on the coffee table.

"Let's skip the show about unsanitary kitchens this time."

"The slimy chicken is part of the reason I ordered veggie pizza."

In the end, he settles on *The Fugitive*. By the time it's over, our pizza is gone, our drinks are empty, and we're lying side by side on the couch with our legs tangled. I turn in his arms, seeing an overwhelming intensity in his eyes. "Why are you looking at me like that?"

"Remember when you asked me what I was afraid of?"

I nod against his chest, pressing my lips to his soft shirt.

His hands grip the side of my face, bringing my eyes to his. "You. I was afraid of losing you again."

"I don't think I ever left you."

"You did," he whispers, his voice edged with pain. "When you started seeing him, it felt like I'd lost you, because all I'd ever wanted was you."

I swallow, wanting so badly to wrap him in my arms and tell him I'm not leaving him for anything. "I now believe things happen for a reason. If you'd asked me years ago to be with you like this, I don't think we'd still be together. I made a lot of mistakes, but I learned from them. You're getting a better version of me."

"I liked the old version of you, and I like the new. That's how I know this is something special I never want to be without. I've loved you for so fucking long, Rachel." He tenderly presses his lips to mine, still holding my face in his hands. His teeth gently tug at my lower lip before releasing me. "Do you feel that when I kiss you?"

"What?" I whisper, staring down at his lips.

"It means something." He takes my hand in his, placing it over his heart. "When I kiss you, it's coming from here. I take my time because I plan on doing it with only you for the rest of my life; I'm not scared of losing you again."

"Sam, you promised slow."

"And I'm giving you slow," he says, cupping my chin in his hand. His mouth traces the line of my jaw, down my neck, to the sensitive spot below my ear. It feels amazing, sending a warm tingle down my spine.

There's this little voice in my head that says we're taking things too fast, but my body is screaming a whole different story. I'm inclined to listen to that voice.

Before I even realize what he's doing, I'm being hoisted into his arms and carried to his bed. Warning bells should be sounding, but they don't. I want this. I want to feel what he does to me without all these clothes between us.

He sets me down on my feet, the back of my knees hitting against the mattress. "I know you want this. I feel it in the way your heart beats against my chest. But if you want to stop, you need to tell me now. It's not going to be possible to hit pause once I start."

This isn't just turning the page; it's a whole new chapter. With Cory, I waited a whole year before I took this step and, even then, I wasn't this sure of how I felt about him. For twelve years I've been getting to know Sam, his strengths and weaknesses, his thoughts and struggles. For twelve years I've loved him … not always in the same way, but I've loved him.

I'm in love with this beautiful boy, even if I'm too afraid to tell him.

I nod. "I want this just as much as you do."

His fingers come up, making quick work of the buttons on my white blouse. His eyes hold mine in quiet contemplation. In all seriousness, the way he looks at me is almost enough to make me cry. Some girls wait their whole life for their fairytale to come along, and mine is standing right in front of me.

He slides his hands down my shoulders, taking my shirt right along with them. I stand in front of him in nothing but a nude bra—definitely not what I would have picked if I'd known this was happening tonight. "You're so damn sexy. I've dreamt about this happening over and over, but even then, I didn't envision you quite like this."

I snake my fingers underneath his shirt, running them along his toned abs. When it's not enough, when I want to feel more of his skin on mine, I pull his shirt over his head, fully exposing his strong chest and taut stomach.

His hands cup my neck, his thumbs coming up to caress my jawline. "When I look at you, I see everything my life is meant to be. It's my turn to show you just how good yours can be."

His lips slowly descend on mine, his hooded eyes fixed on me. He's warm and tender, pulling each of my lips between his before fully covering my mouth. I'm not nervous about the intimacy of what's about to happen—he's familiar enough to me—but I'm worried about not knowing what he likes or dislikes. My experiences probably don't match his, but I hope the level of feelings we have for each other is enough to make up for it.

Gaining more confidence from his warm touch, I slide my fingers down to the button of his jeans, fumbling to pull it loose. When I'm successful, I tug on his zipper and push his jeans down his hips. Turns out, he's a black boxer-briefs man … it's pretty much what I imagined, knowing as much as I do about him.

"You're smiling," he says, lightly brushing his knuckles along my collarbone.

"You make it easy," I reply, standing on my tippy toes to kiss the cleft of his chin. He holds me there, placing his fingers under my chin to bring my lips up to his. There's no need to show me how good life can be, I feel it. Deep down in my chest—it resides there.

He undoes my jeans, easing the tight denim down my legs.

His long fingers come back up, expertly dancing against my sides. "Lie down on the bed, baby."

My chest pulses up and down as I sit back along the edge of the mattress, slowly moving backward against the soft cotton sheets. Sam stands at the foot of the bed drinking in my mostly naked body. We stay just like that for a while. Each of us staring. Each of us feeling. There's no going back now.

My eyes stay on him as he walks to the nightstand and pulls a small foil packet from the top drawer. Maybe I'm a little nervous. This isn't my first time but, in a way, it feels like it is.

The side of the bed dips as he crawls toward me. He might as well be moving on air because he's all I see. "I'm going to kiss every inch of your skin, and then, baby, I'm going to make sure you feel me inside. Especially right here," he says, kissing the spot on my chest right above where my heart beats.

Reaching up, I tangle my fingers in his hair. "Sam. Please."

His mouth doesn't just kiss me there. He makes love to my skin with every touch. He blazes a path down my stomach, inside each thigh ... all the way down to the top of my feet. It's slow, sensual, and has me begging for more by the time he makes his way back up to my lips.

The nerves have dissipated again, and when he sits back on his heels to pull his boxers down, only anticipation fills me. I watch as he rips open the package and carefully rolls on the condom. His whole body is so damn beautiful.

"I'm going to go slow," he whispers, leaning over my body. As he kisses me, I feel him at my entrance. And when he finally breaks away, his eyes gaze into mine as he enters me. Slowly. Completely. I almost want to cry ... it's never been quite like this.

"Okay?" he asks.

I nod, lifting my head to brush my lips against his. It's the reassurance he needed. So far, it's perfect ... one of those moments I'll remember forever. He slowly pulls out until only the tip of him remains inside me, then slides back in, much the way he did the first time. It's a pattern he repeats with soft kisses spread in between, but as my muscles relax, he thrusts harder, faster. I feel every movement, every emotion, communicated between us.

Just when I get to that point where I think I never want this to end because it feels too damn good, the tension builds in my core. Each time he buries himself all the way inside me, I come closer, the tingles intensifying. Before long, I'm having the strongest, most amazing orgasm I've ever had. Toes curling. Back arching. All control is lost. I'm all his, no one can argue otherwise.

"Oh my God, baby. Do you know how fucking amazing that feels?" He groans, and with three quick motions, he follows me to bliss. He buries his head into my neck and moans my name over and over. I didn't know how sexy my name was until just now, rolling off his lips when he's most vulnerable.

For what seems like forever, we stay just like that. Two bodies covered in a layer of sweat, shaking from the aftermath of amazing sex.

Sam slowly withdraws from me, holding himself up over my body. "I feel like we were always meant to get here, Rachel. It may have been a long road, but I'm glad we've finally made it. You were meant to be mine."

I run my hands along his strong biceps. "I'm not going anywhere."

CHAPTER
twenty-five

SOMETIMES, AFTER YOU'VE SEEN all the ugly parts of life, it's hard to believe beauty still exists. And if you live in the ugly long enough, you become convinced the beauty never really existed. Living in the darkness plays with your mind and drains your soul, and when the light finally starts to shine through again, it takes a little while before the trees become green and the flowers begin to grow. Darkness to light is like winter to spring.

With Sam, I'm blossoming again. He's exactly what I need, and that feeling is etched in stone as his lips travel down my bare chest. They're soft against my skin, like a rose petal tracing a path between my breasts.

"Rachel," he breathes against my skin. "Do you know how good you taste?"

All I can manage is a moan as he continues his journey down, placing feather light kisses around my belly button.

"Your skin tastes just like a strawberry." His voice purrs with lust, like a man who's about to get a taste of something he's craved for years.

My back arches when his warm mouth moves between my legs. I've been touched there many times, but not like this. It's intimate, sexy, and frees me in a way I never thought possible.

It feels like it's just us, drifting on a cloud with no weight under or above us. I wrap his hair between my fingers, pulling just enough to reassure him that what he's doing is well received. And when his tongue strokes my clit, I feel that cloud climbing higher. My body releases, walls clenching. He sees it through, punctuating it with the brush of his lips.

When his mouth lifts from my skin, I open my eyes and see him looking down at me. Even in the dark room, I see the desire within them. They burn bright through the dull light in the room.

"This time, when I'm making love to you, I want you to look at me. I want you to see what I feel. I want to see what you feel." His lips come down on mine. He tastes like me as he works expertly, making me yearn for the rest of him. Last night he showed me how good things could be, what I've been missing out on by not being with him. My true friend and soul mate.

"Sam," I moan as he travels the line of my jaw. He continues his exploration down my throat, but instead of using his lips, his tongue draws a line back to my breasts, taking a little time to lap each nipple. He's got me on edge, and I'm ready to jump because I know he'll catch me. He always has.

With one long, slow movement, he enters me and, out of habit, I close my eyes. By doing it, I've always thought I'd be able to concentrate on the sensation of skin against skin … that it would make everything better. He proved that wrong last night.

The backs of his fingers caress my cheek. "Look at me."

I obey, opening my eyes to him. It's not until then that he starts moving, creating a delicious friction between our joined bodies. Those gorgeous brown eyes only leave me when his lips travel down my neck. He sucks, bites, and nibbles as he continues to thrust his body into mine.

When he's done tasting, he braces his hands on the bed, looking straight down at me. "Do you feel how good we fit, baby? Your body was made for mine."

I nod, arching my back to take more of him. There's no way he can push any deeper, but I still crave it. When you love something, you want all of it.

My breathing accelerates. I'm so close, riding the euphoria that comes right before hitting the ultimate high. I grip his shoulders tightly, letting him know my walls are about to cave.

"Hold on, baby. I want to come with you," he whispers, running his fingers up my forearms until they're clasped with mine. His pace quickens, making it harder and harder for me to hold back, and he knows it. It's as evident as the passion in his eyes.

"Sam, please," I moan, squeezing his fingers between mine.

He leans in and kisses me, sucking my bottom lip between his. "Let go, but keep your eyes on me."

With one more thrust, he groans, and my walls clench around him. I struggle to keep my eyes open and on him, and from the way his eyes widen, he's struggling with it too.

When my muscles stop clenching, he collapses on top of me, his hands still joined with mine. "I could lie here all day just like this."

"You wouldn't want a repeat of what we just did?"

"We'd fit a few more sessions in."

"Yeah?"

"Yeah," he says, letting go of my hands to comb his fingers through my hair. "At least a few more times."

Rolling off my body, he allows me to flip onto my stomach. He seizes the opportunity, painting my upper back with feather-like kisses. I cradle one of his pillows in my arms, inhaling his scent. This is exactly how every morning should be. Not a thought flows through my mind besides how much I think I've fallen in love with the guy lying next to me. He's shown me that there truly is life after death. It's a different life. I've changed, grown up, quite a bit from the girl I used to be.

Sam lets his lips linger on my neck, then whispers against my ear, "I'll always keep you safe. You know that, don't you?"

Something about what he says and the way he says it causes my eyes shoot open and my heart to beat rapidly. The voices are back, louder than ever, but this time, it's not Cory. It's Sam.

"Hey, why are you running?"

I'm struggling to catch my breath, to see in the darkness. Strong arms wrap around my upper arms, making it impossible to get away. My back is pressed against a large, muscular chest. "Just let me go. I need to get out of here."

"Look at me, Rachel. I'm right here, and I'll always keep you safe. You know that, don't you?"

"Sam," I whisper, not even needing to turn my head to know whose voice it is. "What are you doing here?"

"Right now, it looks like I'm saving you from something. What are you running from?"

I turn, bracing my hands on his chest. I haven't been this close to him in a while. My relationship with Cory came between us. It was a divider. A separator. Sam was my best friend, Cory became my boyfriend, and they hated each other. There was no space large enough for the three of us. Being this close to Sam almost makes me forget I'm supposed to be running.

The scene from a few minutes ago is coming back to me. It hits me hard, like a jackhammer to the heart, and my knees become weak. Sam's arms come around my back to hold me up. "What the fuck happened, Rachel? Talk to me."

Gazing up, it's hard to make out his face under the night sky. I reach up, running my fingers along his square jaw, feeling the light stubble against my skin. "Something the Big Dipper can't fix," I whisper.

Sam brushes a small strand of hair behind my ear. "I'm Sorry. I—"

"Rachel, what the fuck is going on over here? Is this where you've been all fucking night?" a voice screams from the distance. All blood rushes to my head. Cory.

"Rachel! Rachel!" I'm on my back, and Sam's straddling my waist, his hands gripping my shoulders tightly. I'm lost in a daze, the aftershock of the voices. They temporarily hold my body and voice hostage while I process every part of the memory. When I'd tried to envision what happened that night, I never imagined it like that … with Sam. Why didn't he tell me? If he was there, why would he keep that from me?

Things come into focus again. Sam looks down at me, sweat drenching his hair and brow. Worry and panic are written on his face like a horror story.

"You were there," I finally mumble. "You were there, and you didn't tell me."

His eyes widen, his hands easing up on my shoulders. He doesn't need to ask what I'm talking about. He knows ... it shows in every muscle in his body. "Let me explain."

"Get off me!" I yell, pushing against his chest, but even with the rage inside of me, I can't move him. Neither of us has any clothes on, but I don't care. It's the last freaking thing on my mind. Everything I've built my life around the last few months is crumbling, or maybe it was never on solid footing at all.

"Just give me two minutes. Please." My heart aches just looking at him. Not because I'm absorbing his pain, but because looking at him reminds me of the pain he's caused in me. Staring at him reminds me how great things were, and how full he made my heart. Up until a few minutes ago, Sam Shea was the person I trusted most in the world. Now, though, he's someone I don't trust at all.

"I can't even look at you. This was a mistake."

His chin dips to his chest, his eyes pained and frustrated as he moves off me. Why couldn't he have just been honest with me? Is it that hard? He sits, legs hanging off the side of the bed, elbows resting on his bare thighs. "I was trying to protect you."

"Protect me?" I scream, climbing out of bed, picking my clothes up off the floor along the way. "I've been trying for months to remember what happened that night, and all along you've held a piece of that puzzle in your hands, Sam."

"I didn't think it was the part that mattered."

I quickly clasp my bra and put on my blouse, fastening the buttons at record pace. "It matters! It fucking matters! Maybe ... maybe my parents were right about you all along."

He watches me as I step into my jeans, avoiding direct eye contact. His hand brushes through his hair, then down the back of his neck, but he doesn't leave his spot on the bed. "Is this it? Are we over because of this?" He sounds defeated, resigned.

I pull on my boots and search the room for my jacket. "We never started. A relationship can't be built on a lie. If it is, the whole thing is just a big lie."

"Don't push me away, Rachel. I'll do anything you ask me to if you let me explain."

I come around the side of the bed, waving my hands in front of him. I feel one hundred percent crazy right now with no chance for sanity any time soon. "Don't you get it? The reason Cory and I were fighting was because he saw me with you. It doesn't matter why I was running that night. You're the reason for the accident."

After watching his face twist like heated metal, I can't take it anymore. I'm done talking. Done fighting. Leaving Sam behind, I pick up my coat from the back of the chair and hastily walk toward the door. When my hand is on the knob, I look back one last time.

"Just tell me one thing. What were you doing out there that night? You hadn't been to one of those parties in years."

He visibly winces, climbing off the bed with the gray sheet wrapped around his waist. Just minutes ago, I would have been awed by him, but now, I can't even stand to look.

"Before I ran into you, I was with Lidia Mathers."

Lidia's one year younger than me, and she's different than the girls I've seen him with through the years, but still easy enough to become one of his latest conquests. Him being with her seems a little strange, but it's the least of my worries.

"Was this ever real for you?" I ask, letting the first tear slip down my cheek. "Were you just playing me like every other girl?"

He steps forward until he's only two feet away from me. His hand comes out, aching to touch me, but he holds back. The move is painful for both of us. "Nothing's ever been more real."

I nod, turning away to avoid his glossed-over eyes. "When you look back at this years from now, don't think for one minute that I pushed you away. You and your lies did all the pushing. I need to go," I say quietly, opening the door and disappearing through it. I draw some satisfaction when it slams behind me. I want him to know I'm angry. I want him to feel it in the same way I do.

I walk through the shop, not bothering to take a look back to make sure he's not following behind. As I step out into the cold morning air, I wrap my arms tightly around my middle. The walk from his apartment to my house isn't exactly a short one, especially in weather like this, but there's no way in hell I'd accept a ride from him. Besides that, I need time to think, to try to push down the sickness in my stomach. Just when I finally thought things were looking up, that stupid dark cloud formed overhead again. I'm starting to think it's going to permanently follow me no matter what I do or where I go.

My feet move quickly across the grass as I try to push through the soreness between my legs from last night and this morning. I've never felt so close to someone only to have it all ripped away like this just minutes later. It's different than what happened to Cory because Sam's still here. If I wanted him, I could have him. But not after what he did.

As I come closer to my house, I'm relieved to find that Mom's car isn't in the driveway. At least I'll be able to get upstairs and hide away in my room without questions about my tear-stained cheeks. It seems like I'm going right back to the place I was a few months ago. One step forward, two steps back ... or in this case, at least ten back. But this time, instead of guilt, it's overwhelming anger pulling me back. Sam was the last person I expected would ever hurt me.

CHAPTER
twenty-six

LIFE CHANGES QUICKLY WITH the turn of a key. If it's the right one, it can unlock something fantastic, but if it's wrong, it stops you in your tracks. All I ever wanted was to be happy. When I was a little girl, I spent hours watching Disney movies about girls like me who became princesses and lived happily ever after. I want that … the happily ever after part.

When I got home this morning, I took a long, hot shower, attempting to wash the memories of Sam from my skin. I didn't want to remember his touch or scent. I wanted it gone, but even after I climbed out of the shower, he was still there. I'm never going to forget what we shared last night.

I've lain on my soft cotton sheets most of the afternoon, attempting to forget him, but all I can think about is how it felt beneath his naked body last night. He did things to me that I didn't know were possible, things that I felt well below the skin's surface. Things I'm struggling to forget, even with the rage that's brewing inside me.

"Rachel, dinner's ready!"

I've successfully avoided my mom all day because she was helping with a function at church, but that's not going to be possible now. If I don't go down there, she'll come up here. No matter what I do, I'm screwed. I've been walking around like a giddy teenage girl all week; that's over now. I grab my long black cardigan sweater and slip it on over my gray T-shirt. I could care less what I look like.

I straighten my black leggings and take the stairs slowly, trying to delay the inevitable. Mom is not at the bottom like I thought she might be, but I hear her banging dishes around in the kitchen. Inhaling a long breath, I head in her direction, doing my best to force a smile. That's not easy right now either.

"I tried to call you earlier!" she yells as soon as she hears my bare feet against the entryway floors.

"I was asleep." It's a half-truth ... or half lie. It depends on how you look at it. The truth is my phone has been off all day because I wanted to avoid Sam's calls if he tried to contact me. It's still buried deep inside my purse somewhere, and I don't plan on taking it out until I feel sane enough to handle it.

"Do you want to eat in here or the dining room?" she asks as I round the corner to the kitchen. Her back is turned, straining a pot of spaghetti.

"This is fine," I answer, sliding onto one of the barstools that surround the island.

She turns immediately at the sound of my voice. "What's wrong?"

I pause, my hand lying flat on the cool granite. *How does she do that?*

"Wait. Did you come home last night?"

I shake my head, wishing I wasn't so transparent.

Her eyes rake my body. "Is it Sam? Did he hurt you?"

Yes and yes, I think to myself. It's just not what she's thinking. He didn't force anything. He didn't take anything I didn't want to give him. He simply misused my heart, chopping it up and pureeing it.

"We had a fight. It's over." I shrug, having a hard time admitting to that. I was really starting to feel like Sam was someone I'd have in my life forever.

"Really?" she says, scrunching her nose. "I was just starting to like him, the way he changed you anyway. It was nice to see you smile again, Rachel."

A smile—what brings it on exactly? Is it because we feel good? Is it because life is good, and we feel like it can't get much better? Sure, I felt like that, but it's long gone now.

"I was starting to like him, too," I whisper, tracing circles around the little designs in the granite.

"What happened?" She scoops pasta onto two plates, then grabs for a pot of her homemade spaghetti sauce. It's one of her best dishes, but tonight I'm not hungry. Food is the last thing on my mind.

"You don't really want to talk about this, do you, Mom?"

She stops, placing the pot back on the stovetop. "I do actually. I wasn't what you needed after the accident, but I want to be what you need now."

I'm hesitant. Once I tell her, I can't take it back. There are a lot of things I can't take back these days. "I remembered something about the night of the accident," I say, fixing my eyes on the full plate of pasta that she sets in front of me. "Sam was there."

Her eyebrows pull in. "He was there when you remembered?"

"No ... Yes, I mean he was at the party the night of the accident."

"He never told you that before?"

"No. He's the reason Cory was upset with me, Mom. A while back, I remembered the last minutes before the crash. Cory was so upset, so angry with me. He'd reached for the steering wheel, and when I pulled my hand away, the car veered off the road straight into the trees."

"I don't get it. Why was he angry?"

Closing my eyes, I count silently until my heart rate slows. "Because he saw me with Sam."

Mom's lips form the perfect "O" as she drops her fork on her plate. "So you were with Sam that night?"

I rest my elbows on the counter, shelving my chin in my hands. "No, I don't think so. I was running from something and ended up in Sam's arms. I just don't remember why I was running."

She picks up the towel from the front of the sink and wipes her hands. She contemplating, and I can't believe I just told her all that when I've barely let her in my whole life. "I can't believe he didn't tell you," she finally says, slowly sliding into the seat next to me.

"Neither can I," I reply, pushing some pasta around with my fork.

We sit in this awkward silence, staring down at our plates. Neither of us actually takes a bite, but the food serves as a distraction. I'm still too hurt and pissed off to actually put anything in my mouth.

"Can I tell you something?" she asks, finally pushing her plate away.

"I'm not going anywhere."

Mom actually smiles. That's a rarity in its genuine form. "Now you sound like your father."

I wince. "I hate when you say that."

"Sorry. I know he's not your favorite person, and he could have done a better job supporting you these last few months, but he means well. If he weren't a good man, I wouldn't have married him."

"What were you going to tell me?"

"Just that I never thought Cory was the person you were meant to spend your life with. Loving a person doesn't always make them the best forever choice. He didn't seem like the guy who was going to make you the best version of yourself."

"Is that what Dad does for you?"

She looks away from me, and I know the answer instantly. "I should get the kitchen cleaned up. Do you want me to save you a plate for later?"

"No," I say, pushing my plate back. "I think I'm just going to go to bed. It's been a really long day."

"Okay, get some sleep." I slide down off the barstool and tug my sweater across my chest. Dinner didn't go quite like I'd thought it would, but it wasn't necessarily a bad thing. At least now, Mom will understand why I'm moping around the house for the next few weeks or months. This is going to go down as the year I'm always going to want to forget. I loved one guy, no, make that two, and I lost them both. At some point, it's going to prove to be more than I can take.

When I get up to my room, it's completely dark outside. Fall has its positives, and getting darker earlier is one of them. Before I crawl into bed, I go to the window and gaze up at the stars. Usually, when I look up at them, I think of Sam, and this is no different. Instead of making me feel like everything is going to be okay, though, they bring back the nauseous uneasiness I felt this morning. This is definitely something that even the Big Dipper can't fix.

I'm sitting in the passenger seat of my car. Cory's in the driver's seat, his wrist resting against the top of the steering wheel. "Why are you so against going to this party?"

"I don't know. We just got home, and I wanted to spend time alone with you."

His jaw tightens. "We've been away for months, Rachel."

We have. We've been away at college, but it seems like there are always other people around us. Beau. Kate. Emery. Cory's drinking buddies. There's always someone.

"Maybe I'm just tired," I say, sinking back in my seat.

"Look, I'm sorry. Tomorrow, we'll go out to the lake, just the two of us." His hand reaches for mine across the seat, and the annoyed feeling fades. Cory does that ... he always melts me.

"I guess I can compromise."

Within minutes, we're driving down a gravel road and onto a large grass field. It's packed with cars and, in the clearing, my old classmates surround a large fire. When I left for college, I thought I was going to miss them—that they would be hard to replace, but that wasn't the case. I found people I connected with on a deeper level ... people more like me. Coming out here doesn't even sound like fun anymore.

We both slip out of the car, meeting at the rear. Cory wraps his arm around my shoulders and ushers us toward the crowd, breaking his step long enough to kiss the side of my head. "We'll leave early, okay?"

I relax into his side, lifting my hand to clasp my fingers with his. "I'm going to hold you to that."

"I don't expect anything less."

Everyone looks at us as we walk up to the fire. It's always been like that. We're "the couple." I think they're all waiting for us to fall on our ass or get married. I'd go as far as to bet there's a wager going on. I hate the attention; it only brings pressure.

"I'm going to get something to drink. Don't go too far, okay?"

"I'll wait here for you."

"Good girl," he whispers, kissing me one last time.

That's how this one ends, with him walking away from me. There's a sinking feeling in my stomach because deep inside, I know that was our last kiss.

I toss the sheets off the bed and stumble to the bathroom, needing to fully wake up from this dream. I turn on the dim light above the shower, which is just enough to see my reflection in the mirror without bothering my tired eyes. Cold water ... that's what I need to escape this.

Turning the faucet on to the coldest setting, I fill my joined hands with water. I wait until it's to the top and splash it across my face. I feel more alive, but it's still not enough. I place my hands under the cool water again, and repeat the whole process multiple times. When I finally stop, my hands are numb from the water's temperature.

This recollection reminds me how much Cory and I had grown apart. We used to be salt and pepper. Popcorn and butter. Ice cream and hot fudge. Things shifted slowly until I wasn't so much afraid to lose him but rather the idea of him. No one should hold onto an idea that long; it either needs to become a reality or be abandoned, because ideas are just thoughts without effort or belief behind them.

For the first time I realize that if I could turn back the clock, I wouldn't just go back to the night of the accident. I'd go back to the first semester of college and let go of the idea.

CHAPTER
twenty-seven

NORMAL FEELS GOOD. I wear it like a designer coat as I step into Ms. Peters' shop. Two days spent moping around the house, drowning in my own guilt is all it took for this to feel like a corner of heaven.

"Hey Rachel, how was your weekend?" Ms. Peters smiles, having spotted me while stepping out of the cooler.

"It was okay," I lie.

"Isn't that how they all are? I wonder if I've already had my best or if it's yet to come."

I think about it. She makes a good point, but she also gets the wheels in my head turning again. Are my best days already behind me? Are guilt and anger all I have left?

"What do we have going today?" I ask, tying my apron. I need a distraction now.

"Well, I have a few deliveries ready for you in the cooler. I think there's two for the hospital and one office delivery."

"Do you want me to run those now or wait?"

She looks up at the clock. "Why don't you take them now. If anything else comes up, you can take it later."

"I'll do anything to keep myself busy," I say, heading to the cooler. On the second shelf are three beautiful arrangements with the Peters's touch. One is a huge bouquet of red roses. It's probably for the office delivery. I'd guess an anniversary. The other two are brighter, a mixture of fall yellows, oranges, and reds with a hint of green and white—an elegant mixture of roses, carnations, and daisies.

I place them all in a box, careful not to damage the delicate petals. After loading them into my backseat, I grab the delivery tickets and start toward the hospital. It's not my favorite place. It's never going to be.

Today, I make it through the lobby without running into anyone. The delivery is quick—in and out in less than two minutes. Back in the car, I turn the key back, and out of all songs, "What Hurts the Most" by Rascal Flatts plays on the radio. I'm frozen in place, white knuckles gripping the steering wheel. My mom listened to this song all the time when I was younger. It was literally always on when you turned on the radio one summer. But now, after living through so much, the song holds the key to unleashing my heartache. The words sink into the pores of my soul, freeing the emotions I'd tried to lock up. Pouring rain would be the only thing that could increase the sensations of this moment.

'*And having so much to say*' repeats over and over. Every time I think of what I would say to Cory if he were here right now. If he were sitting in this car next to me, I'd set him free. I'd let him go. Tell him that I love him, that I want the best for him, but that I think he'd have better luck finding what's best without me. He is an important part of what I've become, and for that I'll never forget him.

I thought by holding on to him, the mad, deep, consuming love would come back. I thought our relationship had encountered a bump. Now, though, I know what it feels like to fall out of love. There's a difference between being in love and loving someone because they've played such a big part in your life.

I swipe away the warm tears as I listen to the last verse. The song ends. A new revelation begins.

I should have let him go. I felt the distance growing in my heart, and Cory … I think he felt it, too. Our relationship became too comfortable until it wasn't comfortable at all.

This doesn't necessarily make me feel better or worse about what happened, but it fills in holes. When I compare how we were in my older memories of us to the final ones, the difference is a glaring red light. If only I'd seen it five months sooner.

I pull a travel-size package of Kleenex from the glove compartment and dab it lightly under each eye. By now, the makeup I applied this morning has washed away. The best I can do is clean myself up—make myself presentable enough to walk into an office where everyone is probably dressed in suits and drop off a vase of roses.

Checking the address, I recognize it as the car dealership on the outskirts of town, not too far from my house. I roll down my window, hoping the cold air will help remedy my blotchy, red face.

As I pull back on the street, I press the power button on the radio. One musical therapy session is enough for today. While I head across town, the wind blows through my blond hair, whipping it across my face. I push it behind my ears while I attempt to keep my mind free.

A few minutes later, I'm pulling onto the short frontage road that leads to the one and only new car dealership in town. It's nothing like the massive ones in the city, but they stay busy with farmers buying trucks for their farms, and the town's elite trading in for a new model every year or two.

I glance at my reflection in the rearview mirror, taking a few seconds to slide my tissue-covered finger under my eyes again. Waterproof mascara is wonderful until you try to clean it from your skin.

I get lucky on this one. The young lady who greets me at the door is also who the flowers belong to. I recognize her. She was a couple years ahead of me in high school. Turns out, she's married and has a kid on the way. It's interesting how our lives fork in different directions.

As my car starts back down the road, I see Sam's property in the distance. That stirs something else inside of me. Something more like slow burning anger. The flashback started it, but when he didn't even try to contact me, it spread. Slowly, taking little pieces of hope right along with it. I didn't want to talk to him. I wouldn't have answered, but I wanted to know he was thinking about me. I wanted to hear the pain in his voice as he begged me to give him another chance. I basically wanted to know he felt as shitty as I did—still do. I've never been a vengeful person, but these last few months are testing that. Maybe this is just the world's way of getting revenge on me. I just didn't think he'd let me go that easily.

I pull in front of the flower shop and slowly count to ten, inhaling a deep, refreshing breath after each number. *One ... two ... three...* Cars pass by as I hold on to the top of the steering wheel like it's my lifeline. I attempt to read the expressions on the faces of the passersby. Are they having a good day, bad day, or just indifferent? We encounter people every day without giving much thought to what's going on inside their heads. It's a full, yet lonely, world.

After I-don't-know-how-much time passes, I climb from the car, taking a few extra seconds to soak in the fresh air. Cool and refreshing ... it's exactly what I need. This has definitely been an emotionally taxing few days.

As soon as I open the door to the shop, I'm halted in my tracks. I haven't seen her in months. She hasn't called or stopped by to see me. All contact ceased after she visited me in the hospital, but now she's just a few feet in front of me going through a catalogue of floral arrangements with Ms. Peters. She's got the same shoulder-length brown hair with caramel highlights. I'd recognize her anywhere.

I quietly walk up behind her. I'm afraid she might just run away if she sees me, because that's what she has been doing. I never really tried to chase after her, because she obviously didn't want to be a part of my life. Rejection fucking sucks.

Ms. Peters says something I can't quite hear and pats Madison's shoulder, disappearing into the backroom. Madison's back is to me. It has been since I walked in, but now that Ms. Peters isn't holding her attention, her eyes scan the display of balloons around the shop before landing on me. They actually shoot a little ways past me before snapping back.

"Rachel," she mouths, crossing her arms over her stomach. What I couldn't see from the way she stood before was her swollen stomach. Not as in ate-too-many-cookies swollen, but more there's-a-real-live-baby-in-there big. All I can do is stare at her, not her face, but how the rest of her has filled out.

There's this horrible black hole in the middle of my chest. Why would she want to go through something like this without even telling me? That's probably the worst part. She was my best friend, and I thought I was hers. Sisters. We were like sisters.

"What are you doing here?" she finally asks, regaining her composure. The black hole grows larger. There's no *'How are you?'* or *'What have you been up to?'* She's nothing but a stranger with a familiar face.

"I work here," I choke.

"Oh, I didn't know." She's acting like it's the worst thing that we're here together in the same room.

"I tried to call you a couple times. You never called back." My mom would say that a nice Midwestern girl should just let it go, smile, and move on. But Madison hurt me. I was sick and sad and helpless, and she just left me to heal on my own. That's not a best friend. That's not a friend at all.

She takes a step back until her back hits against the counter. "I didn't know what to say, Rachel. What do you want me to say?"

"I didn't need you to say anything. I just needed you to be there for me. That's what friends do, you know?"

Her eyes cast downward, and when they come back up to mine, they're full of unshed tears. The blood of the soul. "I'm sorry for everything," she cries. "There are things we all wish we could take back, and for me, what I did to you will always be one of them."

"What are you talking about? Help me understand because, right now, I don't. How hard is it to pick up the phone?" My face looks like hers now, tears streaming down. I swear someone took a spikey ball and inserted it in my chest. Every time I turn, it cuts deep into my heart. Each time it hurts a little more. There's not much more that can go wrong in my life. There's not much left inside me to shred.

"I don't want you to hate me. Besides, I heard you're with Sam now," she says softly, smoothing her hand over her stomach. "You deserve to be happy."

The painful ball in my chest just moved a little bit more. A deep, excruciating cut. "I was with Sam. Turns out some people aren't what they seem."

"What do you mean?" Her eyes narrow on me. I'm noticing how much talking they truly do for a person.

"Do you even care?" I ask, crossing my arms over my chest. I sound like a bitch, but I think I've earned it.

A single tear slips down her cheek. "God, I care more than you'll ever know. Don't you get it, Rachel? That's why I stayed away. Because I care."

I'm so freaking confused. Someone spun me around and around then turned me loose here. This whole day just needs to evaporate. "He lied to me, okay? He was there the night of the accident and didn't tell me."

Her eyes widen. "You remember?"

"Just parts. I remember driving to the party. I remember running through a field and straight into Sam. Cory found us. That's why he was so upset with me that night."

She swallows visibly, bracing her hands against the counter. "You don't remember why you were running?"

After everything I told her, that was the last bit I expected her to focus on. "No, I don't remember that part. I don't know that it really matters anyway."

She looks toward the window. Her whole body trembles. "I'm sorry."

"It's not your fault."

Streams of tears fall from her eyes. It saddens me, even after everything. "I should probably get going. I have a doctor's appointment this afternoon."

I nod, coming around the counter to set my delivery tickets in the drawer. "When are you due?"

There's a pause—a long but audible pause. "February."

"I didn't know you were dating anyone."

"I wasn't really." She laughs, but yet she cries. It's one of the saddest things I've ever heard. It almost makes me want to forgive her for everything that happened, or didn't happen, the last few months. I have my shit, and she has hers. I just don't know who's buried deeper.

As I come back around the counter to where she stands, I spot Ms. Peters peeking through the small window between the showroom and backroom. I wonder how much of this she can hear, or if she's just waiting for us to clear out. It doesn't matter. I think she already knows my life is a hair below the level of normal.

"For what it's worth, it was good to see you. I only wish we could have done it sooner," I say.

"Yeah, me too."

Months ago, if we'd had this conversation, I would have hugged her. That doesn't feel like the right move anymore. I'm not sure what's right.

"I'll let you get going. Don't be a stranger, okay?"

"I really have to get going," she cries, walking past me to the door.

I'm speechless. Another person gone. Another disappointment. Another dark cloud of memories covering my sky.

CHAPTER
twenty-eight

THE FIRE CRACKLES FROM across the room as I pull my favorite fleece blanket up to cover my legs. Mom's already gone up to bed, and the house is quiet. This hasn't always been my ideal Friday night, but it's my new Friday night.

The only way to escape to a guaranteed happy place is get lost in a book. If I want to laugh, it's easy to find a book to make me do just that. In the instances I want a good cry, I can find a book to make me do that, too. A well-written book is as powerful as a hug at the end of a long day. My mom swears by a book and a glass of wine before bed. No wonder she always looks well rested.

I made it through the week without any more surprise visitors. Madison and I haven't spoke since Monday, not that I expected our confrontation to change anything. Our friendship is too far-gone. The trust is gone. The feeling that we'll be there for the other no matter what sailed a long time ago. It's better this way.

And Sam ... still radio silence there. Some of the anger has faded away, but where that's gone, loneliness seeps in. When I told him I didn't think I meant anything to him, I didn't mean it literally. I was trying to hurt him like he'd hurt me, but now it's more of a belief. If our relationship was more than just another fling for him, wouldn't he be fighting, even if he thinks there's no chance I'll take him back?

That's the part I don't get. Why he isn't coming at me with gloves on. Cory never fought for me either. Maybe there's nothing about me worth fighting for.

This is when I feel the most alone. When I think way too much. This is when I know it's time to open a book and fall right into the drama of someone else's life. It's always better as an observer.

My phone buzzes on top the coffee table. Besides Mom and Ms. Peters, it barely rings anymore.

"Hello," I answer, folding my book over my leg.

"Did I wake you?"

I straighten at the sound of Kate's voice. "Oh, no, I was just reading a book."

She laughs. "Control yourself on a Friday night, Rachel."

I can't help but relax. She has that power over me. "There's not much to do here this time of year. Actually makes me wish I could return to school right now."

"Aw, don't talk like that, or I'm going to have to come up there and get you. Are you at least cuddled up to Sam?"

Hearing his name sends my heart plummeting. A long, steep fall. "We broke up. Actually, I don't know if we really even broke up, because I'm not sure we were ever really together."

"Oh my God, what happened?"

"I've been remembering little bits and pieces of the accident. Anyway, he was there. He was at the party that night, and he's the whole reason Cory and I fought."

She gasps loud enough I hear it over the phone. "What? You're kidding right? Why wouldn't he tell you that?"

"I wish I knew."

"Wow. I don't know what to say." Her voice is quiet, almost too low to hear clearly.

"I'm trying not to think about it right now."

"He's not an 'it,' so I don't think it's going to be that easy."

She's right. I know she is, but the only way I get through each day is to tell myself that this is just another bump I have to get over. I have to believe there's still something or someone out there for me. That loneliness isn't my destiny.

"I know. I thought if I pretended everything was okay, it just would be. You know?"

"Oh, I know, but things don't really work that way. You can face them, or you can bury them. But let me tell you, when they come to the surface, and they will, they're so much angrier. So much louder."

It would sound ridiculous coming from anyone else, but Kate's like the encyclopedia of devastation. She's lived through so much, and to see her now, you'd never know it.

"I'll work through it eventually. I just have a lot on my mind right now. So much, it's hard to even see straight."

"Is there something else going on?"

I sigh, sinking back down into the couch cushion. "I finally ran into Madison. I think she's an even bigger mess than I am. Pregnant and all."

"That's crazy! Do you think she thought you'd be disappointed in her? I mean, Emery was worried about telling everyone for that exact reason."

"I don't know. Everything seemed off, like I wasn't even looking at the same person."

"That sucks, but the people who stay in your life through your struggles are your true friends. She should have been there for you."

"Like Beau was for you?"

"Exactly!"

"I don't know. I just feel like things have to get better at some point. At least they can't get worse."

"Do you remember the napkin I gave you when you came into the diner? Remember those words no matter what happens," she says quietly.

I'd completely forgotten about the napkin until just now. Too much happened after we left the diner that day, and I never took it out of the pocket of leather jacket. "I will," I reply, trying to remember where I put that jacket. I haven't worn it since then.

"Hang in there. I'll take a look at my work schedule and see if we can do another girls' day soon."

"I'd like that."

"Anyway, I need to get going. Beau just walked through the door. He says he has a surprise for me."

"You're so lucky. Don't forget that."

She's quiet. It's a rare occasion. "You better call me if you need anything."

"I will. Have a good night."

"You too. I hope your book is good."

As I hang up the phone, I stand up from the couch and run upstairs, hoping the napkin is still tucked away in my jacket. Luckily, the coat is right where it should be, hanging behind my door. Sliding my fingers into the right pocket, I breathe a sigh of relief when I feel the paper against my fingertips. I pull it out, unfolding it carefully. The words take my breath away.

> Everyone deserves happiness, no matter what they've done or what's been done to them. A great person once told me every day should be worth at least one smile. It's not always easy, but it's true.

I pin it on my bulletin board and head downstairs to finish my book, realizing my lips are turned up for the first time this week.

"Rachel, why don't you go up to bed?" I must have drifted to sleep at some point while reading because Dad stands over me now. He's still dressed in his suit, but his tie hangs loosely from his neck.

I yawn, noticing the small flame that still burns in the fireplace. That's not going to make him happy. "What time is it?"

"A little after twelve," he replies, kneeling down to extinguish the flames. "Has your mother been in bed a while?"

"She went up a few hours ago."

He nods, his body completely unmoving. I've often wondered what he's really doing when he's out late. Can there really be this much to do at the office, or is there something else that keeps him out late at night? Sometimes, when I actually see him come home, there's something like guilt written on his face. One night, I swear there was even the scent of a woman's perfume. Mom doesn't see it, or she doesn't want to. Even I denied it for the longest time.

"Are you holding up okay?" he asks out of the blue.

"Things can't get any worse," I say honestly.

He looks back over his shoulder. "Your mom said you remembered part of the accident. That should help if the police ever decide to press charges or any lawsuits are filed."

Guess that ball wasn't done twisting. Everything always comes back to the legalities with him. It's not about me. It's not about Mom. We're just part of a package. One he needs for his presentation of the perfect man.

Sitting up, I let my feet fall off the end of the couch. "I'm going up to bed."

"Okay," he mumbles, turning back to the small flame.

My thick wool socks make little sound against the wood floors. This house feels like nothing more than an oversized, empty box. It's never felt much like a home. Sometimes, when Dad's not here, Mom and I pretend it is. But it isn't. It never will be.

CHAPTER
twenty-nine

THE THING ABOUT FLOWER shops in the fall is business slowly dies down. Weddings become fewer and far between. There are still anniversaries and funerals, but those don't require as much work on our part. I miss being busy. It helped keep my mind where it needed to be.

"If you want to head out early today, you can!" Ms. Peters yells from inside the cooler.

Do I want to? No. Do I think I'm a good use of her money right now? No.

"Is there anything you want me to do before I leave?"

"If you could sweep in the showroom, I think I can handle the rest," she says, coming out with an armful of roses. With the swing of her hip, the cooler door closes. I've never seen anyone work quite as hard as she does, even my dad.

"Will do."

Sweeping isn't my favorite thing to do here because of all the little thorns and pieces of glitter that always seem to find their home on the tile floor. If it were up to me, I'd probably run a vacuum over it and make quick work of my little enemies.

I'm halfway done with my last assignment for the day when the door buzzes. That's another thing about flower shops.

Customers don't come in and out like they do the grocery store or gas station. You can go hours without seeing anyone.

Looking up over my shoulder, I spot Madison standing right inside the door. "Hey Madison, can I help you with something?" I ask.

She walks to me like a cat to a mouse. "I was wondering if you have time to talk. Somewhere private."

I'm taken aback but interested all the same. "I'm off as soon as I finish this. If you want to just wait."

"Yeah, I can do that." She sounds scared and vulnerable, like all the ways you don't want someone to sound when they ask to talk to you.

"Is the baby okay?" I ask. Her baby bump is apparent under her black trench coat, but that doesn't mean a whole lot.

"The baby's fine," she says, smiling weakly. "I'll wait outside."

I watch her, afraid she'll leave before she says what she came to say. It's the quickest sweep job in history. If Ms. Peters thought my behavior to be off, she didn't say anything. When designing an arrangement, she loses herself in it. Her eyes narrow with every flower she places, then she steps back to look at it. She repeats these steps over and over again until her vase is full.

She's definitely not paying any attention to me.

I quietly clock out and pull on my puffy black jacket. Tonight brings our first chance of snow. I hate the cold, but I love to sit inside my warm house by the fire and watch the little white flakes fall.

When I step out onto the sidewalk, Madison's back is pressed against the brick building. She's watching cars go by, but I don't think she's actually seeing them.

"I'm ready," I announce.

"We should probably go somewhere private." Her voice shakes like a wall near a passing train. It's scaring the shit out of me.

"Like coffee shop private or my car private?"

"Car," she answers, pushing off the wall of bricks.

Reaching into my pocket, I pull out my keys and press my thumb against the unlock button. I glance at her, noticing she's already heading for the passenger seat of my little car. Whatever this is, she can't wait to get it out.

I step off the curb, looking both ways before entering the street. As I pull the car door open, I have no idea what I've gotten myself into, but I already feel sick to my stomach.

"We're not going anywhere, are we?" Madison asks, interrupting my trance.

I look down, feeling the seatbelt buckle in my hand. Either nervousness or habit caused me to grab ahold of it. "No. Just a habit, I guess." I let it fall back and fold my hands in my lap. "What did you want to talk about?"

She focuses her eyes out the window and clears her throat. "There are two things actually." Her bottom lip quivers.

This is like watching cars collide, or maybe the car is coming at me. "Okay."

"I'm going to start by saying I'm sorry. It's not going to be enough, but I'm so, so sorry."

All I can do is stare.

"I was there that night at the party. I never joined the crowd, though, so no one saw me. Well, except for two people." She pauses, covering her mouth with her small, bony hand. "I went with Sam. I hung out with him every now and then when I just wanted to have a good time."

My eyes fixate on her round stomach. Sam's baby. She's carrying Sam's baby.

"Why didn't Sam tell me?" I cry, feeling the weight of months of heartache weighing on me. Was this some sort of sick joke between them? If they were on a mission to hurt me, they've succeeded.

She shrugs. "I don't think it was a big deal to him. It was all about fun, you know?"

"What does he think about the baby?"

Her brows pull in as her fingers run over the top of her rounded belly. "He doesn't know about the baby."

That fact shouldn't comfort me, but it does. At least I know he didn't sleep with me knowing he was having a baby with my former best friend. After that potential anger toward Sam is wiped away, my disappointment in Madison boils over. "How can you not tell him he's going to be a father?"

Her eyes double in size. "It's not his. It's not Sam's."

"It's not?" Those conversations where you feel like you're talking in circles ... this is one of them.

She folds her elbows onto her lap, burying her hands in her hair. Not an inch of her face is in my view. "That night ... you saw me. You looked so broken ... that look in your eyes. I'm so sorry."

She must be talking to the wrong person. I'd remember being upset at Madison. I would have felt it when I saw her in the hospital. "I still don't understand."

"I was with Cory ... in the woods. We were messing around, and you must have come looking for him. I saw you, but he didn't. When you ran off, I texted Sam and told him he needed to find you."

My heart's gone. It has to be because I swear it's not beating. My lungs must be missing, too. I can't breathe. I feel, but not alive. I'm too broken to even feel broken. My boyfriend and my best friend. The one who'd promised me so much, and the one who I'd thought would be my sister for life. This is not all right. How the fuck did they ever get it in their minds that it was?

"How long? How many times had you 'messed' around with my boyfriend?" The words escape me before I even have time to think about them.

She sobs. Flat out sobs into her palms. I don't feel sorry for her, not even one bit. "A few months. Since the Christmas before when we ran into each other at a party. It only happened a few times when you weren't around."

I'm upset.

Hurt.

Furious.

Pissed off.

"Thanks for keeping it behind closed doors," I groan, every last bit of sarcasm dripping from my voice.

"I didn't mean it like that. Cory was committed to you, but one night we were talking, and he said things were different. He said he'd asked for a break. I knew you were still together, but it was Cory. I'd had a crush on him since high school." She's still crying. She doesn't deserve that release of emotions.

"Why are you telling me this now? Why not just let it go?"

"Don't you get it? The baby is Cory's. I'm not going to be able to hide it for much longer. My mom thinks I've been sleeping around because I won't name him. She sent me to stay with my aunt so people wouldn't talk, but I'm back now. They're going to talk."

I heard her, but I think I stopped listening when she said *'The baby is Cory's.'* This crap doesn't happen in real life. It's a scene scripted for one of those trashy soap operas. Not me. This can't be meant for me.

"Please tell me you're lying," I plead, shaking my head wildly.

She lifts her head back up, revealing her swollen, red eyes. "I'm sorry. So sorry."

That's why I was running that night. I was running to get away from them, to escape the ugliness. And Sam, he was there to save me. Cory and I weren't fighting because I was in Sam's arms ... we were fighting because I'd caught him with my best friend. He ran me off, and I landed safely with Sam. It's not my fault. It's not.

"Get. Out. Of. My. Car. Get out!" My whole being shakes with anger.

She jumps, fumbling for the door handle. This isn't just a two car wreck ... it's a multi-car pile-up. When her door finally clicks open, she takes one more look back at me. "I never slept with Sam. I think you should know that."

"Just go. Please." My voice is lighter, calmer. There's only one place I want to go right now, and I can't get there with her leg dangling from my car.

"I'm sorry," she whispers, disappearing under the dull light of the early evening. I sit and stare straight out the windshield, watching the first of the white flakes fall from the sky. They're not much if you look at them from a distance, but up close, they have more of a pattern. They say no two snowflakes are the same, which is amazing if you really sit and think about it.

I attempt to lose myself in their design, their intricacy, but it doesn't work. After every snowflake is a vision of Cory, then a vision of Cory and Madison together, and it makes me sick. So freaking sick. How can two people who are supposed to have your back do the worst freaking thing imaginable? I could never, ever do something so callous. What would be the freaking joy in that?

Cars are starting to disappear. Once everything closes downtown, it becomes a ghost town. The few people still lingering are looking at my car sideways. I haven't looked in the mirror, but I probably look like hell. I feel like hell.

After what feels like hours, I start my car and put it in drive. Maybe I shouldn't be driving, but I know exactly where I'm going, and the path to get there is etched in my memory. That's one of the best parts of living in a small town; you can drive almost anywhere on autopilot.

CHAPTER *thirty*

THERE'S A SHORT DIRT road that leads to the fields. It's easy to travel on right now, but once the snow becomes a weekly thing, it'll be impossible. My feet aren't too tired to walk out here, but my mind is. I'm drained. I've been sucked of all life. I don't feel human anymore.

I put my car in park and turn off the engine. Mindlessly, I walk to the line of trees, sliding down against my favorite oak. The air is bitterly cold, but it doesn't faze me. Nothing can right now.

I have no hat. No gloves. No boots. But I want to be out here more than I want to be anywhere else. The cold awakens me. Makes me feel like I'm anything but dreaming.

I rest my head back against the rough bark and glare up at the night sky. The stars are hidden behind the clouds, which is a shame because I could spend hours identifying them. Since that's not an option, I let my eyes drift closed, and my mind starts to wander … I should have kept them open.

This party is exactly what I wanted to avoid. A bunch of my old high school classmates falling over drunk, slurring their words, and even a few hook-ups. Cory disappeared more than twenty minutes ago to find us drinks. If I had a few drinks in me, I could ignore it, dull my senses, but I can't now. I just want Cory back so we can leave.

"Hey Rachel, where's Cory?" It's Kyler. He's someone who Cory hung out with a lot in high school. A nice guy but he lacks some common sense.

"He went to get us a drink. How's Northern Iowa treating you?"

"It's good. It's good," he says, rubbing the back of his neck. "Look, I have everything for lemon drop shots over by the cooler. You want one?"

I scan the crowd again. No sign of Cory. "Why not." At least the alcohol will help me tolerate this scene.

Following Kyler to the back of his pick-up truck, numerous sets of eyes follow me. It's not abnormal ... it happens a lot, especially when I'm with Cory. Tonight, they just feel different, though, and I can't put my finger on why.

"Don't tell anyone I said this, but the only reason I bring all this shit is to get girls to talk to me. I give them a couple, and they tell me just about anything I want to hear."

I watch him fill one of the tiny, cheap shot glasses he always brings with him. "Nice, Kyler."

"Some of us haven't been dating the same person since freshman year in high school. We need all the help we can get."

"Some things never change, do they, Kyler?"

"You haven't," he remarks, looking deep into my eyes. "Wrist."

This isn't the first time I've taken a shot from Kyler. I know the drill. I lick my wrist, and he uses a small shaker to pour sugar on it. He places a lemon slice in my left hand and the full shot glass in my right. "If you weren't Cory's girl, I'd let you do this off my abs."

"I'm sorry I'm missing out on that," I say, licking the sugar from my wrist. I quickly chase it down with the shot, then take the lemon between my teeth. I wince. These things aren't my favorite, but they're still better than the beer they usually have on tap.

He grins. "Want another?"

"No," I reply, handing him back his shot glass. "I need to find Cory."

"Rachel, I—"

I raise my hand and walk away. "Bye, Kyler. It was nice seeing you."

After walking the perimeter, I still can't find him so I head off toward a grove of trees. He's probably not in here, but I've looked everywhere else. It's dark. Too dark. I walk around the edge, scared that if I walk between the trees, I'll trip over branches or God knows what else people left in here.

When I'm on the far side, the one you can't see from the party, feminine moans fill the otherwise quiet night. I step in past the first line of trees, more curious than anything. The moans get louder, and now, I hear a male whisper accompanying them. Step through one more line of trees, I tell myself. One more.

I immediately wish I'd stayed back. Cory is wearing the light blue polo shirt I bought him for his birthday, but it's pulled up along his waist. His shorts and boxers are down at his ankles. I can't see his face, but I know it's him. Thin bare legs are wrapped around his waist.

Whoever she is, I hate her. I want to rip all the hair from her scalp and shove it down her throat. Tears well in my eyes, and I take a couple more quiet steps. Then, he moves his lips to her neck, giving me a perfect view of her face. I'm shocked. Sick. Stunned. Of all the people on this world, I never thought it would be her. Never.

Under the little bit of moonlight that shines through the trees, I see her eyes are closed. I want her to open them and see me. I want her to see what she's done to me.

His betrayal hurts.

Her betrayal kills.

I never in a million years thought this could happen.

She wraps her arms around his shoulders and opens her eyes. I'm waiting, and it doesn't take her long to find me. I bet my face looks a lot like the one she wears right now. Shocked. Sad. The only difference is mine has a thick layer of disgust over top.

Her lips part. She's either going to fall into euphoria or call me out from the shadows. Neither one is something I want to hang around for, so I run. Not toward the parked cars or the party itself, but in the opposite direction. Far, far away from everything. Far from the life I'd been living.

The last hole has been filled. The sequence of events all lined up, even if they don't necessarily make sense. She said it started around Christmas. That's always a busy time, but this last year, I took a short ski trip with my mom's side of the family. Three days ... that was all.

I thought I knew him. I thought I knew her. I've never been more wrong. Never. The depth of betrayal runs through my skin into my veins. I don't think I'll ever get over this. Our relationships are built on trust, and almost every relationship I had has been broken. How am I supposed to come back from that?

"What are you doing out here? It's freezing." I don't answer. I don't open my eyes. I'm trying too hard not to feel, and if I look at Sam, that's exactly what will happen. Sam didn't come out to the field that night with malicious intent. He didn't come out there to ruin my relationship with Cory. He was there with Madison, and ultimately, he was there to save me.

Sam protected me for months ... from this. Maybe I should be grateful, because this would've been impossible to handle on top of Cory's death.

It doesn't mean I'm going to forgive him for keeping things from me for so long ... I can't.

His strong arms reach me, lifting me up against his warm body. My eyes remain closed, too tired and swollen from crying to even look where we're going. His shoes crunch at a rapid pace against the fresh snow.

"What happened?" he asks, never breaking his quick pace.

Something tells me if I just say her name, he'll understand. He'll get it. Maybe he doesn't know about the baby, but he knew about them. I wonder if he was ever going to tell me? Does he get how stupid this makes me feel? I should have seen it. Maybe I did, and I just didn't want to admit it.

"Madison," I whisper, burying my face in his black leather jacket.

For the first time since he picked me up from the ground, his footsteps slow. If it's even possible, his arms tighten around me. I was right. He knows, and not only that, he feels. His heart beats the rhythm of mine. He knew how much this would hurt me. He caged me to protect me. He tried to protect my ideals about love, and by doing so, he may have actually strengthened them. Cory could have broken every ideal I've ever had, but Sam saved them by sacrificing himself for me.

The relationship we had, the one we built on, was important to him. He finally had me, or at least most of me. He had to have known that by holding the truth from me, he was putting all of that at risk. Don't get me wrong … I'm pissed at him. I almost wish I'd heard the truth from him, not Madison, but it's easy to say that now. After the initial shock wears off.

My anger shifted from Sam to Cory to Madison … to myself. How could I not see what was going on? I was basically on my way to becoming like my mom. To becoming the type of woman I didn't want to be.

We move quickly through the snow again. The cold no longer bothers me; I'm too numb, too exposed.

I must have drifted off for a little bit. My mind gets a temporary reprieve, and when I wake up, he's walking up a flight of stairs. Heavy boots hitting against the metal staircase. The smell of cedar. I should've known he wasn't taking me to my house.

He kneels, turning the knob and pushing the door open. "We need to get these clothes off you. You're soaked."

A shiver runs through my whole body. My feet and hands are numb. My energy drained. I'm not in a place where I can argue. If I were, I'd ask him to put me down. I'd tell him that just because I understand what he did, doesn't mean I forgive him. Trust is delicate. Once broken, it's hard to put back together.

He sets me down on the edge of his bed. I'm so weak, but he uses his torso to hold me up. First to go is my soaked coat, followed by my sweater. I think my bra joins them, but I'm not sure. I'm so tired. So weak.

"Okay, I'm going to lay you back. We have to get these wet jeans off you." He gently guides me back, removing both shoes, and peeling back my soaked jeans. His soft comforter lulls me ... I just want to sleep. And sometimes, like now, I never want to wake up.

"Stay with me, baby. We need to get you under the blankets." I hear him moving around the room, but all I want to do is curl up into a ball and let the day drift away.

The bed shifts beside me, then I'm back in his arms again. This time, he doesn't take me far, lying me down on the center of the mattress. I expect him to throw the comforter over me and let me go to sleep, but the mattress dips behind me. His chest feels like fire against my back. His legs feel the same as they tangle with mine. The only thing separating the two of us when he wraps the comforter around us is his mesh shorts.

"Go to sleep," he whispers against my hair.

And I do. I drift to sleep just as quickly as I fell apart earlier.

CHAPTER thirty-one

I WAKE UP IN the same position I was in when I fell asleep. Sam's warm body is still locked tightly with mine. His lips are pressed to the back of my neck. They're just there, lingering, providing an extra form of comfort—not really kissing me. But he's letting me know he's here, in case I have any doubts.

I run my feet along the cotton sheets, feeling the sensation of the smooth threads against my skin. My fingers tingle as they brush against Sam's forearms.

"You awake?" he asks, lips still against my skin.

"Hmm, kind of," I murmur, trying to pull away from him. I won't deny that I still feel things when Sam touches me, but I can't act on them. Too much has happened.

His grip on me tightens, clamping me to his chest. "What do you think you're doing?"

"I'm going home." I wiggle with no luck.

"You're not going anywhere until we talk."

Frustrated, I quit fighting him. I don't have the energy anyway. I'll listen like he asked, but then I'm leaving. "Talk," I say, rolling his sheets between my fingers.

"I couldn't tell you," he blurts. "Think about it, Rachel. If I would have said, 'Oh, by the way, I was there the night of the accident and the reason you were upset that night was because

232

you found out your boyfriend and best friend were sneaking around behind your back,' what would you have said?"

I shrug. Honestly, I would've had a hard time believing him without seeing it myself. It would have been a difficult one to swallow.

"I've given you your space, but now, you're going to listen to me." He inhales a deep breath. "What we had, what we *have*, means everything to me. I hate that you even thought for a minute that it doesn't. I would never do what Cory did. Just the thought of it makes me sick. I was going to tell you … that morning when you remembered I'd been there that night. There was just no easy way to say it." His voice is laced with tremendous sadness and regret. I don't feel bad for the way I reacted that morning, but he should have told me a long time ago, no matter what the outcome might have been.

"How long had you known … before that night?" Holding my breath, I count the seconds it takes him to answer. This is going to be the deciding factor between us moving forward together or moving on apart. If he knew long before that night and didn't tell me…

"I didn't," he replies, gripping me tighter. "I swear to God, I didn't. Madison called me, and I could barely make out a word she said except your name. Then, she said something about you catching her with Cory, and I was so pissed. Not for myself but for you."

Closing my eyes, I let out a pent up breath. "You were never with Lidia, were you?"

He laughs nervously. "I talked to her that night, but that was it. I didn't want to explain the whole Madison thing without explaining everything else first."

I hate that he was ever with Madison in any way. Did he care for her like he's caring for me right now? Did he tell her about his mom and dad, his struggles? Did he have feelings for her?

His hand slides up over my hip, his warm fingers caressing my side. "I know what you're thinking … Madison and I hung out a few times. We were sort of friends with minimum benefits. It was about fun … nothing else. I never slept with her."

"I don't need to hear anymore."

"Yes, you do." He scoots back just enough that he can press me on to my back. For the first time this morning, I'm seeing his face. His gorgeous, yet very tired, eyes look down at me. "The way I'm laying here with you right now, I never did that with her. No one has ever been in this bed. No one has been in here." He grabs my hand, resting it on his chest. "The way my heart is beating … that only happens when I'm with you. I love you, Rachel. I'm in love with only you."

He's so sure, and I think I am, too … sure that I love him. When someone's seen the worst of you, but looks at you the way he's looking at me right now … that's love in its purest form. I love him because of the way he loves me. The way he's brought me from where I was to where I am. I love him because of the way he is—kind, protective, always there. I just love to love him.

"I love you, too."

His head lifts from the pillow, his warm lips touching my shoulder. He draws a line to the base of my neck. It tickles just enough to make me squirm in his arms. "You really scared me last night," he says, kissing below my ear. I let him.

"I didn't realize how long I'd been out there. I was so freaking mad, I thought I was going to totally lose it."

He splays his hand against my bare stomach, fingertips tracing my belly button. "You should have called me. I would have come for you."

My heart aches in the worst way after I spoke with Madison yesterday. With all the voices screaming in my head, it was impossible to hear reason. I don't even know if it exists anymore. "I wasn't thinking clearly. I couldn't."

He leans in, gently brushing his lips across mine. He pulls away slowly, his eyes never leaving my face. I never thought I'd be with him like this again. "I really thought you were gone for good. I thought we were done."

"I don't think that's possible. I always come back to you in some way or another, but Sam, I have to be able to trust you. If there's anything else—"

His large hands cup my face. "There's nothing else … not that pertains to you or us. I only kept things from you to protect you. I knew the reason you were running, and I didn't want to be the one to tell you. As much as I wanted you, I didn't want to tarnish how you felt about Cory. Not when he wasn't here to defend himself."

What he's saying makes sense. I think if the tables were turned, and I knew the same thing about someone Sam loved, I would have a hard time coming clean. What would be the point if the person who'd done wrong was no longer here? It just becomes another layer of pain to deal with, and no one wants to see someone they love going through that.

There's one thing I haven't remembered about that night. I can't think of a reason why I would've let Cory into my car. I'm a different person now than I was back then, but I think I would've told him to find his own way home. In fact, I'm pretty sure of it.

"How did Cory end up in my car? Were you still there then?"

"After he found us, he tried to fight me until you blurted that you knew about him and Madison. Everything stopped then. He became really quiet, and you asked me to walk you to your car. God, Rachel, I tried to talk you into letting me take you home, but I didn't try hard enough. You've always been so stubborn," he says hurriedly, brushing his thumbs along my neck. "I made sure you were in the car, and you slowly started to pull away. I thought everything was good and I'd just call the next morning to check up on you. I watched as you stopped at the end of the dirt road, and he jumped in the passenger seat. I didn't expect you to pull away with him, but there was nothing I could do."

Closing my eyes, I nod into his hands. My whole world revolved around Cory. From everything I remember, I was completely broken that night because of what he did, but I loved him. There wouldn't have been any second chances, not after I saw him with Madison, but I would have wanted an explanation. I would've wanted to know why.

"There are so many things I wish had happened differently, or not at all, but I think the ending would have been the same. I think the ending would have always been me and you."

He kisses my forehead. Each cheek. The cleft of my chin. The tip of my nose. "I hope you always feel that way."

I truly believe we all have one person we're meant for. There's a reason I always come back to Sam. Knowing what I know now, I wonder how long it would have taken Cory and I to break up. Would I have found my way back to Sam? Would he have come after me?

I remember when Madison was in my car, and she was telling me how she'd been hanging out with Sam. I couldn't stop thinking about the baby she was carrying, and how I hated that it was Sam's. Honestly, it hurt more thinking about Sam making a baby with her than it did thinking about Cory and Madison together. Maybe it's just because of where I am now in life … the relationships I've rekindled.

"Can I tell you something?" I ask, combing my fingers through his long bangs.

"You can tell me anything."

"When Madison started telling me that she'd been seeing you, I thought the baby was yours. That thought pretty much crushed me."

He climbs on top of me, our bodies perfectly aligned. "Oh, baby, I couldn't even think about that with her. Besides, I think to her, I was nothing but a distraction."

"From Cory?"

"Yeah," he says, kissing the tip of my nose. "We distracted each other."

I still haven't gotten over the fact that Sam liked me all these years. I wonder how long he would have waited. It doesn't matter now, I guess, because we're here. "Thank you, Sam."

"For what?"

"For getting me through all of this."

He kisses me deeply, pushing his tongue between the seam of my lips. His movements are urgent, but we're in sync, our tongues dancing to the sweet song in our hearts.

The second he backs away, I miss his touch. "I'm going to say this again and hope you take it differently this time." He pauses, allowing our eyes to connect. "I'll always keep you safe."

He will. I know he will.

The key to a happy, fulfilling life is to be able to forgive when the devil makes himself known through others. I've had a couple weeks to work through what I learned about Cory and Madison. My anger faded, and an overwhelming sadness took its place. A baby, who will never know his father, is going to be born. And as much as I want to hate Madison, I can't. She's going to be someone's mother—a young mother without anyone to help her.

For some reason, I need her to know that I don't wish anything bad on her. What's done can't be undone ... I realize that, and I'm pretty sure she does, too.

"Are you sure you want to do this?" Sam asks, covering my hand with his.

I smile, albeit a little forced because of the crazy butterflies in my stomach. "I think I have to."

As Madison's house comes into view, my heart rate picks up. Like me, she's lived in the same house since she was born. A one story, baby blue colonial with black shutters. I've always thought it was cute, like one of those perfect homes from a half-hour sitcom, but real life things happen here.

Sam parks along the street but sits quietly at my side. He knows how I work, thinking everything through. I've rehearsed what I want to say over and over the last couple days, but I know the minute I see her, that will all go out the window.

"Just wait here," I say, grabbing the manila envelope from the back seat. "I should only be a few minutes."

"Take your time."

I step onto the curb and slowly make my way up to the white door. I have to tell myself to keep walking, to do what I came here to do.

Before I think too much, I knock against the wood door, praying she's here so I don't have to go through this whole process again. When I'm about to hit my knuckles against the wood again, it opens.

It's Janet, Madison's mother. Her mouth falls open when she sees it's me, but she quickly recovers. She knows. "Hi, Rachel, it's been a while since I've seen you."

"Hi, Janet. Is Madison home?"

She hesitates, her chest moving up and down at a visible pace. "Let me check. I'll be right back."

Instead of inviting me in, she closes the door. Janet knows Madison is home and, right now, they're probably talking about whether or not it's a good idea for her to come out here with me. I don't know if I'd come out in this situation.

A couple minutes later, the door opens again. It's not Janet this time … it's Madison. She looks terrified, and if I had to bet, I'd say she's been crying.

"Hi," I say, trying to break some of the tension. Maybe it will never break, but I might crack it.

"Hi," she says back, resting one hand on her stomach.

"I came by to give you this." I hold out the manila envelope. She carefully pulls it from between my fingers, eyeing it suspiciously. Before we drove here, I'd decided to take the high road. I'm not going to bring up everything that went wrong, because it's not going to make this right. "I think they might be of more use to you than they are to me," I add.

"What is it?" she asks, running her fingertips along the top.

"You can open it." The way she looks at me, you would think I just placed fire in her hands. "It's nothing bad. I promise."

Biting my lower lip, I watch her unclasp it and pull the photographs out. She thumbs through the first few, her eyes welling with unshed tears. "Why are you giving these to me? Don't you want to keep them?"

My emotions boil over. I was going to try to be strong, to hold them in, but that's not possible. Not after everything that's happened the last several months. There were days I didn't think I'd be able to move on, days I didn't want to move on, but I am. Being able to do this proves how much I've grown up.

"I kept the ones of us, but I thought you should have these … for the baby. He or she should know who their father was. They should see his smile, because it's unforgettable. I know I'll never forget it."

Tears slip down her cheeks, but she quickly wipes them away as she looks through photo after photo of Cory throughout high school. In some he's happy, smiling, and in others, he's thoughtful, pensive. It's how I'd want him remembered. "I can't believe you're doing this ... after everything."

"Whatever happened between us, it's not anyone else's fault," I cry, looking at her swollen stomach.

"I wish I could go back. I'm so sorry, Rachel. I was young and—"

"I'll never forget what happened, but I forgive you. A couple weeks ago, I never thought I'd be able to, but I have to. There's no way to move forward if I'm holding onto this," I say. It's the truth. She was a huge part of my life for so long, and it's impossible to hate her no matter how much she hurt me.

She just stares at me, so I continue, "We can't ever go back to what we were, or even a semblance of it, but I needed you to know I'm not angry. Not anymore."

She nods, slipping the photos back into the envelope. "That's all I ever hoped for ... your forgiveness."

"Anyway, I need to get going. Someone's waiting for me." I motion toward Sam's Camaro parked on the street.

"Again, thank you for this," she says, waving the envelope. "For everything."

"Take care, Madison." Without another word, I walk back toward the car, feeling lighter than I have in months. Everything is clearer to me now, and the best part of that picture sits before me. He's a vision in his gray beanie, blond hair sticking out from underneath, and his signature black leather jacket. No words can describe how much I love this guy.

I open the passenger door, sliding into the leather seat. "How did it go?" he asks, before I even have an opportunity to shut the door.

"Good. I'm just glad it's over with, you know?"

"I'm proud of you. I don't think I could have done that," he says, gently squeezing my knee.

"The most difficult things we do in life can be the most gratifying."

"Waiting for you all these years was the most painful, frustrating thing in my life, but what I have now makes it worth it."

The Camaro pulls up next to the large shop where Sam lives and works. I've been spending more nights here than at my own house, but being with Sam makes me feel at home. "Do you want me to cook you dinner?" he asks.

My lips turn up. "Depends. I'm kind of partial to your veggie pizza ordering."

He leans over the console, placing a feather-soft kiss on my cheek. "Whatever you want, it's yours."

I think God created the stars to make believers out of all of us. But how brightly they shine ... that's up to us.

epilogue

Three and a half years later...

THE THING ABOUT SMALL towns is there's always going to be something you miss about them, even if you convince yourself you want to disappear to a bigger place. During the last three years, I've spent most months in the city, only coming home for the warm summer months. I always looked forward to the last day of school, when I'd get to spend some time in the place I love. And this time, I finally graduated, which means this move is permanent.

I majored in design, and once I showed Ms. Peters the work I'd done, she offered me a full-time job. For now, I'll still be doing deliveries, but I'll also get to help with weddings and special events, which is exciting to me. It's kind of funny how tragedy handed me a career path. Design was the last thing on my mind my first year of college.

I've seen Madison around town a couple times when I've been back. We exchanged a simple hello; it's all we can do after everything that happened between us.

The first time I saw her son, Peyton, my heart dropped from my chest. He looks just like Cory, same dimples and thick, wavy hair. He smiled at me once while his mom held him in her arms; my eyes instantly clouded over as I smiled back.

They seem happy enough ... I think we've all grown up and moved on.

As I put the last of my things away in my room, that familiar engine becomes louder as it nears my house. I haven't seen Sam in two weeks, which is an eternity for us. When I decided to go back to school after taking a year off, Sam was the one thing that held me back. He didn't ask me to stay. In fact, he gave me a gentle push. Not because he wanted me to leave, but because he loved me enough to let me go.

I run down the stairs and step out onto the front porch. We've been talking about this day for months. The day our weekend and summer relationship would finally end ... a huge relief for both of us.

His motorcycle comes to a stop in front of the old wooden porch stairs, his feet planted firmly on the ground. He looks every bit a movie star in his faded, ripped jeans, black T-shirt, and motorcycle boots. Sometimes when I look at him, I can't believe he belongs to me.

I take a few steps to the edge of the porch. We're in a tense stare down, my eyes raking him in, his eyes drinking me in. After all these years, I still get that sensation every time I see him—the take-my-breath-away, he-can't-really-be-mine feeling. Even if it begins to fade or dim, he'll still be my forever guy.

I take one step down as he lowers the kickstand. With the second step, he comes off the bike. His fingers flex. I know he's aching to touch me. And with the third step, he stands right in front of me. He's several inches taller, but with me on the step, we're nose to nose, lips perfectly aligned. If I leaned forward just a little bit, the kiss I've been craving for days would be mine.

"Did you miss me?" he asks, running his fingertips up my bare arms.

Closing my eyes, I lean back, letting my long hair cascade down my back. "Maybe just a little bit."

"Just a little?" His mouth comes down on the base of my neck. It's soft and tender ... making me hungry for more. "That should do then," he murmurs against my skin.

"Truth?" I ask, staring up into his eyes.

He nods, rolling his bottom lip between his teeth. If my mom weren't home right now, I swear to God I'd bring him upstairs. This thing he's doing isn't fair.

"I've been counting down since I last saw you twelve days ago, and if I ever have to go that long again, I think I'll go crazy."

He laughs, gripping my hips to pull me closer. "If you leave me again for twelve days ... actually, no, that's never going to happen."

The sun is starting to set in the background as he leans in to kiss me. He caresses my lower lip between his, then does the same to the top. Even though he hasn't seen me in days, his movements are controlled, savoring my mouth. He does it slowly, the same way he always makes love to me when we haven't seen each other in a while. His tongue slips through my lips as his hands run up and down the length of my spine. I feel every part of him against me, and it makes me wet between my legs. It's been so long.

He pulls back before things go too far, resting his forehead against mine. "We'll finish that later."

"Can't we go to your place now?" I pout, doing my best to sway him.

He groans, putting a couple inches between our bodies. "Don't tempt me. I have something I want to give you before we do anything else."

I lean against his chest, staring up into his eyes. "You didn't need to get me anything."

"Trust me, baby, I think you'll like this one," he says, lifting me off the step. Sam and I have never been big on gifts. That's not what our relationship is about.

I follow closely behind him, and when we reach his bike, I allow him to slip his helmet on me. We've been on this thing hundreds of times since that first day. I think I love it just as much as he does.

"Ready?" Sam asks after we assume our usual positions.

"Let's get out of here," I reply, tightly wrapping my arms around him. I probably don't need to hold on quite like this, but it's one of the reasons I enjoy these rides.

It's late May and the air is humid, but as the motorcycle heads out, the breeze from speeding down the highway cools my exposed skin. It's the most refreshing thing in the whole world—the two of us out here. Sometime this summer, we're planning to take a week and travel across a few states. I'm looking forward to it.

I'm expecting us to start toward the lake or maybe even just ride through a few small towns until we're ready to turn back, but he surprises me by turning onto the narrow dirt road that leads to the fields. He stops, smack dab in the middle of the grass, and we just sit there for a while, taking in the view.

"We could have walked, you know."

He looks back, a huge grin on his face. "Hop off."

I jump off and pull the helmet from my head, smoothing out my hair. He climbs off and puts the kickstand down, then grabs my hand in his. "Come with me."

I want to ask him what the surprise is, but then it really wouldn't be a surprise at all. Besides, knowing Sam, he's not going to tell me until he's ready anyway. It's part of what I love about him—his unpredictability.

The sun has almost completely disappeared in the horizon; only an orange glow remains. It's a beautiful, breathtaking sight, especially when you get to share it with someone who means so much to you.

As we come to the line of trees that border one side of the creek, I spot Sam's tent and a single lawn chair set up by the unlit fire pit. "Are we camping?" I ask, tugging on his arm.

"Just follow me." He pulls me along, leading us closer to the campsite. We spent many summer nights out here enjoying the sounds of the crickets and the light of the fireflies. I'm convinced this is what heaven would look like.

"Take a seat," he says once we're standing next to the chair.

"Okay." My voice is quiet, feeling a bunch of crazy butterflies working overtime in my stomach. This isn't quite like the other times he's brought me out here ... he doesn't seem like himself.

I watch quietly as he lights a fire, standing back to admire his handiwork. One might argue that it's a little too warm out here for this, but the sight of the bright flame and the crackling sounds are worth it.

"Rachel?"

"Yeah?" I ask, watching him sway over to me. He truly is the brightest star in my sky.

He kneels on one knee in front of me, gently squeezing my thighs. My heart jumps in my chest. I've seen this in the movies dozens of times but never thought much about it happening to me. He reaches behind his back, pulling out a rolled up piece of paper ... not quite what I was expecting. "What would you say if I told you these fields are ours?"

"I know they're ours."

His head tilts, a nervous smile playing on his face. "I mean really ours. As in, I bought this land." He unrolls the paper, showing me the deed for this very piece of land, his name proudly displayed across the top.

My mouth falls open. This place signifies happiness. It's the first place I met Sam, and it played a big part in reigniting our friendship. It's a symbol of us. The glue that held us together and keeps us together.

"You're not kidding?" I ask, leaning closer to him.

"I want to build a house out here with you," he says, cupping my face in his hands. "And after that, when there's a house for us to call home, I'm going to marry you and make babies. Lots of star-gazing, firefly-catching babies." He kisses me before resting his forehead on mine. "Will you spend the rest of your life out in these fields with me? We may never be rich, baby, but I promise you, I'll try my best to be everything you ever need."

A single tear runs down my cheek. Living out in the middle of nowhere might not be a dream for many people, but to me, it's what life is all about. "Sam, if it meant being with you always, I'd sleep in that tent every night."

The pad of his thumb traces my lower lip. "There aren't many girls who would say that."

I kiss his thumb, letting my lips linger there. "There aren't any other girls who get to spend the rest of their lives with Sam Shea."

"Stand up," he demands.

I don't even ask why. After everything he just said to me, my heart and mind are a big pile of mush. When I'm up, his arm wraps around my waist and draws me into him. He sits back in the chair, and I have nowhere to go besides his lap. Not that I'm going to complain. "That's better," he says, kissing the back of my shoulder.

My head rests back against his strong shoulder. "Is there a reason why there's only one chair?"

"Maybe." I hear the smile in his voice. His arms hold me a little tighter.

We sit in silence, each looking up at the bright stars. This moment reminds me of so many others.

"We could put a skylight in our bedroom," he says.

"Why?"

"So we can look at the stars whenever we want."

Turning my head, I kiss the side of his jaw. "I'd like that."

"What about babies?" he asks, trailing his lips up my neck.

I close my eyes, relishing in his touch. I swear if we don't find a bed soon, I'm going to strip him naked right here. "What about them?"

"How many?" Another kiss. I'm melting.

I moan as his fingers move their way up my bare thigh. This sundress was the best idea I've ever had. "Two, maybe three."

Another kiss. "At least two," he agrees. "What about a dog?"

My legs spread, and his finger slips underneath my panties. "Yes."

He traces the top of my thighs, exploring everywhere except where I really need him to. "Sam," I whimper.

"Hmm?" He's smiling … I hear it.

"Bed. Now."

He laughs, lifting us both from the chair. Placing me on my feet, he guides me to the tent, carefully pulling back the door. I waste no time climbing inside, waiting for him on the air mattress.

I watch as he crawls inside and quickly zips up the door. He comes to me, like a tiger after his prey, eyes never leaving me. With his body over mine, he leans in to kiss me. "I love you," he whispers.

"I love you, too."

acknowledgements

FIRST, AND FOREMOST, I have to thank my husband and kids for being so patient with me when I need my time with my imaginary friends. Your continued support is what allows me to do what I do.

I'd also like to thank my family and friends who have been more than understanding and supportive. I couldn't have done it without you.

To my beta readers, Autumn, Melissa, Bridget, Jennifer, Toski, Ashley, Lisa, Elizabeth, Michelle, and Laura. You feedback helped immensely on this one, and *Thank You* doesn't seem like enough.

Jessica, you are a rock star. You've helped me so much with my writing and became a great friend in the process. Your turn is coming.

To my editor, Madison, thank you for putting up with me, even when I want to use clichés and such. I promise to cause those elusive butterflies with my next project.

To my agent, Jill, without your guidance, Drake and Emery would not exist. Thank you for pushing me to do more.

And last, but not least, to the readers and bloggers who have supported my work, THANK YOU! I never thought I'd be where I am today, and I owe it to you.

Made in the USA
Las Vegas, NV
02 September 2023

76975141R00144